Praise for *The Maid of Ballymacool*

"Deibel's update on the Cinderella st
three-dimensional characters who at
find their way to one another in this

T0044483

"Deibel once again inventively draws on Ireland's fascinating history as inspiration for a compassionate and compelling, sweet romance with a Celtic Cinderella-like flavor."

Booklist

"Jennifer Deibel has done it again with *The Maid of Bally-macool*, a hopeful historical romance novel about unrelenting faith and new beginnings with just a pinch of mystery."

BookPage

"*The Maid of Ballymacool* by Jennifer Deibel is an emotion-driven novel that will keep you reading until the last page. The story was brilliant and moving."

Interviews & Reviews

Praise for *The Lady of Galway Manor*

"Deibel beautifully recreates Galway's sights and sounds."

BookPage starred review

"Deibel has found her rhythm, delivering a classic boy-meets-girl story that packs a powerful punch and avoids preachiness. The historical tale will ring true to readers looking to examine their own biases."

Library Journal starred review

"An inspirational romance, this superb novel is also an exciting historical journey. Both romance and Irish history fans will love this book."

Historical Novel Society

Praise for *A Dance in Donegal*

"Deibel's descriptions of Ireland's landscape, enticing cuisine, sonorous language, and vibrant culture converge to form a spectacular background for the story."

BookPage starred review

"Deibel's exemplarily executed debut is a touching tale of love and forgiveness that also beautifully captures the warmth and magic of 1920s Ireland."

Booklist

"Heartbreaking, tragic, and full of surprises, this novel was the most engaging one I have read."

Urban Lit Magazine

The IRISH
Matchmaker

Books by Jennifer Deibel

A Dance in Donegal
The Lady of Galway Manor
The Maid of Ballymacool
The Irish Matchmaker

The IRISH Matchmaker

A Novel

JENNIFER DEIBEL

Revell

a division of Baker Publishing Group
Grand Rapids, Michigan

Published by Revell
a division of Baker Publishing Group
Grand Rapids, Michigan
RevellBooks.com

Printed in the United States of America

Library of Congress Cataloging-in-Publication Data
Names: Deibel, Jennifer, 1978– author.
Title: The Irish matchmaker : a novel / Jennifer Deibel.
Description: Grand Rapids, Michigan : Revell, a division of Baker Publishing Group, [2024]
Identifiers: LCCN 2023019394 | ISBN 9780800744854 (paper) | ISBN 9780800745622 (casebound) | ISBN 9781493444762 (ebook)
Subjects: LCGFT: Christian fiction. | Romance fiction. | Novels.
Classification: LCC PS3604.E3478 I75 2024 | DDC 813/.6—dc23/eng/20230427
LC record available at https://lccn.loc.gov/2023019394

Scripture used in this book, whether quoted or paraphrased by the characters, is taken from the King James Version of the Bible.

This book is a work of fiction. Names, characters, places, and incidents are the product of the author's imagination or are used fictitiously. Any resemblance to actual events, locales, or persons, living or dead, is coincidental.

Published in association with Books & Such Literary Management, BooksAndSuch.com.

Baker Publishing Group publications use paper produced from sustainable forestry practices and post-consumer waste whenever possible.

24 25 26 27 28 29 30   7 6 5 4 3 2 1

For Jehovah Jireh, my Provider—
thank You for all You've done in my life.
May this offering bring You glory and honor.

To Matt and Brittany Verlei—
may God's abundant provision cover
your hearts, minds, and homes.

Glossary of Terms

abair liom—[AH-burr LUHM]—tell me

Agus tú fein—[AH-gus TOO HAYN]—And yourself?

amadán—[AH-muh-dahn]—idiot

an aimsir—[AHN AM-shurr]—the weather

an-bhlasta—[AHN VLAH-stuh]—very delicious/tasty

anocht—[uh-NOCKT]—tonight

anois—[uh-NISH]—now

anseo—[ihn-SHAW]—here

ar m'fhocal—[AIR muh-OH-kuhl]—on my word; I swear

babaí—[BAH-bee]—baby; young one

bábóg—[BAH-bohg]—doll/dolly

bándearg—[BAHN-dair-ohg]—pink

bean an tí—[BAN uhn TEE]—woman of the house

Bíobla—[BEEB-luh]—Bible

bó—[BOE]—cow

bodhrán—[BOW-rahn]—a traditional Irish drum

braces—the Irish terminology for suspenders

9

buartha faoi—[BOOR-huh FWEE]—worried about

"Caillaich an Airgid"—[KAH-lyahk uhn EHD-ih-guhd]—a traditional Irish folk song. The title literally translates to "The Hag with the Money."

cinnte—[KINN-chuh]—certainly/indeed/of course

comhghairdeas—[kuh-GARR-juh-huss]—congratulations

conas atá tú—[KOH-nuhs ah-TAH TOO]—How are you (in the Munster dialect)

craic—[CRACK]—fun; good times; fellowship

craiceáilte—[CRACK-ahl-chuh]—crazy

culchie—[KUHL-chee]—slang for one who lives in a rural setting; country bumpkin

cupán tae—[KUP-ahn TAY]—cup of tea

Daideo—[DAH-jo]—Grandfather

Daidí—[DAH-dee]—Daddy/Dad

Dáiríre—[dah-REE-ruh]—really?/seriously?

Dia duit [JEE-uh DITCH]—a traditional greeting; literally "God to you/be with you"

Dia duit, a mhac—[JEE-uh DITCH uh WAHK]—God to you/be with you, son

Dia is Muire Dhuit—[JEE-uh iss MUH-ruh GWIT]—response to "Dia duit"; literally "God and Mary to you"

Donal Óg—[DO-null OWG]—Young Donal/Donal Junior

Éirinn—[AY-rinn]—Ireland

féile—[FAY-luh]—festival

feis—[FEHSH]—festival

go maith—[guh MAH]—good; I'm well

Go n-éirí an bóthar leat—[GUH NYE-dee UHN BOH-hurr

LAHT]—good luck; directly translates, "may the road rise to meet you," meaning may your journey/work be easy.

Go riabh míle maith agat—[GO ROW MEE-luh MAH uh-GUT]—Thanks a million

iontach—[EEN-tahk]—excellent; wonderful

Íosa Críost—[EE-suh KREEST]—Jesus Christ

Maidín mhaith, a stóir—[MAH-jeen WAH uh SHTOR]—Good morning, love

maith an cailín—[MAH uhn KAH-leen]—good girl/good woman

mar dhea—[MAR YAH]—yeah, right

m'dhada—[muh YAH-juh]—my dad

midgie—[MIJ-ee]—a small gnat-like insect with a painful bite

mo grá geal—[muh GRAH GEEYAL]—love of my life/my bright love

Moladh Dé—[MUHLL-oo JAY]—Praise be to God

muise—[MIH-shuh]—oh my; dear, dear

na ba—[NUH BAH]—the cows

nach bhfuil—[NAHK WILL]—doesn't it?

ná dean é sin—[NAH JANN SHINN]—don't do that

níl ann ach amaidí—[NEEL AHN ACK AH-muh-jee]—it's simply ridiculous

oíche mhaith, gach duine—[EE-huh WAH GACK DINN-uh]—Good night, everyone

o mo léan—[OH muh-LAN]—oh, dear me

peata—[PA-tuh]—pet; a term of endearment

pionta uisce, le do thoil—[PIHN-tuh ISH-kuh, LEH duh hull]—pint of water, please.

Sasana—[SAH-suh-nah]—England

seafóid—[SHAH-foyj]—nonsense

seisún—[SEH-shyoon]—an informal gathering involving traditional Irish music

sióg—[SHEE-ohg]—fairy

slán—[SLAHN]—goodbye to you/health to you

slán abhaile—[SLAHN uh-WAH-leh]—safe home/get home safely

slán leat—[SLAHN LAHT]—a traditional parting; "health and safety be with you"

stone—a unit of weight equal to fourteen pounds

uilleann pipes—[UHL-uhn PIPES]— the Irish form of bagpipes, played by pumping a bag using one's elbow rather than blowing into a mouthpiece

1

T he warning came far too late, and before Donal Bunratty could register what his daughter was saying, he
was slammed into with the force of a locomotive. Arms
akimbo, he craned his neck to anchor himself in space while
his feet flew up and over his head. The rustic odor of wet hide
assaulted his senses, and Donal groaned and rolled onto his
back. Wiping the muck from his eyes, he looked up to find *Bó*
standing over him, huffing.

Donal grunted. "Hallo, auld man."

Bó sniffed Donal's hair and forehead and then, as if decid-
ing his master was alright, he snorted heavily and trotted off
away from the barn, the deep timbre of his hearty *moo* trailing
after him.

Donal rested on his elbow and turned to see where the bull
was headed. A chorus of lowing filled the bog. The whole herd
of cattle now roamed as free as jaybirds. Flopping back down,
Donal studied the heavy slate clouds mixing ominously overhead as he seemed to sink deeper into the spongy turf. The

rain had passed—for the moment. But it wouldn't be long in returning.

"*Daidí*!" Sara splish-splashed toward him in her wellies. "Sorry 'bout that, Da. I couldn't latch the gate. It's rusted again."

Suppressing a sigh, Donal sat and squinted up at his daughter. Her sleek brown hair clung in wet strands to her cheeks, which held the rosy glow of childhood. She looked off in the distance—toward the herd, no doubt—and in the waning evening light, and from that angle, she looked just like her mother. He swallowed hard and lowered his gaze. Nearly six years later and he still missed his wife, though the grief was more of a distant foggy ache than the harsh knife to his heart it had once been.

He stretched his hand out to his daughter. "Help an auld man up, will ya?"

She giggled and clasped his forearm with both her hands, then tugged with all her might, her feet slipping on the puddled grass. But at last, she managed to help him up. "C'mon, Da, they're gettin' away!" Off she took like a flash toward the errant cattle.

Donal followed suit, though with much slower, heavier steps than his daughter. The next hour played out like a comedy of errors. The pair managed to wrangle the cows into a group fairly easily, but getting them back to the barn was another thing entirely. If father and daughter both walked behind the animals, some at the front would wander off to investigate an inviting shrub or thistle. But if they both walked in front, the group would break up, and the rounding up would start all over again. The fleeting thought that perhaps he should've gotten a dog after all skittered through Donal's mind, but he shook it free. They could barely feed themselves and keep up with the livestock, as it was. At last, Donal and Sara fell into a sort of rotating dance, circling around the mob of stock—that kept the animals in their places. Confused, but in their places.

As they approached the barn, the skies broke open, and rain lashed down even heavier than before. Tugging his flatcap lower over his eyes, Donal squinted through the deluge.

"Go open the door!" he called.

Sara, her hands shielding her forehead like a shelf, hurried to do as she'd been told.

The wind picked up and whipped Donal's coattails and yanked Sara's hair in every direction. He shouted to the girl again, gesturing wildly in case the storm distorted his words. "Now, stand there! No, no, in the open space. Yes, that's it!"

It took another feat of engineering, and a large dram of luck, to get the excited cattle back where they belonged. Once they wrangled the door closed, Donal and Sara efforted to get the latch to catch.

"We need a new one," Sara shouted over the maelstrom.

Donal nodded, water sluicing down the brim of his hat like Ennistymon Cascades. "This'll have to do for tonight." The hasp was secured, but Sara looked at him, her eyes questioning, doubting. "'Twill hold for the night, at least."

It has to. The uninvited thought invaded Donal's mind despite his efforts to stave it off. He refused to entertain any idea of what would happen should they lose the livelihood of their stock.

Back in the cottage, Sara changed quickly and saw to stoking the fire. Donal lumbered into his bedroom, closed the door, and crossed to the window. Pressing his palms to the sill, he rested his forehead against the cold glass as the storm raged on outside. Still breathless from their pursuits, he watched as the panes fogged and cleared, fogged and cleared. He'd always presumed the farming tasks would get easier as Sara grew and her abilities to help grew with her. Yet, for some reason, it seemed the difficulty was only increasing—compounding exponentially alongside Sara's growth . . . and the Irish pound's ever-shrinking reach.

The thud of iron against iron drew his attention back to the kitchen. By the sounds of it, Sara was starting on their tea. Not yet nine years old and already the woman of the house. It shouldn't be this way. And yet it was all they'd known—it certainly felt that way, at least. The three short years they'd shared as a family of three seemed nothing more than a daydream these days. This farm, this land, this life was all Donal had ever wanted as a lad. And now, if something didn't change, he would have to give it all up. The thought churned his stomach.

Catríona Daly leaned closer to the looking glass. Touching her fingertip to the corners of her eyes, she traced the fine lines making their home there. The frown that slid onto her face only deepened the creases, and she scoffed. Flapping her hand at her reflection, she straightened and then smoothed her hair. Neither blond nor brown, it reminded her of the color of water rushing from the bog after a heavy rain.

The haunting whine of a single fiddle note seeped up through the floorboards of the flat she shared with her father on the second floor of the Imperial Hotel. It was followed by the hollow groan of the *uilleann pipes* and the shrill call of a tin whistle. The *seisún* would be starting soon and Father would be looking for her.

Tightening her apron around her slightly-too-thick waist, she gave herself one more look in the mirror. Too old to be young, too young to be old, and having inherited her mother's "big bones," 'twas no wonder she remained single. She grimaced. Lisdoonvarna's unmatched matchmaker. That ought to draw confidence from her customers this year.

Her eyes slid closed, and she steadied herself with a breath before bounding down the steps.

She burst around the corner into the Imperial Pub, which was nestled on the ground floor of the hotel, then tossed her arms with a flourish and let out a laugh that failed to reach her heart. "What's the *craic* now, lads?"

"Caty!" the musicians called over the din of their warm-up.

Catríona made her way to the bar where Peadar polished the wood to a high shine. "The usual, Caty?"

"Aye." She nodded, her eyes scanning the dark, wood-paneled interior. Reflections from hurricane lanterns hung around the room danced on the tabletops, while the soft glow from the turf fire in the hearth pooled in a golden puddle on the floor. Every table was clean and equipped with no fewer than four chairs. "Expectin' a mob, are ya'?" she asked. "The festival doesn't start for another week."

Peadar shrugged as he set a steaming pot of tea in front of her, alongside a pint of water. "Seems some folk are startin' early."

Catríona poured the molten liquid into her cup, then added a splash of milk as she watched the door. She rolled around the idea of another matchmaking season in which their sleepy little village overflowed with interesting new people from all over. Hope fluttered in her weary soul at the thought. Maybe this would be the year. When someone would miraculously swoop in, ignore all the other perfectly coiffed merrymakers, and whisk her away to a life she could only ever dream of. One of excitement and city life that would take her far away from cattle and bogs and the never-ending loneliness that permeated every nook and cranny of her life in Lisdoonvarna. She lived in the famed home of romance, where people found love waiting around every corner—often orchestrated by Catríona herself.

For everyone else, this village represented all their hopes and dreams of finding their one true love. For Catríona Daly, it was a reminder of all she failed to be.

Scooping up her tea service and water, she shuffled to the side room—not much bigger than a wee closet—that served as office for her and her father. Catríona scooted to the center of the bench that filled the rounded bay window. As she settled in for the long evening ahead and arranged her things on the table just so, a ruckus erupted at the main door. She didn't even need to raise her head. Jimmy Daly's chaos surrounded him like a thundering cloud, and Catríona would recognize its unique cadence anywhere.

"Ah, there she is." Her father's broad smile appeared around the corner. His graying hair stood out in all directions from the strengthening near-autumn wind. Though, in truth, it mattered not if the wind blew. The man's hair had a mind of its own. "The finest matchmaker woman in the whole of *Éireann*."

Catríona scoffed. "Oh, Da."

He scurried around and plopped onto the bench next to her, his well-worn woolen jumper scratching at her elbow. 'Twas true, her father carried an air of utter disarray about him. To look at the man, you'd think he'd lost his marbles long ago, along with any information or documents of any import. But the truth was, Jimmy Daly had a mind like a steel trap and could recall every detail of every deal he'd ever made—whether land, livestock, or love. Indeed, some deals involved all three! Catríona had no idea how he did it. She had to settle for keeping detailed notes when working with a brand-new client. Though she could hold more in her memory banks if it was someone with whom she was already well acquainted.

"Ya all set for *anocht*?" he asked, his bushy brows lifted.

Catríona nodded. "Aye, though I must duck out around ten."

"Ten?" His voice cracked. "Ye do realize 'tis a Friday night in Lisdoonvarna? There'll be plenty o' matchmaking work to be done well into the wee hours."

"Yes, Da, I know." For the locals, matchmaking took place all year long. She pulled out the small notebook she carried in her skirt pocket and flipped through it. "But I've the plucking of the gander with the O'Malleys and the Duncans."

He inhaled sharply. "That's right, that's right." He tapped his pointer finger to his temple. "The auld trap's startin' to slip a mite."

"It is not." Catríona slapped his arm playfully, shaking her head. "Ya just only have enough room in there for yer own deals, that's all."

Jimmy's features softened, and he leaned over and pressed a kiss to her forehead. "Ye're a good daughter, Caty. The best." Movement in the main room caught his eye, and he shimmied off the bench. "There's Black-eyed Jack. He's after me to make him a match."

Catríona followed her father's gaze to Jack. At over six feet tall and nearly sixty years old, Black-eyed Jack had been looking for a wife for ages. None of their matches ever seemed to work for him though. This one was too tall, that one too fat, this one not fat enough. Catríona suspected the real fault lay with Jack and his brusque, heavy-handed ways. But that didn't stop her father. He was bound and determined that there was a love out there for everyone.

She flapped her hand in Jack's direction. "Go, go." As she watched her father approach the giant of a man, her smile faded. Feigning interest in her tea, she couldn't help thinking that Jack wasn't the only one who was beginning to doubt her father's credo of true love waiting for all.

2

The light of the oil lantern in Catríona's hand flickered wildly in the wind as she walked to the house on the outskirts of town. The Duncans lived on a massive farm with hundreds of acres of quality land. Catríona rolled figures and sums over in her mind on her way. Chances were, the O'Malleys were going to try and get as big a piece of the Duncans' pie as they could.

Of all the tasks involved in matchmaking, the plucking of the gander vexed Catríona the most. Once a couple agreed they wanted to wed, the plucking of the gander—which sorted out all the land, legal, and financial aspects of the arrangement—came next. Ensuring the bride and groom were compatible for a lifetime of love seemed a lark compared to bartering all the financial requirements and dealings to see that both parties got a fair shake.

Once she arrived, she was welcomed with great fanfare and ushered into the formal parlor. The room had been impeccably and meticulously cleaned, and one unfamiliar with the proceedings would have thought they'd stumbled upon a wake, or Christmas morning. A steaming cup of tea was pressed into

Catríona's hand by the woman of the house as Mister Duncan guarded the doorway, waiting for the O'Malley clan to arrive.

"They're late, so they are," he grumbled.

"*Tsk*, they are not, ya big moaner, ya." Missus Duncan nodded toward the window. "'Tis ragin' out there anocht. 'Twill take them a mite longer than usual to make the journey."

A low growl rumbled in Mister Duncan's chest as his jaw worked back and forth. Catríona could almost see the figures stacking up in his mind as he calculated how much it was going to cost him to marry his daughter off to start her own life.

When a knock sounded at the door, a squeal emanated from the kitchen and a young voice called, "I'll get it!"

Mary Duncan bounded down the corridor and stopped short at the front door. She straightened her apron and smoothed her hands down the sides of her hair. Her shoulders rose and fell as she took a deep breath before welcoming her guests.

She opened the door. "Hi, Matty," Mary said on a sigh, a grin as wide as the Atlantic Ocean on her face.

"Mary." He removed his flatcap, despite the storm pummeling him and his parents behind him.

"Och! Let the poor lad in, Mary. Ya don't want 'im catchin' his death of a cold before the big day!" Missus Duncan skirted past her daughter and led her guests into the entryway of the modest cottage.

Matty stepped close to Mary. The pair had eyes only for each other. Mary slid her arm through his and pulled him closer. "Hi."

"Hi," he replied, gazing down at her as if she were the crown jewels.

"Mary." Mister Duncan's gruff voice shattered the air. "Kitchen."

Mary startled, her bottom lip protruding in a pout, though her gaze remained pinned on Matty's. "Aw, Da."

"*Anois!*"

Without a word, Matty unwound his betrothed's hand from his arm, bent, and brushed a long kiss to her fingertips. "G'on," he said as he straightened. "I'll see ye in a wee while, *mo grá geal.*"

Catríona dropped her gaze to the floor, unable to watch the tender moment any longer. Swallowing the rising personal doubt and dread—nae, jealousy—squeezing her chest, she returned to the parlor and took her seat for the proceedings, grateful the bride-to-be would remain in the kitchen with the other women of the extended family while the negotiations were underway. 'Twould be nigh impossible for Catríona to focus on the tasks at hand with the couple carrying on in such a way.

The remaining parties of the couple's parents, plus the groom, took their seats as well, the roaring turf fire enveloping the room in its soft warmth.

Catríona straightened her posture and pasted her best business face on as she scanned the group. "Now, shall we get started?"

———————∞———————

Catríona collapsed into bed. A driving beat thumped through the floor, and she knew her father was somewhere down there among the din. She really should be down there with him. What good was a matchmaker if she couldn't manage the nightlife? Never mind that it was already two o'clock in the morning. The festivities would carry on until the sun came up—and the festival wouldn't even start for another week. But tonight she was wrecked. Exhausted. She'd figure out an excuse to tell her father in the morning. But for now, sleep beckoned her.

She rolled onto her side, pulled the wool blanket up over her shoulder, and hugged it close. As her eyes slid closed, the image of Mary and Matty floated across her view, the adoration oozing from their gaze at one another. Catríona flopped onto her other side and whispered a desperate plea for the sweet release of sleep. Instead, she was assaulted with yet another mental image of the besotted couple. She shimmied onto her back and heaved a sigh.

Her heart pounded against her chest, and she pressed her palm against it to steady the thrumming. A dizzying tug-o'-war seethed within her, and she didn't know which way to allow it to pull. *Yank*. The matchmaking festival was starting soon, bringing with it loads of new people, the excitement of being able to successfully make match after match, and all the handsome young men dressed to the nines ready for love. *Tug*. Then again, a month straight of lonely hearts connecting with one another was bound to make tonight's plucking of the gander seem like a family dispute. *Heave*. But with all the suiters coming to town, the chances of Catríona finally finding her own true love match rose exponentially. Excitement fluttered within her as she imagined locking eyes with a stranger across a crowded pub. He smiles and waves. She waves back. Then they slowly close the distance between them. *Jerk*. He walks past her and connects with the beautiful dark-haired lass standing behind her, while a snaggle-toothed *culchie* who wreaks of sweat and manure grabs Catríona's hand and proposes marriage.

She pulled the covers over her head and squeezed her eyes shut. Never mind the generations of her family who had served as Country Clare's finest matchmakers, Catríona had to get out of here. A silent tear slid down her cheek. But there was no way out.

———— ◦∞◦ ————

Donal bit back an oath and tugged the reins for Bó to halt. Thankfully the beast complied. Bending to check the share and moldboard of the plow, he responded to the bull's lowing of protest.

"I don't fancy it any more 'an ye do, auld fella." He shook his head and tsked. The foreshare had snapped and sent a crack right through the length of the moldboard. Barely a week had passed since the latch broke on the barn, now this. "Looks like an early quittin' time today." He straightened and swiped the back of his arm across his forehead. In the distance, Sara was bent over a footed stack of turf. She painstakingly rotated each briquette, taking care not to topple the pyramid-shaped structure. With any luck, it would dry in time to burn during the brutal winter months. The torrential rains of late hadn't helped matters. His chest tightened and he groaned. *God, let it dry in time.* He couldn't fathom having to smear cow dung on the walls and whitewash over it to help hold the heat in. But that would be their fate if they didn't have enough turf to burn to warm their small home.

Donal's gaze drifted back to his daughter. His shoulders rose and fell as a deep sigh pressed from his lips. God bless that girl—footin' turf on her birthday with nary a complaint. His thoughts wandered back to the house and the wee fairy cake that awaited the birthday girl. A slight smile tickled the corner of his lips before the weight of reality pressed down, chasing away any hint of mirth. What kind of father gave his daughter nothing more than a single fairy cake on her birthday? Barely enough for two bites—if they were dainty ones—and no other gifts. He cupped his hand over his mouth and ran it down his chin, his whiskers scratching the skin of his palm. He blinked against the stinging in his eyes. She deserved more. So much more.

Bó stamped his foot, jolting Donal back to the present. He unhitched the leads from the bull and took a firm grip of the yoke that straddled the beast's back. Clicking his tongue, Donal tugged, urging Bó back in the direction of the barn. He glanced at the unmoving plow before calling out to Sara.

She looked up and shielded her squinted eyes with her hand.

"I'm takin' Bó back to the barn," he called.

Even from the distance, he could see confusion flash on her face. Then her gaze flitted to the plow and back, sad realization dawning. She smiled softly and nodded. "Have a cuppa tea while ye're over that way. Ya need the refreshment," she shouted to him.

Despite the frustrations at the day's shortcomings, his shoulders bounced with a chuckle, and he shook his head. "Aye, Mammy." Sara's giggle followed after his as he trudged toward the barn, and then home.

Once there, he followed orders and set the kettle on to boil before peeking in the cupboard to check on the fairy cake. Lifting the overturned bowl that covered it, he breathed a sigh of relief to see the petite single-serve cake still intact. At least the mice hadn't gotten to it. He carefully slid the plate out and set it on the rough wooden table in the center of the kitchen. He frowned. He wanted nothing more than to give Sara a grand party with fancy gifts, glittering decorations, and a veritable feast of all her favorite foods. Alas, he knew dwelling on that would do him no good. But there had to be a way he could make the place look a bit more special.

He scanned the room, looking for anything that would dress up the small table and add even the slightest air of celebration. A tiny bunch of paper flowers on the hutch caught his eye. Smiling, he removed them from their pride of place—Sara had made them last year at school as part of an Easter celebration. He carefully blew the dust from them, slid their stems into a drinking glass, and placed the makeshift vase on the table. Looking around again, he wondered if there might be something else he could do. He hurried to his room and dug through the press. Nothing was there save for his musty woolen jumpers and dungarees. He sighed and as he closed the door to the cabinet, a box on the top shelf caught his eye.

His brow furrowed as he removed the box from its place. When he carefully lifted the lid and his eyes fell on the contents, his breath hitched in his chest. He stared at it for a long beat before reaching in and pulling it out. The sheer fabric was buttery soft and felt almost fragile against his roughened skin. He lifted it to the light and smiled at the memory. Connie had worn the delicate scarf on their wedding day. She hadn't seen the use of spending a large sum on a wedding dress—she was more keen to use what money they had on setting up their home together. But Donal had seen the scarf in a shop window in town and couldn't help buying it for his bride-to-be. He lifted it to his nose and inhaled deeply, his eyes fluttering closed. The scent was faint, almost gone, but still there nonetheless. The herby aroma with a slight hint of mint was distinctly Connie.

"I wish you could see her, Con," Donal whispered to the room. "She's the spit of ye." Careful not to snag it on his callouses, he ran the fabric through his fingers as he sank onto the foot of the bed. Theirs had been a marriage of convenience—nae, necessity. Both were in need of stability, and the financial boost from Connie's dowry allowed him to upgrade the farm and set them up for a comfortable, albeit work-worn life. While never a passionate love affair, the two shared a cordial comfort together, having known one another since they were wee ones. Eventually an amiable compassion formed between them, thus Sara came along. And that had suited Donal just fine. He'd never seen the need for passion and romance—there was no time for that anyhow. What he'd needed back then was a partner, help with the farm and the house, and someone to talk to throughout the long, harsh winter nights. Connie had been the same. And her absence left a gaping chasm in their home, leaving Donal struggling to fill the roles of both man and woman of the house, along with both mother and father to Sara.

The all-too-familiar dread that had been his bedfellow of late settled heavily on his shoulders once again. Somehow the duties of the farm and house seemed to multiply with each passing season. And while Sara was capable beyond her years, he wanted more for her than to be his farmhand. She needed—nae, deserved—a full education and to be able to build her own life when the time came. As it was, Donal didn't see how they were going to be able to last another year, let alone ten years to get Sara grown and flown.

His eyes slid closed. "God, help us. We need a miracle."

Outside, the distant toll of the chapel bells rolled across the fields, signaling the *angelus*. Donal shot to his feet. Six o'clock already? He hurried to the kitchen and tied the scarf into a terribly crafted bow around the back of Sara's chair just as the kettle started to whine.

As if on cue, Sara bounded in the back door, hopping as she tried to pull her muddy wellies off. "I'll just wash up and then I'll start on our tea," she said, breathless.

Her eyes widened and her mouth slowly fell open as she noticed the table and looked back to him.

"*Breithlá shona duit, a stóir.*" Donal inwardly winced at the thickness in his voice.

"Oh, a dhadí!" Her voice cracked and she sprinted to him, wrapping her arms around him with such force it almost knocked him over. He held her tight for a long moment before leading her to the chair.

"Happy birthday, sweetheart," he repeated on a whisper. "Have a seat."

She started to protest. "But dinner—"

"Dinner can wait." He scooted her chair in. "Besides, no princess is going to make her own birthday tea!" He steeped the tea and set a cup in front of her and poured her some, fixing it just how she liked it.

He pulled a match from his pocket, then struck it against the table and slid the bottom end into the fairy cake. He sang the birthday song and ended with a robust round of *hip, hip, hoorays.* "Make yer wish, luhv."

A slow smile slid onto her face, and she blew out the flame, which had nearly reached the top of the wee cake. She tugged the spent match out, set it on the table, and took a dainty bite of the treat. Her eyes fluttered closed, and she fell back against her chair. "*Muise,*" she muttered. "*Go h-alainn.*"

"Good." Donal smiled. "So, what'd ya wish for?"

Sara wagged her head while licking her lips. "Hm-mm. If I tell it, it won't come true."

Donal chuckled. "Fine, then. Keep yer secrets."

She held up the rest of her cake. "Have some!"

He lifted his palms toward her. "Oh, no. 'Tis bad luck to eat the birthday girl's cake."

"It is not!" Her laughter filled the room and warmed Donal's heart.

"Alright, alright. It's not. But that's all for ye, a stoir." He poured himself a fresh cup of tea and fought against the tightening of his throat. "I wish it could be more."

"Da," she crooned.

"I know, I know." He stood and stepped to the basin, looking out of the small square window above it. "I'd shower you with gifts if I could, ya know."

"I know."

Silence stretched between them for a long moment. Then

Sara cleared her throat. "Da, there is one thing I'd really like for my birthday."

He squeezed his eyes shut and braced himself for the crushing disappointment he would no doubt have to deliver. "Oh?" he replied, forcing light into his expression as he turned to face her. "What's that?"

She chewed her lip and played with her fingers. "The festival," she murmured, then met his gaze.

His brows slid high. "Ye wanna go to the festival in town? Ready to get matched up and married off, are ya?"

She giggled and squirmed in her seat. "No, a dhadí." She looked him square in the face. "I want *you* to go to the festival."

Donal blanched and blinked hard. "Sara—"

She stood. "I mean it, Da." She closed the distance between them. "We need the help around here. I know you're lonely. And . . ." Her chin lowered almost to her chest.

"What?"

She shook her head, her gaze still down. "Never mind."

He hooked his finger under her chin and gently lifted her face so she looked at him. "What is it?"

She sighed and her chin sank again. When she spoke, her voice was barely above a whisper. "I'd really like a mother."

Sara stared at the ceiling through the inky veil of the dark night. Pressing her hand to her forehead, she groaned. How could she have said such a silly thing to Da? She should've been more subtle. She smiled in spite of herself, proud of finding use for the word Sister Margaret had taught them last week. "*An indirect way of getting something done,*" the nun's voice echoed in Sara's mind. Yes, she should've been subtle with her dad. Instead, she'd let him see her whole plan. And he'd never go for it now. A wee dram of guilt niggled at her belly. She knew he felt awful about Ma's passing—and he hated that Sara didn't have a mother's gentle influence. She hoped she hadn't added to the weight he carried around in his heart all the time. Sometimes Sara wondered if he thought it was his fault, Ma making the trip to the angels.

A faint memory drifted into her mind. One of the few times she'd heard her parents argue. Da had said something about money and the doctor. Ma had disagreed. Sara hadn't been able to hear all the words, and the entire conversation had gone over her head. But Sara wondered now, in the murky dim of her bedroom, if it had been about Ma's sickness. She knew they didn't have much money, and most of the time that didn't bother her at all. What bothered her more was the way her da's forehead went all crinkly when it came time to buy feed for all the animals, or the sad smile he'd give her on special days. But for the first time ever, it dawned on her that perhaps they hadn't had the money to get Ma the medicine or other doctor things she needed when she got sick. She shivered at the thought. Poor Da. No wonder he got so sad.

She pulled her rag doll closer as determination bloomed in her heart, even as her eyelids grew heavy. "That's settles it, *Bábóg*, we've got to get him to the festival," she whispered to her toy. "We can't give up now." Shifting onto her side, she smiled as sleep pulled her deep into the start of a lovely dream.

3

The final days before the official start of the matchmaking festival were always a bit *craiceáilte*. Between all the pubs and hotels in town rushing to make last-minute preparations, her father's typical frenetic energy ramped up at least twofold, and the steady stream of to-be-merrymakers arriving, the excitement was almost palpable. Catríona sat at a table on the patio of the Imperial Pub and pulled her shawl more tightly around her shoulders. This last day of August certainly held the telling chill of the forthcoming autumn. Steam curled lazily from her teacup as she watched the buggies, carts, and foot travelers rolling into town, turning *an tStráid Mhór*— Lisdoonvarna's Main Street—into a river of people.

Farmers walked alongside landed gentry, laughing and talking like old friends. This was the only time of year the classes mixed like this. Granted, they likely wouldn't be running in the same circles once the matching began—what with the doffs preferring to while away the hours taking the waters at the spas and mingling over fine meals at the Queens Hotel and the farmers choosing to spend their time and pounds at one of the many pubs lining the main road or hawking their livestock during the market days. It made sense, though. The farmers were on the hunt for a good woman who knew how to foot the turf and keep a good house. The gentry, on the other hand, were looking for a match that would improve their social standing or secure their family's station for years to come. But for now, everyone was on equal footing, with the potential for love and happiness putting everyone in an amiable mood.

Catríona took a sip of her tea, savoring the bracing warmth as it trailed all the way down to her belly. Suddenly, she stilled. Over the rim of her teacup, she caught sight of a tall figure on the back of a trusty steed. She lowered her cup to clear the veil of steam clouding her view. It couldn't be. She squinted against the morning sunrise. Blond hair glistened in the muted foggy light and broad shoulders narrowed into a masculine V, accentuating his fit waistline. He was a commanding figure, to be sure, reminding Catríona of a general leading his troops in a parade after a decisive victory on the battlefield.

Without warning, piercing blue eyes flashed in her direction. Catríona dipped her head. It *was* him. He'd come back. Andrew Osborne. Her heart quickened as his name floated into her consciousness. What was he doing here? He'd been matched by Figgy McDougal over in Doolin last year. Some highfalutin, newly titled *cailín* fresh off the boat from England. Catríona scanned the crowd, but the woman was nowhere to be seen. Could it be the match had failed? Or had he simply left the little woman at home while he came to take the rejuvenating waters? She absently tugged at the bodice of her dress and licked her lips, hoping to add even a fraction of the glisten the gentrified ladies always seemed to have upon their lips.

Inside the pub, her father's voice caught her attention. Was that man never tired? She chuckled to herself as she gathered her tea things. If anyone knew Andrew's story, it would be him.

Once inside, she slid her tray onto the bar top. "Mornin', Da."

He turned and his eyes brightened. "Ah, good morn', a stoir." He brushed a kiss on her cheek.

"Tea?"

He flapped his hand. "Ya know ya don't hafta ask me twice!" He laughed.

"*Cinnte, cinnte,*" she said. "Have a seat. I'll bring it to ye."

He floated her a strange look before nodding and shuffling off to their customary table.

"Another tray?" Peadar asked her.

"No, no, I'll get it." Catríona shooed him from behind the bar. "Ye just go sit down and take a load off. Goodness knows ye'll be back here long enough over the next month."

"T'anks, Caty. I could use a wee sec," the bartender said before hurrying off and disappearing around the corner.

Catríona gathered the hot water, fresh teapot, tea, and cup and carried it to her father in their makeshift office. "Here ya go."

"*Maith an cailín!*" he murmured with a smile. "What d'ye want?"

Catríona feigned surprise. "Can a girl not make her da a morning cuppa?"

Her dad laughed. "She can, but *you* don't." He took a sip and winced at the hot liquid. "Not unless ya want somethin'."

Catríona fought against the urge to roll her eyes and protest. He could see right through her. Instead, a laugh bubbled up and spilled out of her lips. "Nice, Da." She lowered herself into the chair across from him and followed his gaze out the window. He seemed mesmerized by the revelers making their way into town.

"Looks like quite the crowd already," Catríona said.

He swallowed a swig of tea and nodded. "Aye."

"Lots of new faces." She studied his profile as he continued watching out the window.

"And thanks be to God for it." He shifted to see more easily without having to twist his neck. "'Tis gonna be a grand one this year, Caty. I can feel it."

She nodded. "New folk, new matches. It's grand, so it is."

They were quiet for a long beat before she added, "D'ya know who I could've sworn I saw a moment ago?"

"Hmm?"

"Andrew Osborne. He was rollin' into town on his horse like he owned the place. And his wee wifey was nowhere to be seen."

Her dad's head whipped around. "Och! Wait 'til I tell ya." He shifted his body to face her and leaned in, resting his elbows on the table. "Ole Figgy McDougal made that match last year."

"I remember." Catríona fiddled with her thumbnail and waited for him to continue.

"*Tsk.* I told 'im it wouldn't work. The gairl was too green." He shook his head and continued, "Anyhoo, she broke it off before they could even see the priest about a weddin' date."

Catríona scooted closer. "Really?"

He nodded. "Oh, aye." He cupped a hand around the side of his mouth. "Rumor has it she fled all the way back to *Sasana*." His hoarse whisper rattled around the room.

Catríona reached across, lifted her father's cup, and stole a bracing sip of his tea. Andrew was single? And looking for another match? She rolled her lips together and forced a deep breath as Andrew's chiseled face floated across her mind's eye.

"I was gonna tell ye," her dad's voice broke through her thoughts. "And since we're talkin' about it, seems as good a time as any."

She lifted her brows, waiting.

"Andrew's folks have already written to me. They've come

to their senses and want us to make the match this year, rather than takin' their chances again on ole McDougal."

Catríona's heart sank. "Oh." Father had never once offered to match her with anyone. She often wondered if the thought had even crossed his mind. What little hope she had of catching Andrew's eye—though a fool's hope it was—vanished with the knowledge that her father would be in charge of matching him. If his family was using one of the other matchmakers in the area, at least there would have been a sliver of a chance she'd finagle a meeting or snag him for a whirl around the dance floor. But not now. Jimmy Daly had impeccable taste when it came to matching potential lovers. Every single one of his matches—and there'd been thousands over the years—had lasted. Not a single split in nearly fifty years. "That's good. Ye'll do well with that match." She tried not to let her disappointment lace her voice.

He tipped his head back and drained the last of his tea. "Och," he said almost mid-gulp. "I've no room in my docket. Lord Wyndham's asked me to match his last remaining daughter. When I'm not dealin' with the walk-up business here in the pub, I've got to be focusing on the Wyndhams."

Her eyebrows soared. "The Wyndhams? As in Thomas Wyndham?"

"Aye." He nodded.

"Earl of Dunraven, Thomas Wyndham?" She pressed her palms flat against the rough wooden table.

"Aye, daughter." He looked around. "I'd prefer to avoid his ire, t'ank ye very much. And I'd prefer to stay on the right side of the ground, if ya please. So, aye, I'll be matchin' his girl, and I'll be doin' it right."

She bobbed her head. "Ya make a good point."

He splayed his hands wide. "I know I do!" He rose slowly and placed his tea service back on the tray. "And that's why ye'll be matchin' young Osborne. Ye're set to meet with him and his folks tomorrow night."

Her father scooted out from behind the table and headed for the bar with his tray—his way of ending the conversation. Her mind spun with all he'd just unloaded onto her. Lord Wyndham was one of the most influential figures in the county, if not the whole of Ireland. He'd been instrumental in orchestrating the granting of limited powers of local self-government to Ireland and her people. Her father was smart to treat him well and stay within his good graces. A man like Wyndham had the power to make or break someone like Jimmy Daly. They'd had to give up their land and farm when her mother left, moving into their flat at the Imperial. Earl Wyndham, if pleased with the match made, could gift her father more land or pay enough that the Dalys could make their own decisions on what to do.

As momentous as that was, it still couldn't eclipse the fact that her father had placed Andrew Osborne's fate fully in her hands. A sly smile lifted the corner of her lips as her heart fluttered. This was even better than Andrew using one of their competitors. This was her one chance to really catch his beautiful eye and convince him to whisk her away from this life full of small-town market days, prying eyes, and just scraping by and save her from the humiliation of being Lisdoonvarna's unmatched matchmaker. Her smile widened into a full grin as she imagined the possibilities. There was much to be done before tomorrow night—starting with her wardrobe.

Donal stared into the murky mirror and tugged at the tweed waistcoat hugging his midline. Would this do for tomorrow night? He couldn't remember the last time he'd worn it, and it didn't quite fit him like it had then. All the manual labor on the farm kept him fit, so it wasn't a matter of midlife spread. It was more that the vest sat on him like a stranger's boots. It didn't suit him. Not anymore. He wasn't the same man who'd last sported the garment. He tugged his Sunday flatcap—the one he used to wear to Mass—onto his head, hoping it would improve the look. It didn't. He ripped the cap off and tossed it onto the bed. It was a ridiculous notion from the start. He wasn't going to that blasted matchmaking festival, and that was all there was to it. As he fiddled with the buttons on the waistcoat, Sara came in and stopped short.

"Oh, Da." She stepped closer, eyes wide. "Ya look . . . beautiful."

He smiled. "Beautiful, eh? Just what every man wants ta hear." A low chuckle rattled in his chest.

Sara rolled her eyes playfully. "Och, ya know what I mean." She smoothed her hand down the front of the rough tweed. "It's perfect for the festival."

When Donal didn't answer, but rather fixed his gaze on his reflection, Sara slid her hand into his.

"Ya are goin', aren't ya, Da?"

He looked down at her, his gut twisting. Now that it had come to it, he couldn't fathom being matched up with someone— anyone, really. He wasn't the man he was when he first wed. Truth was, he didn't know who he was anymore, and that was the bigger part of his problems, if he was honest with himself— which he'd managed to avoid being until this moment.

"Ya promised," she whispered, her eyes glistening.

He pinned her with a look. "I did not."

Her wee brow furrowed, and her shoulders sank.

Donal took a step back and sat on the edge of the bed, pressing his eyes closed. The mix of sadness and eagerness in his daughter's eyes, and the disappointment weighing her down, were simply too much to bear. Supposing he did go, what was the worst that could happen? He didn't get matched? Or would the worst be that he actually was matched? As much as they needed the help on the farm, it was hard for him to imagine reentering a marriage relationship at this stage of his life. But was it fair to make wee Sara live without a mother's influence because meeting the woman might prove to be a mite awkward for her auld man? No. No, it wasn't.

He sighed deeply and met her gaze once more. "Aye, peata." He leaned over and pressed a kiss to her head. "I'm goin'."

Sara squealed and clapped her hands. She wrapped her arms around his neck and squeezed. "Thank you, a dhadí." She stepped back and her smile faded. "Now, what're we gonna do wit' yer hair?"

4

S top it!" Sara yanked the hem of her dress out of Paul's grubby fist, refusing to let the tears stinging her eyes fall. She wouldn't give Paul, Margot, and the rest of their cronies the satisfaction.

Margot circled Sara slowly. "Honestly"—she sniffed haughtily—"ye'd think ye'd dress yourself a wee bit nicer before comin' to school." She flicked Sara's threadbare sleeve.

Sara glared at the girl and tried to sidestep her. She always hated the walk home from school, and this was why. Situated about a mile outside of Lisdoonvarna, the small one-room schoolhouse served both the children of the town as well as those who lived farther afield on the many sprawling farms dotting the countryside. The long piece of road on which the school stood was far enough outside of Lisdoonvarna itself that the bustle of the city was noticeably absent, and passersby were few and far between.

The town kids used the opportunity to pick on the culchies after the school day was over. Many of Sara's neighbors had been absent today for one reason or another—a not-entirely-foreign occurrence the Friday before the festival—leaving her to walk the lonely stretch by herself.

Margot stepped in front of Sara, blocking her escape. The rest of the townies closed in around her in a tight circle.

"Ya really should know better than to show up fer school in such a state," Paul added, tugging at her skirts.

"*Ná dean é sin!* Don't do that!" She tugged her dress back again and stumbled into the person behind her, who shoved her to the next person. Around and around the circle they pushed Sara. She squeezed her eyes shut and begged them once again to stop. But each plea only served to encourage them to continue.

Finally, firm hands gripped her shoulders. She opened her eyes to find herself nose to nose with Margot. "What're ya gonna do? Tell yer mammy?"

The other children erupted into a spate of cruel laughter, and Sara could hold her tears back no longer. She also could no longer contain her anger. With a loud sob, she reared back and slapped Margot across the face. A collective gasp rose from the group, followed by a chilled silence.

Margot pressed a hand to her cheek, and her eyes narrowed into tiny slits. "Ye're gonna regret that one, girlie." She released her cheek and, before Sara could react, reached out and gripped a chunk of Sara's hair and pulled. The others followed Margot's lead, taking turns pinching her, smacking her, and pulling her hair. They kept their ranks in a tight circle to keep Sara from getting away.

"Stop it! Stop!" she cried. They only laughed.

"What's the meanin' o' this?" A woman's voice broke through the din.

The circle slowly released its clutch on Sara, and she gasped the fresh air deeply.

"Why, Margot Burke, what on earth do ya think ye're doin'?" The woman was nearly as tall as Sara's father and almost as sturdy. While not as muscular as her father, the woman's build

Margot flinched and stammered, “Nothin’. Just . . . eh . . .”

“We’s playin’ a game,” Paul said, piping up, and the group chimed in with their agreement.

“Yes.” Margot nodded. “We were just playin’ a game with our”—she swallowed hard—“friend here.”

“I see.” The woman turned her attention to Sara, and her eyes widened. “’Tis an odd-lookin’ sort o’ game that leaves a wee gairl lookin’ torn up like this.” She gestured to Sara’s hair and dress, then crouched down to look Sara in the eye. The scent of tea and vanilla wafted up from the folds of her dress as she squatted. “Are ya alright, luhv?”

Tears stung Sara’s eyes once more at the kindness reflected in the woman’s. The lump in her throat was so big, she couldn’t eke out a single word, so she just nodded.

“Mm. Good gairl.” She smiled at Sara and laid a tender hand on her shoulder before returning her attention to the gaggle of children. “I don’t want to hafta tell yer mammy what ye’ve been up to, Margot Burke, but I will. And I’d be willin’ to bet ye’d be the one cryin’ then.”

Margot’s eyes grew wide, and she grasped the woman’s arm. “Oh please, Catríona, don’ do that. I won’t do it again, I promise.”

“Ye’re right about that, lass, ya won’t.”

Margot nodded emphatically.

“That goes fer you too, Paul Callaghan.”

“Yes, miss.”

“Now, ye all git on home.” The woman pointed in the direction of town. “Anois!”

The group jolted off in the direction she was pointing. As

they did, Paul jabbed an elbow into Margot's side. "That's all yer fault!"

"Ow! Is not!" She jabbed back. The bickering continued as they disappeared over the ridge.

Sara looked up at her rescuer again. The woman was watching after the kids and shaking her head as if they might change their minds and come barreling back over the hill.

"Thank ye so much," Sara said, her voice finally returning, though only just.

The woman's attention snapped back to Sara. "Och. Ye poor thing. Are ya sure ye're alright?"

Sara nodded as her chin sank to her chest.

"If ya don't mind me askin', what was that all about?"

Sara fiddled with a loose thread on the bodice of her dress. "They don't like me."

"Ya seem nice enough to me. What's not to like?"

Sara tossed her hands lightly. "They call me a culchie and make fun of my clothes 'cause *m'dhada* can't afford new togs fer me."

"*Tsk!* 'Magine!" The woman shook her head again before sinking down to Sara's height once more. "Ya live out that way?" She hitched her thumb to the west.

Sara nodded.

"I see." The woman bobbed her head as well. "I use ta live out there m'self, ages ago. I know a culchie when I see one. And, believe me, it's not you."

Sara's lips tugged up in a weak smile. "Really?"

"Oh, aye. And I can assure ya, yer clothes are as lovely as a summer's day." She rose to her full height again and extended her right hand. "I'm Catríona."

Sara shook Catríona's outstretched hand. "Sara. Sara Bunratty."

"Well, Sara Bunratty, I hafta be out this way anyhow. Can I walk wit' ye?"

A wide grin broke out on Sara's face, and she bounced up and down on her toes. It would be so nice to have some company on the walk home. "Tá, cinnte!"

———————⟨∞⟩———————

Donal kept his head down as he clomped up the road toward town. He couldn't remember the last time he'd set foot in Lisdoonvarna. His feed supplier was in the opposite direction down the Doolin Road, and living at Ferry Hill, Donal mostly spent any time away from home—which was as little as possible—in that direction. So, heading to Lisdoonvarna, wearing his tweed waistcoat, felt altogether foreign. And to be heading there for a matchmaking festival? Ridiculous.

How could he have let Sara talk him into such nonsense? Trampling the dirt pathway now, free from Sara's pleading gaze—at least until he met her on the road as she came home from school—Donal's resolution faltered. He jammed his fists into his pockets. Utter nonsense. He was a grown man who'd married once and ran a successful . . . well, mostly successful . . . farm. He was more than capable of meeting his own wife. It was the ridiculous show of it all. The courting, the expectations. That's what had made his marriage to Connie so ideal. No small talk or inane chitchat. Just a simple agreement between two adults to share their lives together without any preconceived notions of sweeping romance or any other *seafóid* of the sort.

Now, he was thrusting himself straight into the eye of the storm by agreeing to attend the festival. And for what?

Sure, he could go under the guise of a livestock deal—the *féile* coincided with several market days. But he knew everyone would see right through him. That's half the reason they held the market days when they did, for Pete's sake. The last thing he needed was the likes of Black-eyed Jack or Fatty Boyle sidling up to him with a wink at the end of a livestock bargain, asking about his real intentions. No, any single man setting foot in Lisdoonvarna in the month of September had only one reason to do so, and everyone knew it.

He ripped the flatcap from his head. Hang it all, he couldn't do it. He turned an about-face and took a few paces back toward home. He'd just have to explain to Sara that it wasn't going to work out this year.

His gaze drifted toward the horizon, and in the distance, white caps adorned the top of the sea like a lace doily. He could hear his daughter's voice in his head. *She's all dressed up with nowhere to go, Da.*

Sara would understand. Wouldn't she?

He stopped short in the middle of the road. Aye, she would understand. But she shouldn't have to. She should have a mother at home to help braid her hair and teach her how to keep a house. Instead, she was learning to be the *bean an tí* from her auld man and had to keep her hair short because, though her da could tie a thousand knots in a rope, he couldn't learn to plait hair to save his life.

He at least needed to talk to her again. He checked the sky. Sara should be on her way from school now. He'd meet her on the road, and they'd have a chat. Tugging his hat back in place, he turned toward town again. And as he crested the ridge, he stopped short once more.

Sara was talking to a woman. His daughter's dress was torn, and her hair disheveled. Was that a streak of blood on her arm?

"Oy!" He hurried to Sara's side. "What're ya like, eh? What've ye done to my girl?" He grabbed the woman's elbow and yanked her away from his child. Then he scooped Sara up and brushed the hair from her face. "Are ye alright, peata?" His eyes searched her face.

Before Sara could answer, he set her down and turned to face the woman. She was nearly the same height as him, and she showed no sign of remorse or anxiousness. "What d'ya mean messin' with a wee girl like this? Eh?" He closed the distance between them. "*Abair liom!*"

The woman held her hands up, palms outward. "Ya misunderstand—"

"Oh, do I?"

Sara touched his hand and he stilled. "She was helpin' me, Da. It was Margot and them."

Donal's head spun to look at his little girl. "Och, peata, what happened?" He knelt down in front of her.

His jaw ached and his gut seethed as Sara told him about what the other kids did to her.

A tear slid down her cheek. "Then they said, 'What're ya gonna do? Tell yer mam—'" Her face crumpled, and she collapsed against his shoulder, sobbing.

"Oh, darlin'." He swooped circles on her back with his hand. "I . . . I'm so sorry. So, so sorry. Shh." As he stood up, his daughter still in his arms, he flinched when a silent hand extended a handkerchief in front of him.

"Oh, thank you." He'd completely forgotten the woman was there.

She nodded. "'Course. I came upon them just after they said that horrible thing. Sara landed a hearty slap on Margot's cheek, and the group pounced." She reached over and stroked a strand of hair from Sara's forehead and tucked it behind her ear. Sara's sobs quieted, except for an occasional double breath as she rested her head on his shoulder.

The woman continued, "I got to her as soon as I could, but not before they got a wee piece of revenge." She twisted her lips to the side and shrugged. "I told that Margot I'd be havin' words wit' her parents if I ever heard of her doing anything of the sort again."

Donal stared at the woman. "Thank you," he managed to say at length. "And sorry, 'bout before."

She flapped her hand. "Don't be. I'd have done the same thing if it were my little girl."

"Oh? How old is she?"

The woman's face crinkled in confusion. "What?"

"Your daughter?"

"Oh, well, I don't have a daughter. But if I did, and she was even half as lovely as wee Sara here, I'd be over the moon."

Sara lifted her head and smiled at the woman. "Yeah?"

The woman gave an exaggerated nod. "Oh, aye! But I bet even she wouldn't hold a candle to ye—so kind and cultured."

Sara grinned at the praise. The woman told Donal how the children had been antagonizing Sara and calling her a culchie—a dig at her poverty and lack of station meant to imply that a person was backward and "too country" for civilized people.

"But we know better, don't we, Sara?" the woman said.

Sara wriggled until Donal set her down. "We sure do, Catríona!" Sara scurried over and wrapped her arms around the woman's hips. Catríona looked surprised for a split second, but then she slid an arm around Sara's shoulders and squeezed.

"Us cultured Clare girls gotta stick together, don' we?" Catríona sent a conspiratorial wink in Donal's direction, and he noticed for the first time how blue her eyes were. His breath hitched in his chest.

Sara giggled. "Mm-hmm!"

Standing there, watching his daughter revel in the embrace

of a compassionate woman who had been kind enough to show his little girl even a tiny spate of appropriate maternal affection, Donal swallowed hard against the lump that formed in his throat. What was the matter with him?

"Well, thank you—eh, Catríona, is it?"

"Yep!" Sara chimed.

"Thanks for all ya did for Sara. I really appreciate it."

Sara poked her thumb in his direction. "He's Donal. Donal Bunratty."

Heat crept up Donal's cheeks at the realization that all his manners had vanished in the span of five minutes.

Catríona extended her hand. "I'm Catríona Daly, and you're quite welcome."

Donal accepted her hand and shook it, trying to ignore the way her skin felt so silky on his. They locked eyes for a brief moment, and he pulled free from her grip and slid his fingers into his pocket.

"Now, I'm afraid I must be off," Catríona said. "I'm late for an appointment."

"Of course." Donal nodded. "*Slán abhaile.*"

Catríona nodded. "Slán. Bye, Sara."

"Bye!" Sara waved wildly as Catríona disappeared over the ridge heading toward Lisdoonvarna.

"Let's go home, peata," he said and turned toward their bungalow. He looked down at Sara and she walked step-for-step beside him, her face turned up at him with a wide grin on her face.

"What?" he asked.

She shrugged and skipped ahead of him. "Oh, nothing."

5

Catríona quickened her pace back to town. She'd hoped to have more time after meeting with Widow Clancy before her scheduled meeting with Andrew Osborne and his parents. Now, her plans to spend all her time preening, plaiting her hair, and the like were cut short. Thankfully she'd pulled her mother's evening dress out of the trunk to air out last night. The wrinkles should be mostly gone now, so at least she'd have something appropriate to wear to the Queens Hotel.

Normally, even when meeting with well-to-do families and gentry, Catríona wasn't expected to match the wardrobe expectations of the class. Her normal frock served its purpose just fine, and everyone understood she wasn't there to fit into the social norms—she was there to broker a deal. But this? This meeting was different. From the get-go she wanted Andrew to see that she could fit into his world . . . and her goal was to make him *want* her to fit into his world.

Wee Sara's predicament on the road had set her behind schedule. Though, if she was honest, she didn't mind. She was glad to be of help. She'd been there—having been called a culchie plenty of times in her childhood by the oh-so-cultured children of Lisdoonvarna. She rolled her eyes at the memories.

Those kids wouldn't last a day in Dublin or London or Vienna. Nowadays, no one remembered that the Dalys used to live out in the country. Or if they did, they chose to overlook it because of what Catríona and her father could do for them. So the sight of the poor girl being pushed around by those bullies had broken something inside of her, and she couldn't help but get involved.

Catríona shook her head to refocus her thoughts as she hastened toward home. Once there, she put on her mother's dress—with no small amount of effort. Though slightly dated in style, it wasn't vintage enough to look completely out of place. Studying herself in the looking glass, she frowned. The bodice was a little too snug, and the fabric pulled in places it wasn't meant to. Sighing, she reached behind to loosen the tie at the back, but it was as loose as it would go. Bother.

She'd just have to focus on her other features. After brushing through her long ash-brown hair, she managed to pin it in an intricate updo. She smiled. All those hours playing with her hair in front of the mirror as a child were paying off, it would seem.

"See, Mother, 'twasn't wasted time, after all," Catríona spoke to the room even as her mother's words echoed in her head.

"What're ya spendin' all that time fer on yer locks? It'll make no lick o' difference when no one'll be lookin' at ye anyway."

Catríona scowled at the memory but shook the thought free when she noticed how the expression accentuated the lines on her face. In the distance, the angelus tolled.

"Muise, that can't be the time!" With a final pinch of her cheeks, she rushed downstairs, while biting her lips hoping to bring a bit of color to them.

Grateful no one stopped her to chat as she scurried through the pub, she approached the Queens Hotel not five minutes later. She slowed her pace. As she waited for her breathing to slow, she admired the columned entryway gracing the three-story building, which was whitewashed to catch the muted light of so many misty Irish mornings. Wrought iron railings in decorative scrolls stretched across the top of the portico and balconies hung over the extended dining areas. Finally, ready to face her clients, she ascended the steps and thanked the doorman as she entered the grand entryway.

Mahogany-paneled walls and floors stretched before her, gleaming in the lantern light of the two-story entrance hall. The foyer gave way to the check-in area, which boasted stone walls and polished wood floors adorned with intricately woven rugs. The commanding front desk was made of the same mahogany as the floor and was flanked by gleaming mahogany pillars, with the grand staircase a little farther to the left.

Catríona puffed out a breath and slowly wagged her head. What must it be like to experience such luxury day in and day out? She lifted a silent prayer that her life might soon consist of such things and entered a small sitting room off the left of the foyer. A group of plush wingback chairs covered in rich, scarlet velvet flanked a stone fireplace. An older gentleman sat in one of the chairs, reading the newspaper. Next to him, a woman who looked to be about that same age stared into the dancing flames in the fireplace grate and sipped tea from a fine china cup. And there, at the large bay window, stood Andrew.

Catríona's breath caught in her chest at the sight of him. Dressed in an impeccably tailored suit, he gazed out at the rolling hills of the Clare countryside, hands lazily lingering in his trouser pockets. A dark shadow of stubble lined his chiseled jaw, and the late afternoon light streaming in bathed him in a golden halo. Catríona could have studied him all day like that. Alas, there was work to be done. Work that required her to be close to Andrew, with Andrew, talking to Andrew. She smiled at the thought.

She pulled her shoulders straight and approached the family. "Good afternoon, Lord and Lady Osborne."

Lord Osborne folded his paper and rose. "Good afternoon, Miss Daly. Good of you to come." He shook her hand. "This is my wife, Lady Ruth Osborne."

Catríona dipped a shallow curtsy. "How do you do?"

Lady Osborne joined her husband at his side. "Charmed, I'm sure." She looked to the window. "Andrew, don't be rude. Do come and introduce yourself."

Catríona looked to Andrew, who now faced her. His eyes registered something she couldn't decipher. Then, a wide grin broke out on his face, and Catríona willed the pounding in her chest to still for fear her clients would hear it.

"Miss Daly," Andrew said as he closed the distance between them.

"Mist—" Her voice cracked, and she cleared her throat. "Mister Osborne."

He reached out and took her hand, then lifted it to his lips and brushed a kiss to the backs of her fingers. In an instant, every inch of her hand came alive with electricity, and she had to fight to keep her eyes from fluttering closed at the feel of his lips on her skin.

He straightened and locked his gaze with hers. "I had no idea Lisdoonvarna's matchmaker would be the loveliest girl in town." His mouth crooked sideways in an enchantingly lop-sided smile. "That must make your job quite difficult, indeed."

Before Catríona could answer, Lady Osborne swatted her son's arm. "Really, Andrew, have some decorum!"

The lady gestured to the chairs. "Please, Miss Daly, have a seat and I'll ring for some more tea."

Once the tray had arrived with their refreshments and they were all settled in their chairs, Catríona began. "Why don't you begin by telling me a little bit about yourself, what you're looking for, and what happened with your most recent match."

"Yes, of course." Lady Osborne shifted in her seat. "We're looking for a young lady who can handle the rigors of gentry life in County Dublin. She must understand the tenuous nuances of both the social and political climate in order to best protect our family's livelihood in the area." She continued on, but Catríona struggled to focus on what the woman was saying. She could feel Andrew's dark blue eyes boring into her like he was studying a map, wanting to memorize every path and trail. Her cheeks warmed under his gaze, and she fought to make some semblance of sense out of his mother's words.

When Andrew spoke, Catríona jolted at the deep timbre of his voice. "Yes, yes, Mother. That's all very well and good. But that's what you want for my wife. Shouldn't we be talking about what I want?" He addressed his mother, but his glance flickered to Catríona, and as it did, his lips flashed the briefest hint of a smile. Gracious, the man was handsome. And charming.

"*Psh!*" Lady Osborne flapped her gloved hand. "After the last disaster, I should think your father and I need be much more involved. This match carries with it far more importance than just your preference of hair color and disposition, Andrew."

"Be a good lad now, son, and listen to your mother," Lord Osborne said, taking a lazy sip of his tea.

Catríona's gaze bounced between the three Osbornes as her mind raced to formulate her own plan. Parents were always very closely involved in the proceedings—in truth, the actual bride and groom had very little to do with any of it if they were still living at home. But for some reason, Catríona had envisioned dealing mainly with Andrew himself, like she did with more-established bachelors who'd already lived on their own. She'd forgotten that single gentlemen often lived at home until they wed . . . and even then, many stayed on the family estate with the rest of the extended family. Catríona would have to be very strategic in how she approached both parents and son. She needed more information.

"Speaking of the previous match, I understand that you were matched during the festival last year?" she asked Andrew.

"A true debacle, the whole thing," Lady Osborne replied.

"She was asking me, Mother," Andrew added. "And, yes, we went through a matchmaker in the next village. Figgy something-or-other."

Catríona nodded. "Figgy McDougal, aye."

"You know the fellow?" Lord Osborne asked. "I assumed he would be worth his salt, but clearly I was mistaken."

There was an unwritten rule among matchmakers to never disparage one another's work. Figgy wasn't a bad matchmaker. He had just gotten sloppy in his later years, taking less and less time to fully vet out potential matches. A few of his pairings had failed in recent years, but Catríona would never say as much to a client.

She shrugged. "Matchmaking isn't an exact science. Even though two people may look perfect for each other on paper, they aren't compatible when it comes down to day-to-day life together."

Lady Osborne sniffed. "Well, that girl wouldn't have been—how did you put it . . . compatible . . . with a rock."

"*Tsk*, Mother." A shadow flashed in Andrew's eyes before he replaced it with his blindingly handsome grin. "She was a lovely girl. It just wasn't the right match." He shrugged sheepishly and turned his attention back to Catríona. "For either of us."

Butterflies danced in her stomach, which she sucked in a

wee bit as she straightened her posture. "Well, let's just make sure we do get the right one this time, eh?" She held his gaze, though it was almost too intense to do so.

"Sounds good to me," he said, not breaking their eye contact. His cheek creased in a heart-stopping dimple as he added, "Very good."

6

The sun was already below the horizon when Donal turned off the Bog Road onto an tStráid Mhór. Lamplight flickered and danced on a sea of flatcaps and ladies' tam o'shanters. Donal's steps slowed as he surveyed the crowd of people. Traditional music spilled out of pub doors and windows into the main street, while lively conversations and laughter mixed together to create a unique, dull roar that seemed to rise through the narrow street up toward the sky.

"*O mo léan*," he whispered. He knew the early days of the festival drew a crowd, but good grief, this was far more people than he was prepared to see. *And Sara wonders why we never come to town!* As he wound his way through the mob, his eyes scanned the buildings. Every pub and open business touted activities for the féile on makeshift banners that hung from windows or on slate signs in the doorways. Where to begin?

He made his way through the center of town, to the square. On the way, places like the Imperial Hotel, the Royal Spa, Lynch's Hotel, and the Ritz were full nigh to bursting with merrymakers dancing, drinking, and presumably people making connections ten times over. Donal stood in the square and spun in a slow circle. How was he to know which establishment to choose? Were the matches formally made or did one simply hope that luck of the numbers would all but guarantee each person would find someone?

When he faced the direction he'd started in, he decided to begin at the first place that caught his eye. The entrance to Lynch's Hotel opened onto the square, and golden light spilled from its many windows. Upon entering, Donal very nearly ran into a young lady with black hair and striking blue eyes. "Terribly sorry. Pardon me," he said.

The woman stopped, looked him from head to toe, laughed, and continued on her way.

Donal watched after her for a moment. "I guess she's not my soulmate," he muttered to himself. After a moment, he turned and headed for the pub. The crowd was so thick from wall to wall, he could hardly enter the room. In a far corner, the pulsing beat of a *bodhrán* pumped out a rhythm while all around, heads bounced in time with the cadence.

"Will ya have a drink?" the barkeep called over the din.

Donal winced and shook his head. "No, t'anks. Was just leavin'."

The man shrugged and went back to polishing the pint glass in his hand.

Donal hurried back out into the fresh night air. This was never going to work. Poor Sara would be so disappointed. But she had no way of knowing what the festival would be like— how many people would be crammed into pub after pub with music so loud you couldn't hold a decent conversation with anyone. He'd just have to find another way to keep his promise that he'd find a companion.

As he hustled down the street toward home, one window caught his eye. The pub attached to the Imperial Hotel had only a few figures sitting at tables in seemingly hushed conversation. Perhaps a wee pint before going home to disappoint his daughter would bolster his spirits and dull the sting. He sidled up to the bar and sat on a stool next to an older gentleman with a shock of white hair standing up in every direction.

"*Dia duit, a mhac!*" the man said after draining the last of his own pint.

Donal only barely glanced at the man. "*Dia is Muire dhuit,*" he muttered the customary response to the greeting.

"What'll ya have?" the man asked, then turned and gestured to the barkeep. "Peadar, set this one up!"

Donal gave the man his full attention and waved his hand in protest. "No, no, that's quite alright. Just stopping in for a pint before I go home."

"No one drinks alone in my pub," the old man replied. "Name's Jimmy. Jimmy Daly." He stuck his hand out.

Donal eyed his hand for a split second before shaking it. "Donal. Donal Bunratty."

Jimmy's eyes twinkled, and his brows hitched upward. "Bunratty, eh? Ya Paddy's lad?"

Peadar slid a pint of dark Irish stout in front of Donal. He took a sip, then licked his lips and shook his head. "Paddy was my uncle. My father was Seán Bunratty."

"Och!" Jimmy slapped his knee. "O'course, o'course, out on the farm at Ferry Hill!"

Donal shifted to face the man more fully. "Aye, y'know it?"

Jimmy lifted his own fresh pint to his lips. "I do, I do. Yer auld man was one o' the good ones. I use ta be at Knocknaguilla. Ages ago."

Donal nodded. His father and this man had practically been neighbors. At least in the countryside way of measuring. "Well, 'tis nice to meet ya."

"Likewise." Jimmy clapped a hand on Donal's shoulder. "I've not seen ya in town before. Did yer work bring ya here?"

Donal rubbed the back of his neck, wanting to dispel the heat that crept up it at the man's question. "Eh, no. Not really." He studied the foam on the top of his glass and wiped it away with his finger, trying to ignore the sensation that Jimmy was studying him.

"Lemme guess, the féile?"

When Donal didn't answer, Jimmy only chuckled and rested his elbows on the bar top. The pair enjoyed their drinks in comfortable silence for a long while until a loud crash outside drew their attention. A patron carrying a tray of drinks had run into the back of a jaunting cart.

"Are, eh, are ye closing soon?" Donal asked.

Jimmy nearly choked on his drink. "At barely seven o'clock? Not a chance. We'll be open until the wee hours of the morning. Often we're going until lunch the next day!"

Donal's jaw fell slack and his brows soared. "Truly? Until midday tomorrow?"

"Ooh, aye." Jimmy nodded heartily. "During the festival, once the sun goes down, it's go, go, go until it comes back up. Many places will have things going on in the daytime—picnics, day trips, t'ings o' that sort. The Ritz even has a noon dance session."

Donal chewed his lip as he considered what Jimmy said. He pivoted on his stool and looked around the room. "If ya don't mind me asking, every other place is packed—a man can't even get in the door. Why is it so . . . quiet . . . in here?"

Jimmy chuckled. "Normally it's chockablock in here, but I just sent the crowd off on a sunset walking tour with one o' the lads that helps me out. They'll be back shortly."

"I see."

Jimmy waved Peadar over. "*Pionta uisce, le do thoil,*" he muttered and then turned his attention back to Donal. "So, ye're here for the matchmakin', are ye?" Jimmy waited until Donal met his gaze. The twinkle remained in the man's eyes, but there was no hint of jest or tease. The warmth from the drink was starting to spread, filling Donal's chest with a bit of resolve and courage. What could it hurt to tell this man why he was here?

He downed the last of his stout and dragged his sleeve across his mouth as Peadar set a glass of water in front of Jimmy. Jimmy drank it down in one go like a man who'd been wandering the desert without a drop to drink for days.

"Go on, lad," he said.

Donal told Jimmy about his marriage to Connie, about Sara, Connie's death, and his financial hardships. "Her birthday was last week," he said, looking at Jimmy. "Sara's. Her one wish was for me to come to the féile."

Jimmy pressed a hand to his chest and tsked. "So you can find a wife?"

Donal ran a hand down his face. "That, and . . . to find her a mother."

"Peadar! *Cupán tae* fer the lad!"

Donal couldn't help the chuckle that rattled his chest at Jimmy's gesture of sympathy. When it came to healing wounds of the heart, most Irishmen turned either to the cuppa or the pint. And some sorrows were simply too strong for the pint and had to be handled solely by the cupán tae.

Jimmy sidled up closer to Donal and lowered his voice. "I'll tell ya, if it's a wife ye're after, ye've come to the right place."

"Have I now?"

"Tá, cinnte. The Dalys are the best matchmakers in the parish." He cupped his hand around his mouth and added in a hoarse near-whisper, "The best in the whole of Ireland, if ya ask me."

"No one ever asks ye, Jimmy," Peadar said with a laugh as he set the tea service in front of Donal. "And yet, ye always tell them anyway."

"Och! Away wit' ye, ya messer!" Jimmy snatched the towel from Peadar's hand and batted it at him playfully.

A true laugh bubbled up from Donal's chest now, and he let it roll through his lips. "You mean to tell me that ye're a matchmaker?" He couldn't help the way his voice hitched an octave as he asked the question. Jimmy Daly looked nothing like he imagined a matchmaker to look. Donal had envisioned an old lady with a broom in her hand and a kerchief on her head or something of that ilk. Not a wild-haired man with a twinkle in his eyes.

"Is that so strange to ye?" He got up, circled the bar, and began washing his pint glasses.

"Well, yes, 'tis, actually." Donal laughed.

Jimmy shrugged. "Maybe ye should get to town more often." He winked as he set the clean glasses on the shelf. He turned and rested his elbows on the bar. "I'd like to help ya. And yer wee gairl."

Donal blinked hard and shifted in his seat. "Ya would?"

Jimmy nodded, then looked past Donal and held up his finger, asking someone to wait. Donal glanced behind him to see a tall, slender gentleman in a top hat and coat in the doorway. "I'll be right with ye, sir," Jimmy said.

"I'll let ya go."

"So ye'll let me make ye a match?"

"T'anks, Jimmy, but I can't."

"Nonsense!"

Donal dropped his gaze to the polished wood of the bar. "I canna pay ye."

"*Psh.*" Jimmy flapped his hand. "Don't worry about that part. It always works out in the end. I promise I'll be fair."

When Donal hesitated, Jimmy added, "Think of wee Sara."

"Now that's hittin' below the belt, Jimmy," Donal said, half in jest.

Jimmy just pasted a sheepish grin on his face and turned his palms up as if to say, "What do you expect?"

"Come back to me here tomorrow night," he said as he made his way to the fancy gentleman in the doorway. "Eight o'clock," he called over his shoulder.

Donal sighed. "Aye."

"Grand, so!" Jimmy clapped his hands once and sent a twinkly-eyed wink Donal's way before escorting his new guest into a small room off the side of the main pub.

"I'll be here," Donal murmured under his breath. "I don't know why, but I'll be here."

7

At eight o'clock sharp, Donal stood outside the Imperial, trying to work up the courage to go inside. He wasn't sure if he was more afraid that Jimmy wouldn't be able to match him . . . or that he would. Sara had gotten a grand kick out of the whole thing and had been trying to get rid of him all evening. But he wasn't about to show up any earlier than absolutely necessary. No matter, he was here now. No sense in standing in the street.

A gust of warm air greeted him as he opened the door to the pub. The inside glowed orange from the lantern light and the fire in the grate. And unlike the previous night, the pub was full wall-to-wall with people.

I guess Jimmy was right about that at least. Chockablock, indeed.

He scanned the throng, looking for a shock of wild white hair. He found it up at the bar, then he heard Jimmy's robust voice telling some story or another to a completely enraptured crowd.

Donal got as close as he could, then waited for the story to be done. Raucous laughter erupted at the punchline, and Jimmy stood, shaking hands and patting backs as he made his way toward the small room off the side of the entrance.

When he caught Donal's eye, Jimmy's face brightened even further—something Donal wouldn't have thought possible—and he held his hands up over his head like the victor in a race.

"Donal! Ya made it!" He turned course and worked his way through the crowd toward him.

They shook hands and Jimmy shouted in Donal's ear over the din, "I'm afraid I canna work with ye tonight, lad."

The sinking in Donal's heart took him by surprise. "Oh, that's grand. It's fine, it's fine."

Jimmy shook his head. "'Tis not fine, but 'tis the life of a matchmaker. I've got a verra important pairing I'm workin' on."

Donal nodded. "Don't give it another thought."

"Remember that fella from last night? The fancy one?"

"Aye."

"That's Earl Wyndham, and he's asked me to match his daughter. I must see to them tonight. But not to worry. My daughter's the best matchmaker in the county!"

Donal's brows drew together. "But I thought you were the best in the county?"

"Who'd ya think taught m' daughter?" He winked and erupted into a spate of laughter.

Donal joined in with a chuckle. "Fair enough."

"Anyway, I'm heading to the Queens Hotel to see to the earl and his gairl." He gestured to the small side room. "My daughter's in my office, and she's expectin' ye. Go on in. It's just as good as if I was makin' yer match."

Donal eyed the entrance to the so-called office. Working with Jimmy was awkward enough, but his daughter?

Jimmy shuffled behind him as he made his way to the main exit. He gently nudged Donal forward. "Ah, g'on, g'on."

Donal rolled his eyes. "Alright, alright. I'll go." As he wove around merrymakers and one couple that was snogging in the center of the mob, he tried to imagine what Jimmy Daly's daughter might be like. He envisioned a female version of the old man, with wild, long hair, weather-worn skin, and a twinkle in her eyes. He smiled at the ridiculous image his mind had created. Maybe this wouldn't be so bad, after all.

But as he entered the small office, he stopped short. Two women sat behind the table in hushed but animated conversation. No wacky hair greeted him. No leathered skin from years of exposure to the elements. Rather, the exact opposite of who he'd envisioned sat at the table backed up to the bay window. While both women were lovely in their own right, his pulse quickened at the sight of one of them, and he inwardly chided himself for the way his breath refused to leave his chest.

"Catríona?" He breathed at last.

Her gaze shot up to meet his. Her forehead creased for a brief second, and confusion clouded her eyes.

"You helped my daughter on the road the other day."

Recognition dawned. "Ah, yes. Dougal, is it?"

He blanched. "It's Donal, actually."

The other woman snorted. "Nice one, Caty."

Catríona shot the woman a look. "That's enough outta you, Maeve. Out ya go."

"Fine, fine," Maeve said, laughing. "I was just leavin' anyway. Good night to ye, Donal." She emphasized his name loudly in Catríona's direction.

"Slán," he murmured as she brushed past him.

Catríona rolled her eyes at her friend before turning her attention to him. "Right." She winced. "Sorry, Donal. Please do come in."

Catríona fought to keep from crinkling her nose at the hint of manure that wafted up from Donal's boots as he rounded the chair and sat down. Craning her neck, she strained to see the mantel clock on the shelf over the bar. Eight o'clock. She bit back an oath. She'd hoped to spend the evening helping Andrew find a match at the dance over at the Queens Hotel. Well . . . that's what she would say, anyway. And, in truth, she *was* hoping to help him find a match. Just, perhaps, not the match anyone was expecting.

But, no, her father had sprung Donal's case on her just before she could head out the door. God bless her auld man. He had the softest heart of any man she knew. It served him well in his matchmaking, but it was also his Achilles' heel, leading him to take people on for pairing when he had no time to do so. Then again, that's what this whole festival was all about. They always overextended themselves.

"Sure, 'tis only a month," her father had always said. "We can do an'thing fer a month."

Perhaps he was right—it was their livelihood, after all. But that fact didn't help her now, sitting across from the Farmer in the Dell when she could be spending her evening with Prince Charming. The sooner she got the particulars out of the way with Donal, the sooner she could get over to Andrew before someone else could catch his eye.

"So, Mister . . . eh"—she checked her notes—"Bunratty, is it?"

"Aye." He shifted in his seat, his cheeks pink. "But Donal is fine. Never was one to stand on ceremony."

She studied him for a beat. His clothes were clean and tidy yet worn in places. He clearly took care of himself, but one would never mistake him for a titled man. Yes, it did seem odd to address him so formally. "Very well," she said. "So, Donal, what are ya lookin' for in a wife?"

He blanched for a moment. Catríona couldn't help the smile that tickled the corner of her lips. His inexperience and unassuming nature were a refreshing change of pace from the typical farmers who traipsed into her office. He cleared his throat. "I . . . I don't really know. I hadn't expected you to ask that question." He chuckled and his dark stubble creased in his cheeks. "Which seems silly, given yer occupation."

Catríona laughed. "Good point." She glanced at the mantel clock again. "I know it can be a mite . . . uncomfortable . . . to have conversations like these. But needs must, I suppose. Aye?"

His stoic countenance returned, and he scratched at his jaw. "So it would seem."

"Let's try this, tell me about yer job." Though she needn't have asked. It was clear.

"I'm a farmer." Then he added, "For now." But he'd said it so quietly, Catríona wasn't sure she'd heard him correctly.

She looked up from her paper. His head was down, and he was picking at a thread on the edge of his sleeve. When his gaze met hers again, his eyes held a sadness that made her pause. For a split second, she wondered what sort of heartache he'd endured to bring him to this point. She cleared the thought with a sip of tea from her now-tepid cup, nodded, and scribbled *farmer* on her notepad next to his name. "And are ya lookin' for help on the farm?"

When he didn't answer, she looked up at him again. His hazel eyes were boring into hers, and he seemed at the same time lost in thought.

"Are ya?" she asked again.

He blinked and shifted in his seat. "Help. Aye."

She made another note. "Right, so we need someone who's familiar with the processes of farming in the West—or at the very least willing to learn and get her hands dirty."

He shrugged. "I s'pose."

"And what about looks? What're ya lookin' fer there?"

"Doesn't matter."

Her scribbling stilled. "I beg yer pardon?"

"I don't care about looks or an'thing like that." He raked his fingers through his hair and crossed an ankle over his knee.

"No preference whatsoever?" Catríona was used to all manner of blokes coming in with a list as long as their arm of what they were lookin' for—and it wasn't about a woman's personality.

He shook his head.

Who was this man? She pressed her brows high. "But if there's to be roman—"

He stood so fast he nearly knocked the chair over. "Look, I'm not here for romance or passion or whatever ya wanna call it. I made a promise to my daughter . . ." He held up his hand, and a long pause stretched between them. "Look, I need a partner for the farm and a mother for Sara. That's why I'm here. But now I say it, *níl ann ach amaidí.*"

"It's not ridiculous," she said.

"T'anks for yer time." He turned for the door.

"Donal, wait." Catríona stood and rounded the table to stand next to him. "I know this must be very difficult, but ye obviously came here fer a reason."

He flapped his hand. "A silly birthday wish."

She laid her hand on his arm. "Just give it a chance."

He curled and uncurled his fingers, and Catríona tried to ignore the flex of his muscle beneath her hand. She dropped her touch and attempted to infuse some levity to her voice. "Besides, I think ye're underestimatin' the power of a wee girl's birthday wish."

He looked at her from the corner of his eye.

She smiled, hoping to ease the tension creasing his face. "Look, I have a coupla lasses in mind that might be a good fit fer ye." She paused, Sara's face floating across her mind. "And good fer Sara. Will ya at least agree to meet them?"

The mantel clock chimed the half hour as Donal nodded.

"Grand, so." She snatched her cloak from the bench behind the table. "I'll be in touch soon to set things up."

He sighed deeply and lifted his hands in surrender, then stepped back as she brushed past him, heading for the door. She tried to ignore the look of confusion on his face at her hasty retreat, but if she had any hope of seeing Andrew tonight, she had to leave now. A wee dram of guilt niggled at her gut, so she paused at the doorway and turned back.

"It'll be alright." When he didn't respond, she added, "Okay?"

"Okay," he replied. And with that, she hustled out into the chilly September night, feeling his gaze follow her all the way.

8

When Catríona returned to the Imperial at one in the morning, it was just as full as when she'd left. Her father was at the bar with a young fella she'd not seen before. Many people had paired off and were dancing together or sitting at a table chatting over a pint. She wove through the crowd toward the office. When she saw Maeve sitting at her table, she grinned.

"Och, there ya are! I thought ye'd never come back." Maeve yawned. Like Catríona, she was still single. But unlike Catríona, she held no interest in being matched. Having been friends with her since childhood, Catríona had no doubt Maeve would find her love eventually. But Maeve had always had to do things her own way.

"G'on with ye," Catríona said. "It's not that late."

Maeve pinned her with a look. "So, are ya gonna tell me how it went or do I hafta guess?"

Catríona sank down next to her friend and leaned her head back against the seat. "'Twas lovely."

"Aye?" Maeve put her elbow on the back of the bench and rested her head in her hand.

"Mm." Catríona nodded. "When I got there, he was chattin' up Shannon Beehan."

At the mention of Shannon's name, Maeve mimicked tossing her hair over her shoulder and released a girlish giggle.

"Exactly." Catríona rolled her eyes thinking of Shannon's overly flirtatious ways. "But wait'll I tell ya. When he saw me come in, he ended his conversation with her and invited me to sit and have a drink wit' him!"

Maeve's eyes widened. "He did not!"

"*Ar m'fhocal* he did!"

Maeve puffed out a breath. "Well, miracles never cease." She shifted to lay her head against the backrest of the bench and closed her eyes. "What'd ye talk about?"

Catríona sat up straight. "That's the best part! He spent the whole night asking after me!"

Maeve's eyes slid open, and she pursed her lips at Catríona.

"I know." She shook her head. "I wouldn't have believed it either if I wasn't there. In fact, I'm not sure I believe it now." Her mind drifted back to sitting at that table, Andrew's sapphire eyes fixed on her. It was like they were the only two in the room.

"Did he dance wit' ye?"

Catríona's shoulders sank. "No, he said he hates dancing. Something to do with all the balls and cotillions his mother forced him to do as a lad."

"Makes sense." Maeve cracked her eyes open once more. "And it gives you a chance to convince him otherwise." She winked and a low, guttural laugh rumbled in her chest.

Catríona swatted her friend's arm. "What're ya like?" Though she had to admit, she liked the idea. She imagined asking Andrew onto the dance floor for a slow waltz. He would refuse at first, but she'd manage to convince him. His movements would start stilted and awkward, but then they'd lock eyes. His arms would tighten around her, and they'd dance and dance, pulling one another closer with each song.

Her lips crooked up in a smile.

"Oy," Maeve said, shattering the fantasy. "Where'd ye go off to just now?" Amusement laced her voice.

"Oh, nowhere." She turned a sly grin to her friend. "I just like the way you think."

The pair erupted in laughter, even as the images played in Catríona's mind over and over.

"Och, Caty, I'm wrecked," Maeve said when their laughter died down.

"Wanna just stay here tonight? Da won't mind." Catríona gathered up her notepad and cloak.

"Eh, sure, why not." Maeve groaned as she pushed herself up to stand. "It's a mite closer than my house, that's fer sure."

The friends linked elbows and headed up toward the flat, knowing full well the merrymaking downstairs would stretch on until after the sun came up.

⊸◯◯⊷

Donal stared through the dark at the ceiling. He'd been home for hours but sleep still eluded him. Things had been set in motion that he couldn't stop now. And even if he didn't find a suitable match, simply looking for one felt like a turning point after which nothing would ever be the same.

Perhaps that was a good thing. It had been almost six years since Connie's passing, but they'd been living as if it were only yesterday. Maybe it was time to move forward. Yet the thought set such a heavy rock of uncertainty in his gut. He rolled onto his side, facing the empty half of the bed. "It would be nice to have someone to talk to about all of this," he whispered to the pillow.

"Then talk to me."

Donal flinched at the sound of Sara's voice coming from the doorway. "What're ya doin' awake, pet?"

She padded over and crawled into the bed next to him. "I could ask ye the same thing."

He smiled at the gravelly sleep-laced sound of her voice. "Fair enough."

"Did ya meet her?" she asked.

His brows pulled together. "Meet who?"

Sara pulled the covers up over her and yawned. "My new mom."

Donal's chest tightened. "Oh, peata." He tucked a strand of hair behind her ear. "I'm afraid it doesn't work like that."

"Mm." Her voice was drifting quieter. "Maybe tomorrow."

Donal smiled and leaned over to kiss her forehead. "Aye, luhv." He lay back on his pillow and closed his eyes. "Maybe tomorrow."

———∞———

Sara stirred and stretched, willing her eyes to open. The sky was still dark, but her body just knew it was time to get up and start the farm chores. She looked over at her dad, who snored softly. She smiled at his profile and studied it for a minute. She always liked watching him sleep. The sadness went away, and his forehead wasn't crinkled with worry. She was about to brush a light kiss on his cheek when he sucked in a deep breath and slowly released it while he shifted onto his side, pulling the blanket up higher.

In the distance, Sara heard Bó lowing. The poor thing was hungry. Feeding the stock was usually Da's job, but she didn't have the heart to wake him just yet. It was rare that he wasn't up before her, so she decided to let him sleep.

At the back door, she slid her wellies on and buttoned up

her coat. Outside, a silver mist hung in the air, muting all the sounds of the world. This was Sara's favorite kind of morning. She liked to pretend the vapor held magical powers, sprinkling everything and everyone with fairy dust and bringing joy and good luck to them all.

Mooooooo.

"I'm comin', Bó. Hold yer horses!" Sara giggled at her own choice of words, the image of Bó holding the reins of a horse flashing in her mind's eye.

Once in the barn, she greeted all the cows and horses by name and set to work filling their feed troughs with grain and hay from the stash in the corner. Then she went to the well and drew a few bucketsful of water to fill their drinking trough. By the time she started mucking out the stables, the sun had begun to peek over the horizon.

A soft glow in the kitchen window told her Da had woken up and was fixing his morning cuppa. Sara's mouth watered at the thought of tea and toast. She'd head in for her breakfast soon.

"Hello?" a woman's voice called from the barn entrance. "Mister Bunr— er . . . Donal?"

Sara poked her head out from one of the stalls. "Catríona!" She ran over to greet her new friend.

Catríona's face brightened, and she rewarded Sara with a wide grin. "Sara! How are you?"

"I'm grand now!"

Catríona scanned the inside of the barn.

"Da's inside. Makin' breakfast." Sara picked up a strand of hay and broke it into pieces.

Catríona looked to the house and back. "Oh, right. I wondered if I might be a bit early."

"Nah." Sara flapped her hand. "We're always up early. Wanna meet my cows?"

Catríona chuckled. "Of course I do."

Sara took Catríona's hand and led her to the first stall. "This is Bó."

"Nice to meet you, Bó," Catríona said, stroking the bridge of the bull's nose.

"And this," Sara said, tugging Catríona to the next stall, "is Bó a Dó."

Catríona laughed. "I see. So, we have Cow and Cow Two?"

Sara beamed. "Mm-hmm!" She pointed to the next beast in line. "And that's Bó a Trí."

"And let me guess," Catríona said, gesturing to the last one in line. "Bó a Ceathair?"

Sara crinkled her nose. "No, that's Pete."

"That's what I get for lettin' the wee one name the cattle."

Sara and Catríona both spun toward the voice. "Mornin', Da!" Sara skipped over and hugged him.

"*Maidín mhaith, a stóir.*" He bent and kissed the top of her head, then scanned the barn. "Did ya already feed 'em?"

Sara grinned and nodded, pride swelling in her chest. "You were still sleepin', so I thought I'd surprise ya."

Her dad knelt down and held her shoulders. "Ye're somethin' else, ya know that?"

"Yep!" Her dad and Catríona both laughed, and Sara's stomach growled. "I'm hungry. Can I get breakfast?"

He nodded. "Oh, aye, I'd say ye've earned it. In fact, have two pieces of toast."

Her mouth formed into an O shape, her eyes pulled open wide. "Really? T'anks!" She kissed his cheek and ran off toward the house, calling over her shoulder, "Bye, Catríona!"

9

Donal watched Catríona pet Bó's head. "She's very sweet," she said, gaze trained on the cow.

"Eh, that's a boy," he said as he stepped closer, humor lacing his voice.

Catríona looked to him, confusion painted on her face for a moment before recognition dawned of what he'd said. "Och, I was talkin' about Sara."

A deep chuckle rumbled in his chest. "I know." He joined her in front of Bó's stable. "And, yes, she is."

"It is very clever naming yer herd Cow One, Two, and Three." She smiled and met his gaze. Her eyes, the color of sea glass, sparkled with delight.

"Don't forget Pete," he said.

Catríona threw her head back and laughed. "No, how could I forget Pete."

Donal warmed at the sound of her laugh and couldn't help but match her smile. It reminded him of sunlight on the sea. The thought arrested him, and he turned suddenly to grab a pile of hay. Never mind that Sara had already fed the cattle, he needed something to bring him back to his senses.

"I presume you didn't come here to discuss my daughter's

pet-naming habits?" he asked, shoving too much feed into the already full trough.

She sighed. "Alas, I did not, though I do believe it's a topic I could discuss at length now I think about it."

Donal bit his lip to keep from smiling as he moved down the line, gifting Bó a Dó, Bó a Trí, and Pete with extra food. The poor beasts wouldn't know that meant they'd get less tonight. He winced at the thought. "How can I help ya, miss?" He straightened and wiped his hands on his trousers. "I've a lot to get done today."

"Of course." She stepped away from the stall and clasped her hands at her waist. "I wanted to see if you might be free for a midday meal?"

He stilled, a shovel in his hand. Was she asking him to lunch? His heart quickened, but he efforted to keep his face stoic. "I have to eat one way or another, so I suppose I could manage."

Catríona grinned. "Grand! She'll be here at one o'clock, with all the trappings for a picnic."

Donal blinked. "She?"

"Aye!" Catríona nodded. "Máiréad Bailey. She's one of the lasses I was tellin' ye about last night."

"Right." Donal tried not to huff as though he'd been punched in the gut. "Of course."

Catríona stepped closer, her brow creased. "Is that alright? Do ya already know her?"

He shook his head. "No, no, 'tis fine." He knew this was what Catríona was going to be doing. What would possess him to think she'd be matching herself with anyone? He didn't know much about the matchmaking trade, but he was fairly certain that wasn't how it worked. Never mind the fact that he felt betrayed by his own self that he would even hope she would want to spend time with him in that way. *Amadán.* This was exactly why he didn't want to mess with any of this romance nonsense. It pulled his attention away from what really mattered—saving the farm and giving his daughter the mother she deserved.

"One o'clock," he repeated. "Grand."

"Brilliant!" She flashed him an equally brilliant smile. "Ye're gonna love her. I know it."

Donal could only nod.

"Well, I must be off." Catríona headed for the door. "I'll be in touch again to see how it goes with Máiréad." She scurried from the barn, but then stopped and turned back. "Tell Sara I said goodbye."

"I will." He lifted his hand in a wave goodbye and watched as she headed across his property to the road and disappeared.

———————⟨∞⟩———————

One o'clock arrived all too soon, and just as the bells finished tolling, a remarkably tall woman with a shock of bright red hair—and equally bright red cheeks—came up the front walk to the cottage. Donal ducked behind the entrance to the barn, feeling every bit the foolish schoolboy.

"Da!" Sara's voice called from the back door of the cottage. "Someone's here ta see ya."

Donal squeezed his eyes shut and muttered to himself, "Sara. You're doin' this for Sara."

Drawing a long, deep breath through his nose, he ran his fingers through his hair and set a determined pace across the yard to the house. Before he even entered, he could hear the stranger's voice carrying through the closed windowpanes. His pulse quickened. Was she yelling at Sara?

He took the three stairs to the back door in one long stride and burst into the kitchen. "Sara, ya alright?"

Sara was at the hob, waiting for the kettle to boil, one finger wiggling around in her ear as she nodded at him. "Da, this is Miss Máiréad." She gestured to the woman who seemed to fill the entire room with her presence. "Máiréad, this is my da, Donal."

"Dia duit, a Dhónaill." She approached and stretched out her hand. While not an overly large woman, except for her height, she seemed to have enough personality—and volume—for at least five women.

He shook her hand and returned her greeting. "'Tis nice to meet ya."

"Likewise," she nearly bellowed. "Catríona sent me with the fixin's for a picnic." She held up a basket. "Shall we?"

Donal glanced at Sara, whose face registered a look that seemed to say both "have fun with that" and "better you than me," and he couldn't help the smile that tipped the corner of his mouth.

He gestured to the front door. "Yes, of course. There's a large oak just at the bend in the road that might be nice."

"Grand, so!" She turned to Sara and called over her shoulder as she sidestepped out the front door, "Lovely to meet you, Tara!"

Donal blinked hard. How difficult was it to remember the name Sara? A quick glance at his daughter showed her shaking her head.

"Don't correct her," she seemed to say with the gesture.

He smiled at her, yanked his scarf off the peg near the door, and shot one more helpless look at his daughter while Máiréad's voice bounced around the walls of their sitting room. Sara hid a giggle behind her hand and then waved him off.

⎯⎯⎯⎯◦∞◦⎯⎯⎯⎯

Two hours later, Sara scurried away from the front window to pour a fresh cuppa when she saw her father trudging up the front walk. The door creaked open, and she heard his boots scuff the floor as he dragged himself inside. He didn't usually lumber that much except for at the end of the harvest, poor man. She came around the corner with a steaming cup in hand just as he flopped onto the sofa and closed his eyes.

"Hi, Da." She held the tea out to him. "How'd it go?"

His face scrunched up, and he pressed a finger to his lips. "Shh. No. More. Words." His eyes slid open, and her heart clinched at the exhaustion she saw behind his gaze. A vision flashed in her imagination of what it would be like having that woman in the house all the time. Seeing that tiredness on Da's face all the time. No, this wouldn't do 'tall. He needed someone who lifted him up, not weighed him down. No, Máiréad Bailey was clearly not the woman for them.

She set the cup on the side table, taking great care not to spill any on the doily Da had once told her was a wedding gift, then she bent and kissed his forehead and crept from the room.

10

"Can ya do no better than that?" Donal asked, his gut churning.

Willie grimaced from behind the counter and slid the secondhand clasp toward Donal. "'Fraid not, Donal." He shrugged. "What I quoted ya already includes a steep discount."

Donal tugged his flatcap from his head and ran his hand down the back of his neck. "Would ya take a barter?"

Willie's lips pursed. "What'd ya have in mind?"

Donal's thoughts tumbled over what little he had to offer. Perhaps some butter from Pete, but that wouldn't cover half of the price Willie'd given. He silently counted the footed stacks of turf standing out in his bog right now as he pictured them in his mind's eye. He and Sara would need them for the winter, but if they were judicious in their use, they could perhaps spare a stack or two.

"How's yer turf stash?" Donal asked.

Willie's head waggled. "I'm alright there, though a man could always use a mite more turf." He swiped at his nose with a handkerchief, then stuffed it back in his pocket. "Almanac is callin' fer a wild winter."

Donal winced but forced his expression to steady. "Will ya take a stack o' turf for the clasp?"

"Eh . . ." Willie sucked in a long breath through his teeth, his chin lazily swinging back and forth in thought.

"G'on, Will." Donal fisted his hands on the countertop. "I canna have the stock roamin' free again." He couldn't lose another one to the elements. Though, at least he'd not had one run through town and tear up a pub like his da did. Or have one eaten by a lion that escaped from a traveling circus like his *Daideo*. But losing one to a broken leg from getting stuck in a divot in the turf, and another to a run-in with a horse and buggy, was bad enough. "I gotta have this clasp."

Willie glanced around the shop as though he was about to spill a state secret, then he sighed. "Throw in some butter and ya have a deal."

Willie Baggott always drove a hard bargain, but butter was easily replaced—so long as he could keep the cattle fed, which he couldn't do if they ran away. Better some butter and turf than money he didn't have.

"Deal," he ground out at last, extending his right hand to the man.

Willie took his hand and shook it once. "Grand, so."

"I'll bring yer goods by week's end," Donal added.

Willie nodded and held out the clasp. "Take it wit' ye now. I know ye're good for it."

A fraction of the weight on his chest released. "T'anks."

Willie moved toward the back of his shop. "'Sides," he called over his shoulder, "if'n ya don't bring it, I know where ya live." His robust laughter filled the room.

"Ye're welcome anytime." Donal tipped his cap and slid the clasp into the baggy pocket of his dungarees. He turned to leave but a familiar profile caught his eye through the dingy window.

Catríona stood on the far walk in a dress far fancier than he'd seen her wear before. Her posture was taut, her movements calculated as she threw her head back in an exaggerated laugh. She set her hand on the arm of the tall, blond man next to her. Donal stepped closer to the window and squinted. The man seemed familiar, but Donal couldn't place him.

He reached up and tucked a strand of hair behind Catríona's ear. Donal's spine stiffened. Just then, a slightly older gentleman rounded the corner in a topcoat and hat. Not the fancy man Jimmy had spoken of, but one nearly as posh looking. Catríona's countenance pinched slightly. She straightened her posture even more and tugged on the bodice of her dress.

Donal stepped outside just as Catríona turned. Their eyes met, and he froze for a beat. Then he offered a tight smile and tipped his cap as he quickened his pace.

"Oh! Mister Bunratty," she called.

He stopped and greeted her, and she waved him over.

"Lord Osborne, Lady Osborne, Andrew. This is Donal Bunratty."

The earl raised a single brow, then tipped his hat so slightly with his index finger, Donal almost missed it. "Mister Bunratty is another one of my clients," Catríona added. Her full, thick Clare accent had disappeared, and her words had a smooth roundness to them that didn't fit her at all. Donal wondered if she tried to match the stations—or at the very least, personalities—of those she was matching, but that didn't make any sense. Especially since the stilted, antiseptic persona she currently embodied couldn't hold a candle to the easygoing nature and compassion he'd seen her display on the road with Sara and with him in the barn the other day. No, this was altogether strange indeed.

She reminded Donal of the wooden peg game he'd made for

Sara when she was a wee tot. Sara would try to jam the round peg into the hole for the triangle piece. No matter how much she twisted or shoved, it never would fit. Matter of fact, Donal felt like one of those pegs himself, given the current company.

"Nice to meet you," he said.

Andrew stepped closer, his pointer finger wagging at Donal. "I say, have we met before?"

Donal paused, his brow knitted. He studied the young man's face, and recognition finally dawned. "Ah, yes, I believe we have. You purchased some livestock from me last year around this time." It hadn't been a terribly pleasant experience. Donal had found the gentleman overbearing and demanding. Then again, that was par for the course with much of the gentry, so he'd forgotten the lad after the deal had been struck.

"Ah, yes." Andrew snapped his fingers. "That's right! Two of the finest heifers we've ever had."

"Indeed?" Donal's chest warmed with pride. "I'm glad to hear it." He had half a mind to suggest they broker another deal, but truth be told, he couldn't spare another heifer. He'd not been able to breed them this year like he'd done previous years. The financial toll of the two he'd lost had affected every aspect of the farm—from not having the stock available to sell and trade to being unable to afford the extra feed needed for the expectant mothers and eventually the calves.

Andrew shrugged. "At least that's what my man at home tells me. Personally, I can't stand the beasts. I'm more than happy to let him deal with them."

Next to Andrew, Catríona's lips twitched in a half smile before returning to their put-on pious state.

Donal swallowed the smart-aleck retort that formed on his tongue and managed to reply only with, "Yes, well, to each his own."

"Indeed," the earl said with a sniff. "Now, I believe we've an appointment?" he added, turning to Catríona.

"Yes, we do, in fact." She smiled tightly. "Good day to you, Mister Bunratty."

Donal regarded her for a long moment, then bowed slightly at his waist. "Miss Daly. Lord and Lady Osborne. Mister Osborne."

The trio headed in the direction of the Queens Hotel, while Donal went the opposite way. As he made the short trek to the plowman's shop to see about repairing his moldboard, he mulled over the encounter with Catríona. The younger Osborne's actions suggested an intimacy to their relationship that seemed strange given Catríona's profession. Donal had assumed she was making a match for the lad, but perhaps he was mistaken. While the Dalys and the Osbornes certainly didn't seem to be on equal footing socially, who was he to say who would be a good match with whom? That was Catríona's world in every respect. Though, from what Donal remembered of the lad, he seemed to be a mite *too* familiar with the fairer sex. It seemed he'd seen Andrew with a handful of different girls throughout their dealings last year—usually out in the countryside. Alone.

Granted, all during a matchmaking festival. Chances were, those were outings set up by whoever his matchmaker was. Just like Donal's picnic with Máiréad. He shuddered at the memory and absently tugged at his ear as though her strident voice still rang in it. A few days had passed and Catríona had yet to present him with any other ladies. That was just fine with him, though he knew it wouldn't be with Sara. As he approached the plowman's work shed, Donal's eyes flitted to the sky as he sent a silent prayer winging heavenward. *Lord, let the right woman be out there. And bring her to me in Your time.* He didn't make his desire that that timing be sooner rather than later so he could leave all this matchmaking nonsense behind part of his official prayer. He had a hunch the Lord was aware. The fact that a prayer had surfaced at all was a shock. His faith had faltered a bit of late as he struggled to reconcile the idea God was good and loving with the idea that He allowed His children to suffer, go hungry, even homeless. Nevertheless, a wee plea to the Auld Man Upstairs could hardly hurt. Could it? With one more glance upward, Donal slid the heavy wooden door open.

The earthy scents of sawdust and hot iron hung in the warm, damp air. In the corner, Owen Madigan looked up from the plow he was sanding.

"Donal Bunratty, as I live and breathe!" He rounded the workbench, hand extended, his leather apron covered in fine dust. "I've not seen ye in a dog's age."

Donal took his hand and shook it. "Aye. Been busy."

Owen grunted. "That seems to be goin' around, fer sure." He brushed his hands down the front of his legs. "What can I do fer ya?"

Donal explained about his cracked and broken plow, sharing exactly what had broken and where.

"Och!" Owen flapped his hand. "I can fix that fer ya, no problem."

Donal winced. "Thanks, but there's just one other thing."

"Oh? Wha's that?" Owen crossed his tree trunk arms over his broad chest.

Donal's gaze drifted to his feet as he shifted his weight back and forth. "It's just . . . well . . . I can't pay ye." He couldn't bring himself to look the man in the eye, so he kept his gaze trained at the ground.

"Hmm," Owen said, and Donal could hear the man's stubble scratch against his calloused palm as he stroked his jawbone. "Well, I'm sure we can come to some sort o' arrangement." He stepped past Donal and through the open door. He turned and examined the outer walls of his work shed.

Donal watched as the man studied the building as if he was considering buying it. After a long moment, he patted the weathered wood and nodded. "Outside o' my shop needs paintin'." He closed the distance between them. "You do that fer me, and I'll fix yer plow."

Donal's eyes widened. Painting a building of this size would take ages—and pull him away from all his own duties on the farm. The harvest already past, that would cut down on the workload some. And he'd have no harvest at all next season if he wasn't able to plow the ground. Even fifty years on, the land was recovering from the famine, and it took a certain sort of finesse to coax it to grow much of anything still. He needed a good plow.

"I've already budgeted fer the supplies. I'll get those, not a bother. I just need ya to paint it. Aye?" Owen dipped his chin, his eyes pinned on Donal expectantly.

The supplies. Donal hadn't even considered that. If Owen had expected him to procure those as well, there'd be no way. But given that he would take care of those, he really had no reason not to accept the very fair terms.

Donal nodded. "Aye." The men shook hands, and Donal added, "Thanks."

"You scratch my back . . ." Owen turned and headed for his workbench. "Bring me yer plow at week's end, and I'll fix it up fer ya. You can start paintin' then as well."

Owen, already engrossed in his work, didn't look up when he mumbled his parting. "Slán abhaile."

"Slán." Donal lifted his hand as he turned to go. Closing the door, he tried to work out when he would have time to run the farm, raise Sara, and paint a work shed. Oh, and find a wife. He rolled his eyes. *What've ye gotten yerself into, Donal Bunratty?*

11

The next day, Catríona was up and out of the flat before her father had even gone to bed. Rather, she'd discovered as she scurried out into the misty morning, that he'd fallen asleep on the bench behind the table in their office. Tempted to just go on her merry way, she stopped short in the doorway of the pub and turned back. Hastening into the small room off the side of the main pub area, she crept in and slid her father's coat off the peg and draped it over his sleeping form. Things would be quiet for a while, with the merrymakers having either retired to their own slumber or moved their party elsewhere. Peadar stopped serving drinks between eight and nine in the morning to give himself time to wash up, take his own breakfast, and just let the pub rest. The room was just as much part of all the matchmaking as Jimmy, Catríona, Peadar, and the patrons, and Catríona always felt it seemed to sigh in relief when the church bells tolled eight o' the clock and it could rest a wee while.

Catríona smiled to herself as she slipped outside as silent as a prayer during Mass. She had a few errands to run and clients to check in on before meeting Andrew for the organized walking tour of the village and surrounding areas that culminated in a hillside picnic for all the participants.

This particular walk was being hosted by the Queens Hotel, so the food promised to be especially delicious. Catríona didn't always attend the events herself—in fact, she never did. But she'd not matched Andrew with a specific lady for the day, instead telling him that the picnic itself was a mixer designed to orchestrate meeting new people. It was technically the truth. But she chose to keep to herself that many came with a partner already set and used the walking tour and picnic as a chance to get to know them, rather than spend half the time trying to find a good match for the day. True, that left a chance that Andrew would actually meet someone at the event, but she had more control this way and guaranteed herself at least a little bit of time with him to herself. She hoped her plan would serve the intended purpose.

She mulled over the path the tour would take, winding through the town, then southwards toward the Aille River. Where Main Street forked with the Bog Road and Kilfenora Road at the bottom of Sulphur Hill, they'd veer east toward Kilfenora. But at the thought of the Bog Road, Catríona's thoughts turned to wee Sara. And Donal. She wondered how Sara was faring with the kids at school. While decent children at heart, they could be downright cruel at times when their current worldview seemed threatened. Something they'd learned from their parents, no doubt. She'd not heard any more of her trouble, so she hoped that one day was the end of it. Sara was such a sweet girl. She deserved the best. Catríona's heart twisted at the reminder that Sara was growing up without knowing the warmth of a mother's love. Much like Catríona had. She shook the thought free as quickly as it had come and forced her mind to focus on the matters at hand.

She'd been swamped with clients all day yesterday after meeting with the Osbornes and had sent Maeve with a message for Donal about the walking tour. She knew his schedule had precious little room in it, but she did hope he'd come. If for no other reason than wee Sara's sake.

───────◦◦◦───────

An hour later, Catríona was hustling to the Queens Hotel feeling like a duck on a pond—smooth and graceful on the surface, but underneath, her heart just raced away. At least she hoped she appeared calm and collected while her pulse quickened at the sight of Andrew in a dashing day suit, walking cane in one hand and a porcelain cup in the other. She absently patted her hair and tried to steady her nerves with a deep breath.

"Why, Miss Daly, you're looking as lovely as ever," Andrew called, the morning sun glinting in his deep blue eyes. He closed the distance between them and pressed a genteel kiss to each cheek.

Catríona hoped he didn't feel the warmth that flashed in them at his touch. "Good to see you again, Mister Osborne."

He pinned her with a look, and she chuckled.

"Sorry. Andrew," she corrected herself.

"That's better." He looked just past her, ticked his head, and held his cup aloft.

As if from nowhere, a dainty maid appeared and took it from his hand. Her head remained low as she bobbed in a shallow curtsy.

"Thank you, dear," Andrew said, his eyes trained on the maid. She kept her gaze on the ground, but before leaving, glanced briefly up at his face, her own expression taut.

Did he just wink at her? No, he couldn't have. The light caused him to squint, surely. The maid dropped her head low again and hurried inside.

Andrew turned his attention back to Catríona. "The service here truly is remarkable."

"Is it?" Catríona's brows arched. "I'm glad to hear it! Only the best for Lisdoonvarna's finest guests." The heat returned to her cheeks, and she looked away. What sort of malarky was she speaking? She wanted to win the man, yes, but with her dignity intact. She couldn't afford to be too forward and risk offending him.

Just then, a short, roundish man appeared on the front steps and clapped his hands twice. "Ladies and gentlemen, might I have your attention, please?" Frank Devlin was the current patron activities director at the Queens. Catríona smiled at the sight of him. He'd grown up in the area, the son of one of the poorest farmers in the county, but had somehow managed to finagle this position. He was very good at his job, but Catríona couldn't help feeling like he looked like a lad playing dress-up with a fancy man's things.

The group gathered closer, and Catríona studied the crowd. A strong number and seemingly a fair mix of singles and pairs. She searched for Donal's tweed flatcap, but he was nowhere to be seen. But just as she glanced behind her, he appeared over the crest of the hill, slowly coming up the walk looking every bit the lost puppy. His brow furrowed, eyes darting this way and that as he chewed his lip. When his eyes met hers, he paused for the briefest of moments, nodded slightly, and moved forward to join the back row of guests.

Catríona lightly touched Andrew's arm. "I'll be right back. One of my other clients just arrived, and I must check in quickly."

Andrew glanced around, then leaned down until his lips brushed her ear. "Not Lisdoonvarna's finest though, aye?"

Grateful for the long sleeves hiding the chill bumps skittering across her skin, Catríona laughed. "Oh no," she whispered. "There's only one of those."

He puffed a mock sigh of relief and pretended to wipe drops of worry-filled sweat from his brow. "Thank goodness," he said, his lips once again deliciously close to her ear, her neck. "I was worried there for a sec." When he'd finished speaking, he remained close and pressed nearer still. It wasn't a kiss on her ear—more like a nudge—but it set butterflies loose in her stomach, and her eyes drifted closed as their wings fluttered in her belly.

She steadied herself with a breath and replied, "Be right back."

As Donal approached the crowd, a sense of dread gnawed at his gut.

A gaggle of ladies and gentlemen several steps above his own station stood gathered around the front steps of the Queens Hotel. What on earth was he doing? And how many times was he going to have to resign himself to this quest? At least once more, it seemed.

Then he stopped short. Catríona stood there in a lovely day frock—one that suited her much more than the ridiculous get-up she'd been wearing the other day but still fancier than he'd seen her wear in their previous interactions. The morning sun had managed to burn away the mist, and her hair gleamed in its gentle light. Donal's pulse quickened, and a smile tickled the corner of his mouth, even as the relief that washed over him at the sight of her took him by surprise. She noticed him and smiled. Then, the gentleman she'd been with in town leaned in close and whispered something in her ear. Donal's gaze narrowed, and his lips instinctively tightened into a thin line. Donal had whispered many a time in his life, but there'd never been a need to get *that* close to the other person. Catríona, however, seemed to be eating it up. She laughed—nae, giggled—at whatever he said. Though Donal didn't think it possible, the man leaned in even closer and said something else. More giggling. And blushing. Hang it all, why was that man so infuriating? And why did it bother Donal so much to begin with? Andrew Osborne had been no picnic to deal with in their livestock dealings last year but had done nothing that grated on Donal's last nerve as much as the young man did now.

Catríona patted Osborne's arm and then turned in Donal's direction. His heart lurched a beat, and Donal tugged on his waistcoat. The blasted thing would never feel right.

"You came! I'm so delighted." Catríona extended her hand as she approached.

Donal took her hand and shook it cordially as the thought that her soft skin reminded him of the scarf he'd used on Sara's birthday danced into his head like a leaf on a breeze. "Mornin', Catríona." He hoped his face didn't betray his thoughts. He tugged his hand from hers and jammed it into his trouser pocket before the traitorous thing could cause any other mortifying thoughts that had no place taking up residence in his brain.

She glanced back at Frank Devlin, who seemed to be wrapping up some sort of speech or instructions, then settled her gaze on Donal. "Today's a walking tour of the town and then we'll head down the Kilfenora Road to the hillside for a picnic provided by the hotel," she whispered, presumably not wanting to interrupt Frank any more than they already had.

Donal nodded and eyed the crowd. Some stood on their own, including one lass who appeared to be taking stock of every gent present. He'd examined heifers the same way on market days, and before a chuckle could rumble in his chest at the comparison, the lass's eyes pinned onto him. He pretended to study a very interesting speck on his shoe. When he sensed she'd moved on, he looked up, relieved to see his senses were correct. He then finished his scan of the crowd. A fairly even group of singles and pairs alike were present, and Donal wondered how long this endeavor would take.

As if reading his thoughts, Catríona continued, "Some have come already paired with someone, so as to become better acquainted with one another. Others have come on their own or with a friend, hoping to make a connection at some point during the day."

"Alright" was the only response he could muster. And yet, he couldn't help but wonder . . . "So . . . did ya have a plan fer me? Like, a person, or . . ." No one ever accused Donal Bunratty of being eloquent.

Her gray-blue eyes widened for a split second as panic seemed to flash behind them. But before Donal could truly register the expression, her confident facade returned. "No." She shook her head. "No set plan. I'd just hoped ye'd have fun, and perhaps fate would lead you to the right lucky lady."

"*Psst!*" Catríona didn't seem to notice the hiss that came from behind her.

"I'll be around most of the day, so if anything comes up, or ya have a question, just let me know."

"*Psst! Psst!*"

Catríona turned toward the sound. Osborne was gesturing for her to go to him. She lifted a finger and turned back to Donal. "I'm sorry, I need to see to another client." She shrugged. "Ya know how those gentry folk are like."

Donal nodded. *Indeed, I do.* "Who is he paired with today?" *What are you doing, man? That's none of your business!*

Her cheeks flushed and she shrugged again. "Oh, no pair

there either. It seems like it's the day to let luck have her say."
She smiled, and Donal warmed at the sight. He also decided
in that moment, match or no match, he'd make sure Andrew
Osborne lived up to his title of gentleman when it came to
Catríona Daly.

12

As the group set off on their tour, they naturally seg-
regated themselves so that those already paired with
someone were toward the front of the group while the
singles were in the back. Donal absently wondered if someone
already matched up ever discovered someone they preferred
more among the group on these sorts of outings. What happened then?

"Penny fer your thoughts." The soft voice broke his reverie,
and he realized a tiny wisp of a woman had started walking
next to him.

"Pardon?" he asked.

She smiled sweetly and studied his face for a beat. "Ya just
seemed a mite lost in thought."

He chuckled. "Yes, I suppose I was."

She shrugged and pulled her shawl tighter around her shoulders. "We've a long day ahead of us. I'm all ears if you're inclined to share." She turned her attention to the front of the
group where Frank was explaining the history of the spa wells.
Donal took the moment to study the woman at his side. Ebony
hair framed a face that at first glance appeared practically porcelain, but closer inspection revealed signs that perhaps she'd

95

not had such an easy life. Either way, her hair glistened in the morning light and dangled in a dainty plait down her back, over her Galway shawl. It didn't seem cold enough to warrant such a heavy covering, but she also had no meat on her bones. In fact, she was so petite, if he didn't know any better, Donal might have thought her to be a *sióg*. He smiled at the thought of telling Sara he'd met a real-life fairy, but his smile faltered at the weight of the responsibility that lay before him. Not only was he choosing a life partner for himself but the woman who would be shaping the woman Sara would become.

Donal suddenly became keenly aware that he'd been staring at the poor woman, and before he could look away, her gaze swung about and met his. The bare hint of a smile twitched at the corner of her mouth.

"What? Cat got yer tongue?" The kindness that shone in her dark eyes disarmed him, and he allowed a small grin to crack.

"I'm just not in the habit o' bearin' my soul to a stranger. That's all." He shrugged sheepishly, hoping that was enough to change the course of their conversation.

She stopped and jutted out her hand. "Deirdre O'Malley."

Donal took her hand and shook it. "Donal," he said. "Donal Bunratty."

She nodded decisively. "There. Now we aren't strangers anymore."

Unbidden, a hearty laugh bubbled up in Donal's chest and tumbled out of his mouth.

Her nervous laughter joined in, and she pressed a palm to her forehead. "I'm terribly sorry. I'm not usually so forward, but this whole matchmakin' business has me a bit flummoxed."

"You too?" Donal puffed out a breath he hadn't realized had been weighing on his chest. "I thought it was just me. Everyone else seems so . . . comfortable."

"Don't they, though? I don't see how." She chewed her lip, and they hurried to catch up with the group who had moved on down the road. As they walked, Donal noticed the beauty of this area for the first time in ages. The spa wells were tucked into the hillside along a bend in the Aille River. The bathhouse gleamed like a jewel in green velvet, surrounded by lush trees and other flora and fauna. The sound of the water trickling along its banks brought a hint of whimsy to the place, and the air was thick with the rich scent of damp turf, fresh water, and the tangy, slightly minty aroma of gorse bushes and elm trees. 'Twas no wonder the place was said to hold healing properties.

"So, how did two folk like us get here, of all places?" Deirdre asked.

Donal shook his head. "I've been asking m'self that question since the festival began."

Deirdre nodded knowingly. "Did ya travel far?"

"No, didn't travel 'tall. I have a farm down the Bog Road." He glanced at her. "You?"

"Oh, aye." She sighed. "I'm from down Killarney way. My mam sent me up here since there's not much to choose from in the way of good men at home."

Donal's brows lifted. "Killarney? That's a far piece!"

Deirdre huffed a breath. "Yes, yes, it is."

As the crowd meandered through the town of Lisdoonvarna then back out and down Kilfenora Road, the pair chatted amiably about their experiences at the festival so far. Deirdre had laughed heartily as he relayed the story of his picnic lunch with Máiréad.

"I know that gairl!" Deirdre cried. "She's stayin' in the same guesthouse as me, and I can assure you, she never gets any quieter."

They came to a bend in the road, and the group turned

sharply and trekked up a grassy hill. At the top, several long tables were set up, their crisp white tablecloths swaying softly in the breeze. An army of hotel staff was lined up behind the tables, which were laden with all manner of food. Donal's stomach rumbled, and his hand clutched at his belly in an effort to silence it.

All across the ground, blankets and quilts had also been spread out for people to sit on, transforming the telltale patchwork emerald fields into an actual patchwork of fabric, food, and folk.

"It's been lovely chatting, Donal. My roommate at the guesthouse is over there and is asking for me to sit with her." She gestured to a younger woman who was settling down onto a blanket and smiling in their direction.

Donal nodded. "Thanks. I enjoyed talking wit' ye too."

She smiled and shrugged. "Perhaps we'll meet up again later."

He matched her smile. "Perhaps." He jammed at the grass with the toe of his boot. "I think I might enjoy that."

Her grin widened, and she nodded once more before scurrying off to join her friend.

Donal's gaze followed her, and he allowed himself to ponder if she was the kind of woman he could spend day in and day out with. Her quiet but confident demeanor put him at ease straightaway. And chatting with her had been almost as comfortable as it had been with Connie, though the two women had completely different personalities. Of course, it was far too soon to know if he'd want to marry the lass, but she was the first one so far that he had any sort of interest in seeing again. Then, just beyond where Deirdre and her friend were sitting, Catríona caught his eye, causing his pulse to quicken. She was talking with a young couple. Her familiarity with the woman made Donal think it must be one of her other clients.

Or a friend from town. Either way, he couldn't help the smile that spread across his face at the sight of her.

Then, movement in the corner of his eye stole his attention. He spotted Andrew at one of the tables, talking to a waitress. The girl's head was down, and she fidgeted with a serving spoon as she nodded. Andrew grazed a finger down the girl's arm from her shoulder to her fingertips, and she stiffened and froze as though she'd come across a mad bull. Donal glanced back to Catríona, who was still talking with the couple, plus another few people who'd joined in their conversation.

He looked back to Andrew and the waitress just in time to see the girl jump slightly, her eyes wide. Had Andrew smacked her botto— No, he couldn't have. He wouldn't dare. As Andrew lifted a cup of punch from the table, he quickly blew a kiss to the girl with his free hand. It was so quick and so small a gesture, Donal couldn't be sure anyone else would've seen it. Donal himself wasn't sure what he saw. But the twisting in his gut and the tightness that ached in his jaw told him Andrew needed to be watched.

"Are ya enjoyin' the day?"

Donal spun to find Catríona smiling up at him. "Aye." He swallowed hard and nodded.

"Good." She grinned wide, and Donal tried to ignore the way her dimples punctuated her smile like a jewel in a crown. "It seemed like ye and Deirdre were havin' a nice chat."

Donal chewed his bottom lip. "Aye, we did. She's very nice."

"I'm so glad to hear it, Donal." She patted his arm and every nerve in his body sprang to life. "I was so worried ye'd be miserable."

"Well," he said as a chuckle rumbled deep in his chest, "the day's not over yet."

She laughed and it was like music to Donal's ears. Not the

forced, demure laugh he'd seen her emit so often around Andrew. No, this was a natural, mirthful sound, and Donal loved it.

"That's true enough, but let's hope it's all smiles from here on out. Aye?"

He searched her eyes for a moment before answering. "Aye."

Andrew approached, and Catríona's posture instantly straightened. And . . . was she holding in her stomach? Whatever for? Andrew held out his elbow toward Catríona. "Shall we sit?"

She looked at Andrew, and the admiration Donal saw in her eyes sucked the air from his chest like the time Bó a Dó had kicked him in the stomach. *Don't tell me she truly is enamored with this oaf?*

"Me?" she said, stretching the word long and smooth in that strange accent he'd heard her use the other day.

Andrew shrugged and scanned the crowd, most of whom were already settled in their places with plates full of food. "I've not found another lass I'd rather sit with among this lot."

Her cheeks flushed, and she batted her lashes playfully. Donal couldn't help the crease of confusion that flashed to his brow.

"Excuse me, Donal," she said, her eyes trained on Andrew as she slid her hand through his offered arm. "We'll catch up again later."

---∞---

Catríona's heart raced as she and Andrew made their way to the only empty blanket left. Could it be? Out of all the ladies present, he wanted to have lunch with *her*? Keeping her steps dainty, she rounded the edge of the quilt, and when Andrew held out his hand to help her lower herself to sit, she held her breath as she took hold of it. His hands were softer than she expected. Softer than hers, she feared, and as soon as she was seated, she snatched her hand back. She couldn't very well have him thinking her work-worn hands an issue.

Arranging herself on the ground was more difficult than she anticipated. If she was by herself, or just with Maeve, she would have sat with her legs crisscrossed over one another, or she would've lounged back on her side. But with Andrew, she had to ensure she maintained the highest sense of decorum at all times. Pressing her knees together off to one side, she bent her legs so her feet tucked in behind her. She had to support herself with her right hand on the ground in order to keep her posture straight and tall. Eating like this was going to prove a challenge. Not that she'd eat much in front of him, anyway. Her mother's voice echoed in her mind.

"No man is gonna want ya if ya keep shovin' tea cakes in yer gob. Ya got my big bones, gairl. Ye'll have to watch yerself and keep a tight figure if ye're gonna land a man of any quality."

She picked up a small, triangular cucumber sandwich and nibbled the corner before placing it back on her plate. She could always eat later.

"So," Andrew said around a mouthful of smoked salmon salad. "What've ya got for me?"

Catríona took a sip of her punch, her mind spinning, trying to decipher meaning from his words.

He must've read the question on her face, because he added, "For my match."

She slumped under the weight of his request, but she righted herself immediately.

Andrew licked his lips as his gaze bounced from woman to woman in the crowd. "Do you have any ladies in mind?"

Yes, me! Catríona shifted her legs around to the other side, biting her lip before she could blurt her thoughts out loud, ensuring she kept her belly sucked in while doing so. She'd made a plan for this moment. All she had to do was implement it.

"Actually, I do. I've arranged a dinner for you at the Ritz tomorrow night with a young lady. Seven o'clock."

His eyes danced with glee. "Brilliant."

"Her name is—"

He held up a hand, his palm to her. "Don't tell me a thing. I want to be surprised."

Catríona smiled and nodded. "Very well." *Oh, you'll be surprised, Andrew. Don't you worry about that.*

He picked up his empty cup. "I'm going to get some more to drink. I'll be right back."

As he stood, she took her own cup and extended it out to him, but he was gone, halfway to the table already like a moth to a flame. *Never mind*, she told herself. He probably just didn't notice. *He didn't offer either.* She swatted the thought away as she swatted a *midgie* that hovered around her face.

She glanced up at Andrew, but he was nowhere to be seen. Instead, Donal stood at a distance, his eyes trained on her, his stare filled with intensity. She tried to drop her gaze, but she couldn't bring herself to look away.

13

So, are ya betrothed yet?" Maeve's voice boomed through the small office of the Imperial Pub.

Catríona scowled. "*Shhh*! Wouldja be quiet?"

"Bah!" Maeve flapped her hand. "No one's payin' me any mind. I could say I was gonna marry the Pope and no one would care." She turned and eyed the crowd filling every corner of the pub. "See?"

Catríona rolled her eyes.

"No one in their right mind would take ye on fer a wife, Maeve Scanlon!" a man's voice called over the din.

Maeve winced. "Okay, so maybe I'm a mite loud." She rounded the table and sat on the bench next to Catríona. "But ya still haven't told me how it's goin' with yer knight in shining armor."

Catríona ignored the niggle of doubt that washed over her at the idea of Andrew as a knight and, instead, forced a smile onto her face. "He asked me to have the picnic with him on the tour yesterday."

Maeve's brows soared. "Did he now?"

"Aye."

"And I'm sure ya put on all yer best airs for the lad?" She sat up straight, a pious look plastered on her face.

"Of course," Catríona said. "I know what I'm doin'."

Maeve flopped back against the bench. "If ya say so."

Catríona crossed her arms over her chest and twisted her body toward her friend. "What's that supposed to mean?"

"Nothin'." Maeve scratched at a decades-old stain on the table. "It's just . . . ya know ye're gonna have to send him out with real girls, like?"

A sly grin snaked its way onto Catríona's face. "Oh, aye." She checked the clock on the wall. "In fact, he's out with one of Lisdoonvarna's finest ladies as we speak."

"Is he?" Maeve sat up again. "And who might that be?"

Catríona pretended to busy herself looking through the ledger her father kept all his matchmaking records in. "Hester."

"Hester?" Maeve slapped her palms onto the table. "Hester McGowan?"

"Aye." Catríona flipped a page in the ledger and ran her finger down a column.

"Hester who perpetually looks like she just took a big bite o' lemon, Hester?"

Catríona feigned nonchalance. Next to her, Maeve erupted into a spate of laughter.

When her guffaws died down, Maeve wiped her eyes and pressed a hand to her stomach, trying to regain her breath. "You don't actually think they'd be a good match, do ya?"

Catríona pinned her friend with a look. "Well, of course I don't! That's the whole point!"

Maeve shook her head. "Hats off to ya, lassie."

The pair were quiet for a long moment, both happy enough to let the din of the pub crowd wash over them.

"Caty?" Maeve asked quietly.

"Hmm?"

"Are ya not worried that makin' a poor match on purpose will wreck yer reputation?" She scooted forward to rest her elbow on the table and pressed her fist against her temple. "I mean . . . is it not a mite . . . risky?"

"Maeve Scanlon, I've never known you to be one to back down from a scandalous challenge." She hoped the humor lacing her voice would mask the swirl of doubts that had taken up residence in her gut. Of course it was a risk. To intentionally make a bad match—especially for one's own gain—went against the unwritten code of matchmaking. Not to mention the damage it could do to her father's business.

"I know," Maeve said, her voice quiet. "I just . . . I don't want to see you get hurt. Or lose yer livelihood." She reached over and clasped one of Catríona's hands.

For all her crazy whims and wild ways, Maeve really was the best of friends, with a heart of gold. Catríona knew what she was doing was risky—unethical, even. But she saw no other way. Her other options were to continue on, business as usual waiting and wondering for her marital status—or lack thereof—to drain every ounce of credibility from her matchmaking. Or to marry a local man—likely a farmer, because all the men who weren't farmers married off long ago or weren't worth giving the time of day. She thought back to her days in their farmhouse—having to smear dung on the walls to hold the heat in during the winter, forever smelling of cow hide and turf no matter how hard one washed, never knowing if they were going to make it through the winter, if the livestock would survive, if the turf and tea would hold out. She couldn't do that again. Wouldn't do it. She didn't care how many unwritten rules she had to break, she had to get out of this place and go where she never had to think of such things again.

"Maeve," Catríona said around the lump forming in her throat, "I can't."

Although she knew it was impossible, Catríona was certain Maeve knew exactly the thoughts she'd just been mulling over. The two could practically read each other's minds after decades of friendship. "He's my only way out."

Maeve wrapped an arm around Catríona's shoulders. "Right, then. What can I do to help?"

―――――∞―――――

Catríona tried to stifle the frustration brewing in her chest as she made her way to Owen Madigan's shop the next day. She'd trekked all the way out to Donal's house only to find both him and Sara to be gone. The air was chilled, and mist hung suspended like a curtain of tiny diamonds. But she was in no mood to admire the muted beauty surrounding her. Instead, each new drop that settled on her nose or cheeks or forehead was like new kindling to the fire of her annoyance. Not that she had any real right to feel thus—Donal had as much right to go about his business as any other person in Lisdoonvarna. She just wished there was a way to know he was away from home before making the half-hour journey down the Bog Road out to Ferry Hill.

Upon returning to town, she'd seen Owen heading into the market. He'd overheard her asking another patron about Donal. "Donal Bunratty?" he'd asked. "He's out paintin' my shop."

Now, as Catríona approached the shop, her steps slowed, and she forced herself to take a steadying breath when an angelic voice caught her attention. She rounded the corner to find Sara singing a jaunty tune while she mixed a bucket of paint. A small chuckle rippled through Catríona's lips. *"Caillaich an Airgid"* was a funny song to hear such a wee girl sing—with lyrics about a young man who supposedly fell in love with a woman old enough to be his grandmother because of her money. In the end, he married someone else. Strange lyrics aside, Sara sang with gusto as she stirred in time with the beat, no doubt accompanying the music in her head. Every now and then, she'd punctuate a phrase by jabbing the stir stick at the bottom of the bucket.

As Sara finished her song with a flourish, Donal appeared from behind the building, a fresh paintbrush in his hand. He glanced at Catríona briefly at first and then stopped short. "Hallo there." His face alternated between surprise and amusement, neither one seemingly willing to take over the expression in earnest.

Sara's gaze shot up from her bucket, and she jolted to her feet. "Catríona!" She ran over and slung her arms around Catríona in an embrace.

"Hello again, Sara. It's lovely to see you." She returned the girl's hug, surprised by the emotion that welled up in her chest as she did so.

"Have ya come to help?" Sara asked, peering up into her face.

Catríona blinked the moisture from her eyes. "Help?"

"Wit' the paintin'!" Sara looked to the shop and back. "Da's the best painter in County Clare!"

Catríona met Donal's gaze then, and he gave her a sheepish look and shrugged. "Can't argue with that. Sara's the leading authority on paint quality."

Catríona laughed. "I don't doubt it. Sadly, no, I didn't come to help with the paint. I came ta help with somethin' else."

Sara sighed. "Alright." She went back to her bucket, humming a new tune quietly to herself.

Catríona stepped over to Donal. "I just came to let you know that there's to be a dance tomorrow at the square."

Donal's eyes clamped shut, and he drew a long breath in. "A dance?"

"Aye, and it's one of the best of the whole *feis*."

"Oh?" Donal's brow had furrows as deep as if he was planting barley.

"Of course! It's become one of the most beloved traditions of the matchmaking festival, as it is the only daytime event that is hosted by all the vendors and pubs in town."

He scratched the back of his head. "I see." He bent and took the bucket from Sara and made his way to the front wall of the shop. Dipping his brush in, then taking care not to have too much excess on the bristles, he methodically swiped up and down on the wall.

Catríona followed him. "And bein' that it's a daytime affair, many folk bring their families with them."

Donal stilled. "Families?"

"Yes, Donal." She closed the distance between them. "You're not the only one in your predicament, ya know? And even those who don't have kids come with their cousins or nieces and nephews. There's always a huge throng that shows up, and the craic is mighty."

"Will this be like the walking tour?" he asked, swiping his brush on a new section of wall.

Her face scrunched. "How do you mean?"

"Am I goin' on my own, or do ya have someone in mind fer me to go with?"

Ah, that. It had been nearly a week since she'd set him up with anyone specific, and when she had, it hadn't gone very well. She'd been so focused on Andrew and her other in-town clients that she'd all but forgotten about actually matching Donal. She promised herself to be more intentional with her clients while she was still here. "This one ye're going on yer own, but I'm workin' on some other meetups for ya."

"Mm-hmm." He finished his current stroke before turning to dip his brush in the bucket.

"So, the square is over at the crossroads of Main—"

"I know where the square is," he interrupted her. "It's just over there." He gestured in the general direction of where it would be. Only he gestured with the hand holding the freshly loaded paintbrush, sending a large glob of paint flying through the air and landing directly on Catríona's face.

Catríona gasped and froze, eyes glued shut by the paint, mouth agape, until she felt a drip slide down her nose in the direction of her lips, so she pressed them closed.

"Oh my goodness!" Donal exclaimed. "I'm so sorry, are ya alright?"

"Da! What're ya like?" Sara's footsteps rushed over, though Catríona couldn't see her with her eyes still closed.

"I'm fine. It's nothing. I'm grand." She grabbed the glob of paint and then shook her hand to the side.

"Oy!" Donal shouted again and Sara erupted into a fit of giggles.

Catríona cracked one eye open—partly because she was worried paint would get in it and partly because she was terrified of what she feared she'd just done. Her vision was fuzzy at first, but as it cleared, she saw Donal standing there, jaw slack, hands held out to the sides. White paint speckled his face, hair, and clothes.

"Oh, Donal, I . . ." But words failed her.

"Ya know, I didn't mean ta fling the paint at ye. Ya didn't have to retaliate." Humor laced his voice, but his face was so serious, Catríona's stomach dropped. Meanwhile, Sara was doubled over, still laughing, arm outstretched, her finger pointing at her dad.

"No, I didn't mean—"

Donal took his brush and flicked it in Catríona's direction, sending a shower of mini paint droplets all over her.

"So that's what it's going to be like, eh?" She bent to her side and stuck her hand in the paint bucket, keeping her eyes trained on Donal.

"Now, Catríona, let's talk about this," he said, sidestepping her in a circle, his hands held up in front of him. "Let's just let bygones be bygones. Aye?" A wide grin split his face, and a light she'd never seen before danced in his eyes.

She pretended to consider his offer, then said, "No, I think I want revenge." She lifted her hand from the bucket in a fist. She raised it in front of her slowly, and Donal poised himself in a stance she imagined he used when trying to corral Bó or Pete into the barn after they'd escaped. She quickly flicked her fingers outward, and large splotches of paint landed on his arms and face.

He released a robust laugh. Then they both lunged for the bucket at the same time. Sara squealed as Donal and Catríona flung the white emulsion at one another. In a flash, all three were joined in the good-natured war, and laughter and squeals filled the air.

Catríona grabbed Donal's wrist and swiped a large smear down the sleeve of his shirt. He responded by wrapping his arm around her waist and holding her tight. With his other hand, he slowly ran his paint-laden fingers down her cheek. She sucked in a gasp at the cold, wet goop now covering her face.

"Oh, you've gone and done it now, Bunratty," Catríona said through gritted teeth.

"Get 'im, Catríona, get 'im!" Sara transferred another handful of paint into Catríona's hand. Donal still had her by the waist, so she turned toward him in order to reach his face with her refreshed ammunition. But before she could plant the goop on his face, she stilled. Their eyes locked, both breathless, and they stayed that way for a long moment. Not even the paint sliding out of her hand and down her arm could tear Catríona away from his gaze.

"I think . . ." he whispered.

"Yes?" she said, barely able to breathe.

He blinked for the first time since they'd locked eyes, breaking the trance that had overcome them. He cleared his throat. "I think . . . I think we're out of paint." His arm slid from around her waist, and he stepped back, taking his warmth with him.

Catríona dropped her gaze, and it fell on the bucket, which was, as it turned out, empty. Over her shoulder, someone cleared their throat. She turned to see Andrew, hands on hips, scowling at them both.

"Catríona, a word?" His foot tapped impatiently on the ground, and he flashed Donal a look of disgust.

Taking a steadying breath, Catríona straightened her posture and tugged at the bodice of her dress, fully aware that nothing she did could return the decorum she'd worked so hard to display in his presence up till now. "Of course." A nervous smile quivered on her lips. "Just one moment."

Turning back to Donal, she said, "Um . . . sorry about that." She glanced at the paint bucket and back up to him. "It appears I owe you more paint."

His bottom lip pushed up his top one as he shook his head. "*Ná bac leis sin*," he said. "Don't bother with that. After all, I was the one who started it."

Heat flashed up her cheeks and she smiled. "Well, that's true," she said softly. "But I kept it going. I'll set things straight with Owen."

Donal's face flushed.

Before he could protest any further, Catríona continued, "Anyway, will you come tomorrow? To the square?"

His gaze searched her face for a long moment, his eyes conveying something she couldn't read. "Aye, I'll be there."

Sara stepped up next to him, paint covering her from almost head to toe. "*We'll* be there," she said through a wide grin.

"Right." Donal sighed. "We'll be there."

14

Catríona brushed her hands down the front of the skirt of her dress, more out of nervous habit than in an actual attempt to smooth or clear anything. "Andrew, how are ya?"

As she approached him, he held his palms out toward her. "That's quite close enough, if you please."

She blinked as though she'd been slapped. "Yes, of course. I'm a mess. We had . . . a bit of an . . . accident."

"I saw this so-called accident, but that's not why I wish to speak with you." He yanked a handkerchief from his inside breast pocket and handed it to her, gesturing to her face.

"Thank you." She rubbed across her forehead and cheeks, but most of what was there had already dried on. "What did you want to discuss?"

"How much are my parents paying you for your services?"

Her face twisted in thought. "It depends on the match that's made and the terms that are set with it."

"I see." He tugged his suit coat straighter. "And did you truly believe Miss McGowan and I to be a good match?"

Catríona's mouth bobbed open and closed like a fish out of water as heat crept up her neck. "Hester has lots of good qualities."

"That may be so," he said with a sniff, "but none of the qualities were on display last night. The woman has as much mirth and joie de vivre as an undertaker."

Swallowing a guffaw, she nodded. "Thank you for letting me know. Matchmaking isn't an exact science, and it often takes some trial and error."

"It took McDougal no trial at all. He had my match made almost immediately!" His hand twirled in a flourish as he spoke.

Catríona simply gave him a look that said, "And how well did that work out for you in the end?"

Andrew sighed and slid his hands into his pockets, his ire clearly cooling a bit. "Alright, so it wasn't a perfect match."

Catríona bobbed her head.

"But it was a far cry closer than Hester McGowan," he added hastily.

Now it was Catríona's turn to hold her hands up, but more in surrender than in defense. "Alright, yes, I see your point." She twisted his handkerchief in her hands. "I'm not through with your matching yet, Andrew. I'll be sure the next girl is worthy of the Osborne name."

"Mm." Andrew looked down his nose at her. "Very well. Perhaps you might find someone to accompany me to the dance at the square?"

"You wish to attend? I thought you didn't dance?"

"I don't." He shrugged. "But I hear it's to be great fun, and if nothing else, we can stroll the grounds together or take in a pint at the Ritz." He winked, setting her heart aflutter.

Catríona pulled her lips into a thin line and bobbed her head again. "Of course. I'll see what I can do." She picked at some dry paint in her hair. "Now, if you'll excuse me, I need to clean up for tonight's events at the Imperial."

He looked at her as if to say, "That's an understatement," then gestured to her hands. "Keep the handkerchief."

She smiled sheepishly and waved it at him, both as a gesture of thanks and a white flag of surrender. "I'll be in touch about the dance."

At that, he turned on his heel and strode decisively down the street. Catríona watched his form shrink as the distance between them grew. What had she been thinking setting him up with Hester? Yes, she'd meant to pair him with someone he would never be attracted to, but she should've been smarter about it. Now, if she wasn't careful, she'd lose his trust altogether, his parents would cancel their agreement with her, and she'd be stuck here forever.

Sara skipped along next to her dad as they headed home. They'd have to wash up, and the laundry would be a bear, of course, but she didn't care. This was the most fun they'd had together in a very long time. She slowed her skips and slid her hand into his.

"Did ya mean it, Da?" She peered up at him and giggled at the splotch of paint that was stuck on his ear.

"Mean what, luhv?"

She tugged on his hand. "About the dance, ya silly billy! Are ya really going? And do I really get to go too?"

He stopped and stooped down to look her in the eye. "Is that what ye'd like?" His gaze searched her face.

She nodded. "Aye, a dhaidí, it is."

His lips pressed into a tight sort of smile. Not the carefree one she'd seen on him back at Owen's shop, but the one he used when he was agreeing to something he really didn't want to do. "Then, yes, we'll go. The both of us."

"Yeehoo!" Sara whooped, then jumped up and threw her arms around his neck.

He stood, lifting her off the ground as she clung to him. Then, in one fell swoop, he flung her around so she was riding piggyback. She giggled and pushed his hair from tickling her nose.

"Who knows," he said as he did a little giddyap step, "mebbe ye'll bring me good luck. Ye can help me pick out a nice gairl, aye?"

Sara grinned as she watched the sea appear in a thin line on the horizon before they turned onto the Bog Road. A hint of an idea had bloomed in her mind. "Aye."

———◦∞◦———

The next day, Donal and Sara strolled up to the square a little past one o' the clock.

Sara tugged on his hand, and he squatted low so he was eye level with her. "Now, don't be nervous," she told him. "Ye're a fine dancer."

Donal chuckled and tweaked his daughter's cheek. "Thanks, miss."

"And don't be worried what ya say neither. Ye're a grand chat when ya just relax."

"Am I now?"

Sara bobbed her head enthusiastically. "Mm-hmm!"

"And what makes ya think I'm worrying about what to say?"

She rolled her eyes playfully. "Nine years of experience." Then she scowled at his head and reached up to brush a stray cowlick off his forehead. "But we still need ta figure out somethin' with this hair."

He took her hand away from his hair and kissed it. "One thing at a time, eh?"

She scoffed. "Och! Fine."

"Good gairl." He bussed her cheek, then stood and surveyed the square. Along the south side, a group of musicians played a lively jig. Several couples already bobbed and swayed around the makeshift dance floor while others milled about the perimeter or sat and talked on the benches that flanked the border of the square.

"I'm gonna go see what I can find," Sara said, then hurried off.

"Wait, what are ya lookin' for?"

She stopped and tossed her hands with great frustration. "For yer wife, silly!" She then turned and scurried off again.

Donal puffed a chuckle through his nose and shook his head. "Of course," he muttered to himself. "How ridiculous of me."

"I see ye're still deep in thought," Deirdre said as she stepped up next to him.

Donal startled. "Hello there."

"Is that yer wee girl?" she asked.

He smiled after his daughter. "Aye. She's a blessing." After a pause, he added with a laugh, "And a handful."

Deirdre smiled up at him. "The best ones always are."

Donal scratched at his jaw as he mulled over her comment. "Aye, I suppose they are," he said with a nod.

The band ended their tune to delighted applause before jumping into an up-tempo reel. Donal's toe instinctively tapped to the rhythm, his heart matching pace with the driving bodhrán beat. He used to love dancing, and the traditional music of his ancestors always set his pulse soaring and his heart pounding. There was something in the music that almost seemed part of his own soul, and he couldn't sit still in its presence.

He felt Deirdre watching him more than he could see it. He met her gaze.

"Ya like the music?" A playful smile curved the corner of her lips.

Why did he feel as though he'd been caught skimming the cream off the milk bucket? He bobbled his head side to side. "I can't lie, I really do. I don't get out to hear it near often enough."

"Well . . ." Her eyes flitted to the dance floor and back to him. "Would ya fancy a dance?"

He wanted to turn her down. Not because she wasn't nice or pretty or kind. But because it felt wrong. Nae, not wrong as in immoral. Wrong as in . . . strange. Out of place. He'd not danced with anyone since Connie. Before? Oh, there'd been plenty of dance partners at the pub on a harvest night. But since Connie, all that had just felt frivolous. He'd been so bogged down with the farm and livestock and raising Sara that making time for fun that didn't produce anything felt . . . irresponsible. But he was here now. The harvest was in—what little of it there was. He pushed that thought out of his mind as soon as it materialized. What good was it for him to come if he wasn't going to participate?

At length he smiled. "I believe I would." He poked his elbow out in an offer to escort her into the square.

She slid her tiny hand into the crook of his arm, and they made their way to the floor. The band was in fine form this afternoon and the pace quick. Donal's legs shook. He felt about as steady on his feet as a new calf. But as the dance went on, his muscles began to remember the steps, and he settled into a more comfortable routine. He was so focused on remembering *how* to dance that he was sure he was a horrible partner to dance with. He wasn't able to lead Deirdre as properly as he'd have liked because it took all his energy and concentration not to step on her toes or sweep a foot out from under her.

When the song ended, he nearly collapsed right there on the dance floor. He took a few gasping puffs of air before braving a look at Deirdre's face. When he finally ventured a glance, they both burst into laughter.

"That . . . was . . . quite the . . . reel!" she said, clearly winded herself.

"Sit?" He huffed and pointed to a bench where Sara was seated, arms folded across her chest, lips jutted out in a pout.

"Please," she said with a laugh.

They made their way to the bench, and as they approached, Donal asked Sara what was wrong.

"I couldn't find her." The pout returned.

"Couldn't find who?" he asked, full breaths still evading him.

She pinned him with a you-know-darn-well-who look.

His brows arched, and his mouth formed a circle. "Oh." When Deirdre's back was turned, he mouthed to Sara, "My wife?"

She nodded.

"Ah, well," Donal replied, "I'm sure she's around here somewhere."

Deirdre lowered herself into the seat as she mopped her brow. "Who is it ye're lookin' for?"

"No one," Sara murmured.

"Deirdre, this is my daughter, Sara Bunratty." He gestured between the two. "And Sara, this is Miss Deirdre O'Malley."

Deirdre extended her hand. "It's a pleasure to meet you!"

Sara offered a tight smile and shook her hand. "Likewise."

Donal's breaths were coming more easily now, and he was suddenly aware that his mouth was bone-dry. "I heard rumors that there was lemonade somewhere. Would you ladies like some?"

"Oh, yes, please," Deirdre said.

"I guess," Sara mumbled.

"Three lemonades—or . . . whatever it is they have—comin' right up!" He followed the perimeter of the square. More merrymakers had arrived while they had been dancing, and he had to bob and weave around someone at every turn. Finally, near the entrance to the Ritz, he found a table offering lemonade, tea, and pints of the dark, almost-black stout original to Ireland. While rarely one to ever turn down a cuppa tea, he was far too warm and parched for a hot drink at the moment. He scooped up three lemonades, thanked the keeper behind the table, and made his way back through the gauntlet to Deirdre and Sara—who looked equally as uncomfortable as the other. While Sara was staring a hole into the ground in front of her, Deirdre watched the crowd, a look of growing concern shadowing her face.

"Here ya go, luhv." Donal handed Sara her drink. "This should perk ya right up." He handed Deirdre her glass, and she absently thanked him. His thirst was so great, it took all the self-control he could muster not to down his whole glass in one gulp.

At last, he sank onto the bench between the two, grateful to get off his feet for a few minutes.

"Donal, do you know who that man is?"

Donal followed Deirdre's gaze, but there were at least two dozen men on the dance floor. "Which one?"

"The fancy one." She jutted her chin toward the crowd. "With the blond hair."

At that moment, a few couples spun just right so as to give Donal a clear view of Andrew, holding his dance partner far closer than the song called for. Though the woman didn't seem to mind much—Donal recognized her as the "stockman" who'd been sizing the lads up on the walking tour.

"That's Andrew Osborne," he answered after a long beat. "His family owns land down in County Dublin, and they've come here to match him up with a wife."

Deirdre practically snorted.

"Why do you ask?" He shifted to see her face more clearly.

"There are rumors flyin' about him all over town. Rumors that he"—she leaned forward to see if Sara was listening, then lowered her voice—"that he's been makin' himself far too familiar with the staff gairls over at the Queens. And most of them are none too happy about it neither."

Donal's stomach clenched. He'd wondered as much after seeing Andrew's behavior at the picnic, and the way he played things so hot and cold toward Catríona. On one hand, it felt good to have his suspicions validated, but on the other—and much more disturbingly—he hated that any young woman would have to suffer his fiendish behavior. "That's terrible" was all he could manage in response.

Deirdre shook her head. "And seein' him there now, with that one all snuggled up to 'im. It's disgustin'."

"Aye, it is." He splayed his fingers across his jawline and scratched. "Have any of those other gairls brought accusations forward?"

She shrugged. "Not that I'm aware. As far as I know, it hasn't gone so far as to warrant that, necessarily." She faced Donal more fully. "But if he's allowed to carry on like this, it's only a matter of time before it does. I'm sure of it."

"Quite possib—"

"Catríona!" Sara shouted, startling both Donal and Deirdre. Sara jumped up and bolted across the floor.

Donal watched as Catríona greeted Sara. He smiled at their sweet interaction.

"I'll just be off, then," Deirdre said as she stood.

Donal stood as well. "Oh, you don't have to go."

Deirdre smiled. "It's alright. My friend just arrived and she's waving me over."

"Well, alright then." Donal slid his hands in his pockets. "Thanks for the dance."

She curtsied. "Anytime. The pleasure was all mine," she said, then left.

"Da! Da!"

Donal pivoted on his heel to see Sara running up to him, dragging Catríona by the hand. "Yes, darlin'?"

Sara beamed. "I found yer next dance partner."

Donal looked to Catríona, whose face was as red as a beat. She offered him a sheepish grin and a shrug.

"Oh, pet, I don't think—"

"You promised!" Sara interrupted.

"Whoa, I made no such promise." Then he looked at Catríona and said, "I did not promise her I'd dance with ye."

"Och! Da." She strung the last word out long and whiny. Then Sara stepped closer to him and motioned for him to lower down. When he did, she whispered, "You asked me last night to help you. You said I could help."

He studied her face for a beat, while searching his own mind for a reason to refute her. He did say that perhaps she might be able to help him find someone. Though the chances of Catríona Daly becoming his wife were slim to none. So, what harm could it do to dance one jig or reel? He'd danced with loads of girls as a younger man, none of whom held expectations of marriage.

"Alright," he said, booping the tip of her nose with his index finger. "But only because ye're so cute."

Sara grinned and clapped her hands before turning to Catríona. "Ye're gonna go dance with my dad now."

Catríona's shoulders bounced in amusement. "Am I now?"

"Yep!"

Donal placed his hand on Sara's shoulder. "I'll take it from here." Then he stepped closer to Catríona, hand held out to her. "May I have this dance?"

Catríona's gaze flitted to Sara and back. She smiled and placed her hand in Donal's. "It'd be an honor."

They hopped onto the dance floor, ready to join the fast-paced polka, but just as they got into position, the tune changed, and the fiddle began to play "*An Cailín Bán.*" The slow air was haunting and full. Catríona met Donal's gaze, her eyes wide like a doe startled by a hunter. The same fear gripped Donal, pinning him where he stood. This seemed far too intimate a way to share a first dance.

"Actually, I need another drink. I'm rather parched," Donal said.

Catríona nodded. "Aye, me too. We can dance in a wee while."

Sara grabbed both their hands. "Ah, g'on. It's just a dance. It's not like ye're proposin' marriage." Sara's eyes widened, and she clamped a hand over her mouth. Donal had rattled off that old phrase a million times when Sara tried to avoid doing a particular chore or did not want to work with one of the kids from a neighboring farm. He suspected she realized the old saying hit a little too close to home for their current situation and couldn't help but laugh at the irony of it all now.

"Alright, alright," Donal said. "We'll go." He offered his hand to Catríona once more and led her back onto the dance floor. He gently placed his right hand around her waist, as Catríona slid one hand up on his shoulder. She stepped closer so they could move freely to the music, fitting into his arms like she was always meant to be there, making Donal instantly feel right at home and fully alive all at once.

They joined the swirling crowd, some practically snogging on the dance floor, others stiffly going through the motions. But as the song played on, Donal found himself getting lost in the moment. There was no awkward footing, no shaky legs. The rest of the world faded away, and it was just the music and him and the beautiful woman in his arms. The lyrics of the song floated through his mind, and it tore at his heart how much they matched his own thoughts. His own desires. He couldn't bring himself to fight them anymore. The song spoke of the deep sadness that would fill the man's heart if the woman he loved didn't return his affection. And while it was far too soon to say he was in love with Catríona, the thought of having to release her in a few short moments filled him with dread. So he let his eyes drift closed and allowed himself to be fully immersed in wherever the music would take them.

Donal's grip on her hand tightened ever so slightly as she relaxed into the smooth, slow steps of the dance. At first, the idea of dancing to such a song with a man like Donal Bunratty had terrified her. She worried that he might get the wrong idea. But Sara's gaze was so persuasive—it reminded Catríona of the wee puppy who used to come around the pub. Her dad had told her not to feed him, but she just couldn't say no to those big, pleading eyes. And Sara had had the same effect on her.

Donal seemed utterly lost in the moment, with his eyes closed, his feet leading them effortlessly around the dance floor. And then, from deep within his chest, the humming began. A rich, baritone voice that rumbled in his core and drew Catríona in. She was certain no one else on the floor could hear it. Perhaps no one else in the world. But his voice lured Catríona in like a siren with its almost hypnotic silky tone. Slowly, she rested her head on his chest, her own eyes fluttering shut. His arm slipped tighter around her waist, and she had never felt safer or more protected than in that place, in his arms, his voice reverberating through them both.

Loud applause jolted her out of the delicious trance she'd fallen into. Her eyes flew open, and she stepped back a pace, cold air rushing in to fill the space between them.

"You, eh, you have a lovely voice."

Confusion crinkled his forehead.

She smiled and her shoulders bobbed slightly. "You were humming."

Donal's jaw fell slack and his brows soared. "I was not!" It was more a statement of disbelief than of rebuttal.

"Aye." Catríona nodded. "And you have a very lovely voice."

His cheeks flushed above his stubbled chin, and his gaze dipped to the floor before popping back up to hers. "And you have a lovely . . . well . . . you."

"Och! Daaaa!"

15

Catríona rushed to her flat as fast as her feet could carry her—which wasn't nearly fast enough, given the size of the throng milling all around the square and along Main Street. When did all these people get here, anyway?

"Caty! Wait, Caty!"

Ignoring Maeve's calls, Catríona continued on toward the Imperial. Once there, she stopped briefly as her mouth fell open. The pub was chockablock, wall-to-wall people. In the middle of the day. She pushed her way through the crowd and took the steps two by two, grateful that she knew the way by heart since tears had completely clouded her vision.

At last, she exploded into the flat and collapsed onto the bed. What on earth had just happened? How had a simple, innocent dance made her feel such things? She barely even knew Donal. And while he wasn't hard on the eyes, his looks didn't hold a candle to Andrew's breathtaking features. She forced herself to bring an image of the young Osborne into her mind's eye. His deep blue eyes, sparkling with mischief, his perfectly coiffed blond hair, the chiseled cut of his jaw. Yes, that was what she was looking for. That, and the fact that he wasn't a farmer or shepherd or anything of that ilk.

The strident slam from the other room told her that Maeve had finally caught up to her. "Catríona Mary Daly!"

Catríona groaned, grabbed the edge of the duvet, and rolled herself up in it like a sausage roll.

"Okay, lass, what in the world was that?" Maeve asked as she plopped down on the edge of the bed.

Catríona drew the duvet closer around her. "What was what?" she murmured into the thick fabric.

Maeve gripped Catríona's shoulder and rolled her so they were face-to-face, even though the duvet obstructed any view of Catríona's features. Maeve slowly lowered the blanket from Catríona's face. "Caty. What was that?"

Catríona feigned ignorance. "What? Oh, that? It was nothing." She forced a laugh. "His wee daughter, Sara, she wanted us to dance. We weren't gonna, but she gave us those puppy dog eyes, so we just had one dance."

Maeve blinked hard and looked at Catríona with wide eyes. "That was some dance!"

"It was just like any other dance," Catríona lied.

Maeve settled a look on her. Clearly the woman wasn't taking that for truth, but that wasn't Catríona's fault. Maeve cleared her throat. "In all my years of knowin' ya, Catríona Daly, I've never seen ya dance like *that*. Wit' anyone."

Catríona shot up. "Dance like what?"

Maeve's gaze drifted to the ceiling as if searching for the right words to communicate whatever it was she was trying to say. "Ye looked smitten wit' each other. Ye looked . . ."

"Don't say it."

"Ye looked in love."

Catríona lifted watery eyes to meet her friend's gaze. "I told ya not to say it," she said, her voice barely audible. "I hardly know the man. There's no way we could be in love."

127

Maeve rolled her eyes. "Och! I didna say ye *were* in love. I said ye *looked* in love. There's a difference."

Catríona wiped her eyes and shrugged, unsure of how to respond.

"I'll tell ya though"—she wiggled closer and tucked her feet up underneath herself—"if a man held me like that? Danced with me like that?" She puffed a breath through her lips and shook her head.

"Oh, stop it, wouldja?"

"What?" Maeve tossed a single hand up and let it fall.

"Do ya really not see it?" Catríona's chest burned and tightened. Maeve of all people should know exactly why Catríona could never be with Donal Bunratty. Or any man like him.

"I really don't, Cat. Why doncha enlighten me."

"I could never be with a man like that, Maeve. You know that!"

Maeve gave an exaggerated nod, the corners of her mouth pulled down in a look of mock wisdom. "Oh, yes, that's right. Why would ya ever want to be with a man who is kind, honest, not too bad to look at." She shrugged. "Oh, and then dances with ye like that. How ridiculous of me."

"Maeve!" Her friend flinched at the sheer volume of her voice, but she didn't care. It was the only way she was going to get through to her, apparently. "Donal Bunratty is everything I'm trying to escape!"

Maeve heaved a single laugh, but it was completely devoid of any mirth.

"He's a farmer. He's a single father." Catríona counted on her fingers for added emphasis and clarity. "He can barely afford his farm—that's why he needs a wife. So he doesn't lose his farm."

"Does all that really matter?" Maeve placed a gentle hand

on Catríona's knee. "I always kinda thought that was just . . . excuses."

"Not excuses, Maeve. *Reasons*. They're reasons." Catríona shoved the duvet off and pushed herself past Maeve and off the bed. "And they're bloomin' good reasons, if ya ask me. Is it a crime to want to have a life of stability and ease?"

Maeve just stared back, unmoving.

"Ye forget. I've lived his kind of life once already. And God as my witness, I won't live it again."

She yanked her shawl off the peg and struggled to tie it around her neck.

"So, ye've spent time talkin' to God about this? That's good. Cause it sorta seemed to me ye were doin' this all on ye're own and hopin' He'll catch the message."

Catríona gasped as if she'd been slapped in the face. She pulled the shawl from around her neck—what was wrong with the blasted thing, anyway? It wouldn't tie for the life of her. She wadded it up and threw it on the floor, then leveled a glare at Maeve and stormed out. She wasn't sure where she was going to go, but she just couldn't be here any longer.

She scurried down the steps to find the pub now blessedly empty. Her father must have sent them out on one of his midday adventures. She made for the door, anticipating the cool rush of fresh air once she made it outside, but her father called her before she could make her escape.

"Caty!" he called again.

She stopped, hand poised on the door, ready to swing it open. She pressed her eyes closed for a second as her head fell backward. Taking a deep breath, she exhaled slowly. "Coming, Da."

Sluggishly, she turned and made her way into their office. "Yeah?"

He rubbed at his eyes with one hand and gestured for her to

sit with the other. Catríona complied and noticed for the first time how tired her father looked. Dark shadows ringed his eyes, and his skin was pale.

"Are ya alright?" she asked, reaching across and taking his hand.

He scoffed and flapped his free hand. "*Psh!* I'm grand out. Just need a wee bit o' shut-eye." He shook his head and ran his hands over his hair, which returned to its customary state of jutting out in all directions as soon as it was untouched. "Matchin' Lady Wyndham-Quin is gonna be the death o' me."

Oh, that's right! Catríona had completely forgotten about her father having to match the landlord's last remaining living daughter. His other two had sadly passed away—the most recent one only four years ago. She couldn't imagine the pressure her father was feeling. "Tough goin', eh?"

He let out a puff of air that sent his lips flapping. "I've not had one this tough since Biddy Bridewell wanted me to match her perfect, darling son."

Catríona couldn't help the laughter that bubbled up at the memory of precious little Tommy Bridewell. He could do no wrong in his mammy's eyes, but boy was that lad trouble in just about every way. "Well, ya worked that one out eventually. I'm sure ye'll get this lady sorted as well."

Her father wagged his head. "I dunno, luhv. I've been lookin' at her pedigree, and no one I'm comin' up with is good enough."

"Oh?"

"Her father was in the House of Commons under Queen Victoria. He attended the coronation of King Edward, for cryin' out loud. Tell me, who do we have rattlin' around here that would match that status?"

Catríona drew in a long breath as she mulled that over. He was right. No one from the area would fit that bill. And she'd not heard of any of the gentry who'd traveled in for the festival that would be near to matching their station. "I'll keep my ear to the ground. That's a tough one. But I've no doubt Ireland's finest matchmaker is up to the task."

The smile he offered didn't quite reach his eyes, but he thanked her anyway. She'd never seen him so unsure of a match. And if he was going to have one miss in his decades of matchmaking, this was for sure not the one to mess up.

He took a sip of his steaming tea and that seemed to reset his mood a bit. "So, how goes it with young Osborne?"

"Well . . ." Catríona sighed. "It's goin'."

He took another sip of tea, then poured another cup and slid it across the table to Catríona.

"What's yer trouble there?"

She took a long draw of the hot liquid to hide the truth she feared he might read in her eyes. That her trouble was needing more time to win him over and that Andrew was growing impatient with her matches thus far—or lack thereof. "It's just takin' some time to hone in on his tastes." She wiggled in her seat and crossed one ankle over the other. "He has very specific preferences but isn't great about communicating them clearly."

"Aye," he said around a mouthful of brown bread. "That happens sometimes."

"Mm-hmm." Another sip of tea.

"But the feis is practically almost half gone, so don't dillydally."

"I know, Da!" Catríona immediately regretted her tone, but she couldn't help it. Could no one see that she had a plan? She knew what she was doing. *You'd better hope you do, lass.* She shoved the thought away like a pest, then stood. "Speakin' of, I'd best be off. Lots to do."

Her father eyed her for a long moment, and she could tell he was trying to read her mind. At length, he nodded. "*Go n-éirí an bóthar leat.*"

She smiled. "And good luck to yerself. I t'ink ya need it more than I do." She leaned around the table, bussed her father's cheek, and left.

16

When they arrived home later that afternoon, Donal sent Sara inside to wash up and take care of her house chores while he checked on the animals. His trusty stock lowed softly in their customary greeting as he entered the barn.

"Hallo, lads and lassies," he muttered absently, turning to check their feed. As Donal rounded the corner into the small stall he used to store the grains and oats, his mouth fell open. Where was all their feed? He bent and dug through the little remaining grain as though he'd find more buried underneath. Tipping backward he flopped onto his rump and pinched the bridge of his nose, trying to recount all the feedings he'd done over the last two weeks. *Aye, that's about right.* He just hadn't realized he was coming down to the dregs of it already. Standing with a grunt, he made a mental note to check his coffer at home to see how much more he could purchase. Would that it was summer and he could allow them to graze on the grasses, as was preferred by all cattle farmers in Ireland. The sheep were hardy enough for it, but during these harsher autumn and winter months, livestock had to be housed and their diets supplemented with grain feeds to ensure their safety and the safety of the fields.

To run out now was a horrible turn of luck. Or poor planning on Donal's part. Then he remembered—his harvest had been smaller than previous years due to troubles with his equipment and bad weather, so his income had been less as well. He wasn't able to buy the typical amount of feed and had to settle for a smaller order and hope that he'd be able to make another purchase later into the winter. If he couldn't get his cows' dairy production up, there'd be no chance of that either.

Sighing, he grabbed the wheelbarrow from the corner and headed out to the turf stacks. He needed to get the remaining briquettes in and stored before the weather turned. And if his aching knees had anything to say about it, a storm would be brewing soon.

Maybe it's not the weather but yer dancin' that's the problem. He shook his head at the thought.

When he arrived at the turf stacks, he began checking each one, one briquette at a time. Sara had done a good job with the turns, and all sides were sufficiently dry so as not to mold and mildew while stored. He started loading them into the wheelbarrow, setting a rhythm as he worked, humming one of the jaunty tunes he'd heard that afternoon. Before long, it was full to the top brim. Donal grabbed the handles to head over to the next row, and the next, until all the turf was brought in and ready to be properly stored.

After wrestling the wheelbarrow back to the shed and stacking most of it, he put the rest into an old potato sack and hefted it up onto his shoulder to take to the house. Once there, he loaded the bucket next to the fireplace with what he could and put the bag in the lean-to shelter just outside the back door for easy access later.

Then he went to the kitchen, washed his hands in the basin, and set the kettle on to boil. A quick scan of the cupboards revealed his and Sara's provisions were getting fairly low as well. Because of course they were.

He sighed and rubbed his forehead, hoping to relieve the dull ache that had taken up residence there. The kind that came from carrying the weighted burden of worry upon his shoulders. The kind that tensed every muscle and tendon and refused to let go.

He turned to the press Connie had brought when she moved in. Reaching to Donal's height, the top had open shelves that housed various and sundry cups, teapots, and some of Sara's art projects—including the paper flowers he'd used for her birthday celebration. The bottom half was like a chest of drawers. Sliding open the center drawer, he pulled out his money pouch, cringing at the lack of heft of it in his hand. He silently tallied the amount in his head. There was enough, most importantly, to provide him and Sara food for the rest of the season. But that was about it. No extra for feed, turf, or any other emergencies that may arise.

"Lord, what do I do?" he said on a sigh.

The prayer felt foreign on his lips, which unnerved him even further. Faith in God had been a staple of his life for years— turning to God for favor in the planting and harvest, for wisdom in raising Sara, and the like. But ever since Connie died, his prayers had grown short. Less urgent. Far less frequent. He'd prayed so fervently for God to heal Connie. Not so much, he was mortified to admit, because of his love for her—though he believed they did grow to love each other in their own way—but because he was terrified of what would happen to him and Sara if she died. Connie had done so much, from keeping the house and cooking to helping Sara with her learning before she started school, but also with her connections and relationships in the community. When she passed, rekindling those connections on his own felt odd. Awkward. Like he was an imposter trading on a good name he had no right to. That's why they'd made such a good team. Connie, though quiet, was outgoing and so good with people. She could read them—their emotions, their intentions. Sometimes he wondered if she could even read their thoughts. Meanwhile, Donal was content to keep his friendships to one or two of the lads in the area and chose to confide in his cattle rather than people. So, once it was just him and Sara, Donal had let those connections go, insulating himself—and Sara—more and more each passing year, until it was quite literally just the two of them figuring things out. And it worked just fine for them. Until it didn't.

He'd begged God to heal Connie. And He hadn't. If God was all-knowing, then He knew what it would mean for Donal and Sara to be without the woman of the house, and He still chose to do nothing. So, trusting Him now was challenging and remote.

They just needed a break. Some kind of relief from the constant riptide current of hardships and scraping by. But that's not how it worked for the rural man in Ireland. Donal sighed and resigned himself to the fact that he'd have to come up with a solution on his own.

Sara cracked her door and peeked through the opening as her dad rummaged through his money pouch. She hated seeing his forehead get all crinkly and his eyes dark like that. She hated that there was nothing she could do to help their situation. And while she knew she wasn't a drain on their household, she couldn't help but feel responsible for the bulk of his worries because he worried so much about providing for her.

Just then, a thought drifted into her mind. A faint memory of something Sister Margaret had talked about once. About a talk *Íosa Críost* had given a long time ago. Sara remembered feeling comforted by it at the time and thought maybe her dad—who was now standing at the basin, hands pressed on the edge of the sink, head hung low—might now too.

Taking a deep breath, she slid the door open wider and slipped into the kitchen. She watched him again for another long beat, trying to gather her words before speaking.

"Da?"

His head popped up and he looked over his shoulder. His eyes were red and glassy, though his cheeks were dry. He smiled that sad sort of smile she saw from him all too often. "Hallo, pet. C'mon, give us a hug."

Sara scurried over and wrapped her arms around his waist, relishing in the deep, earthy scent of his clothes that was special just to her dad. He never smelled gross or stinky, despite how hard he worked. Sara wondered how he accomplished that. Today his normal, comforting scent had an added layer to it. The musty, loamy aroma of turf. She inhaled deeply and wrapped herself in it like a blanket. It was the smell of home.

He gave her a wee squeeze and bent and kissed the top of her head, holding a long moment before straightening again. "Best medicine in the whole wairld," he said, his voice thick and husky.

She smiled up at him. "Ever'thing okay with *na ba*?"

He chuckled. "The cows're fine, pet."

Sara nodded and shuffled to the hob as the kettle started to whine. They performed their ritual of making the tea like a well-choreographed dance. Sara smiled at the thought—and at the memory of seeing her father look so happy and so . . . mesmerized . . . dancing with Catríona.

As they settled at the table, she wrapped her hands around her cup and took a stab at what she wanted to share. "Da?"

"Mm?" He stared out the small square window over the basin.

"Have you ever heard of . . ." She paused, her tongue curling around the corner of her lips as she tried to recall what Sister Margaret had called it. "The Serpent on the Mound?"

He turned to look at her, his face crinkled. But not the worried kind. The confused kind of crinkled. "The Serpent on the Mound? Hmm. Can't say I have."

Sara's eyes widened. "Really? Sister Margaret said it's really well-known."

Her dad leaned forward and folded his arms on the table. "She did? Well, why don't ya tell me about it and I might remember a bit." The way the sides of his mouth twitched made Sara curious for a second if he was making fun of her. But he'd never done that in her whole life, so she chose to believe he wasn't now.

"Well," she began, wiggling her rump to a more comfortable spot on her chair. "The Sister says it's one of Íosa's most well-known talks, but I'd never heard of it before that day."

A twinkle in her father's eyes made it seem like he'd figured out what she was talking about, but he didn't say anything. He just waited for her to continue, so she did. "It had a lot of stuff in it that sounded really good to me. Some of it was confusing though."

"Oh? Like what?"

Sara shrugged. "Well, like about flowers wearing clothes and stuff like that."

He cocked his head. "That does sound strange."

"*Nach bhfuil?*"

He nodded. "It does, indeed." He smiled, "But I believe the name of the talk is 'The *Sermon* on the *Mount*.'" He bubbled with laughter.

Sara nodded enthusiastically. "Yes! That's it!" She scratched her nose and wiggled in her seat again. "Anyway, the part that I liked was about how if Íosa loves the birds and animals enough to make sure they have food and places to stay, why wouldn't he do that for us too?"

The smile slid from her dad's face, and Sara's heart skipped a little bit. Had she upset him? "Da? What do you think it meant about the flowers wearing clothes and stuff?"

He reached up and rubbed the back of his neck as he pulled a deep, slow breath in through his nose and let it back out. He stared at an old tea stain on the table for a long time, and Sara wondered if maybe he didn't know.

"It's okay," she added quickly. "It's confusing, that's all."

He looked at her again. "No, it's alright. I think it's exactly what you said."

She scrunched up her nose. But she'd said she didn't know what it meant.

"I think it means that if the flowers don't have to worry about makin' themselves look pretty, and the birds have nests, and animals can find food, then God will provide those things for us too. Because He loves us even more than them."

Sara's mouth opened in a big circle. "He does?"

Her dad nodded seriously. "Oh, aye. That's why the cross happened."

Now it was Sara's turn to study the table. "Wow," she whispered.

"Wow, indeed." He reached over and patted her hand. "Now, why doncha go out and stoke the fire in the grate and I'll get started on supper."

———◦∞◦———

That night, Donal lay in the darkness and chill of midnight and stared at the ceiling. He'd never felt like more of a fraud in his whole life. All that talk about the flowers and animals . . . he couldn't bring himself to tell Sara what he was really thinking. That they needed provision both for their animals and for themselves. And last he checked, manna hadn't fallen from heaven in quite some time, so it seemed unlikely to start now.

He shifted in his bed, rolled to his side, and forced his eyes closed. But they only popped back open. He needed to see it again for himself, so he sat up and let his feet slide over the edge of the bed and onto the ground. He sat there for a moment, unsure if he really wanted to read it. After scratching his head with both hands, he huffed and stood up. As he headed for the sitting room, he paused outside Sara's door and pressed his ear close. Her soft breathing calmed his racing heart and caused a tiny smile to tip the corner of his lips. He didn't deserve her.

Finally, he shuffled into the sitting room, lit one of the gas lanterns, and carried it over to the chest in the center of the room. Opening the heavy lid as quietly as he could, he held the lantern aloft to chase away the inky blackness hiding within. There on the top was the family Bible. Weighing at least half a stone, it had been in his family for as long as he could remember. He wasn't even sure who the first one to have it was. And he couldn't remember the last time he'd looked inside it, let alone read it. In the few years of schooling he'd had, the nuns never encouraged them to read it for themselves. It needed to be interpreted for them, they'd said. Not from Latin to Irish or English but from a spiritual expert so that their feeble minds could grasp it. Though, secretly, Donal had always wondered if that were really true. Why would the Lord give such a thing to His people if not all of them could read it for themselves? Then again, his curiosity on the matter had never been strong enough to drive him to find out for himself—especially in the last six years.

After lifting the book gingerly from its place inside the chest, he set it on his lap and reached up to close the lid. But it slipped from his fingers and fell closed with a loud thud. Donal winced and shot his gaze toward Sara's door and waited. Nothing. That child could sleep through a hurricane.

At length, he set the hefty Bible on top of the chest and put the lantern next to it. He opened it carefully, near the back of the book. He remembered enough from school that if it had Íosa in it, it was toward the back. Moses and Adam and Eve and all them were closer to the front. It took far longer than he'd anticipated, but after flipping through and skimming page after page, he finally came across the subheading "The Sermon on the Mount." He released a soft chuckle remembering Sara's misnomer. In his own mind, it would forever be the "Serpent on the Mound."

He started reading, and the first sentence stopped him in his tracks. "Blessed are the poor," it read. Well, Donal certainly felt poor, what with no way to provide for his family or livestock. But he continued. "Blessed are the poor in spirit; for theirs is the kingdom of heaven."

He dropped his hands to his lap as his gaze drifted around the room. *Poor in spirit, poor in spirit.* The phrase reverberated in his mind. What on earth did it mean to be poor in spirit? He was poor of money, that much was certain. And if his faith was as lacking as he felt it was, would that mean his spirit was also poor—in that it was lacking the richness that a hearty faith could bring? *Boy howdy, Sara was right. This is confusing.*

But he continued, astounded at the contradictions Jesus seemed to make in His statements. Mourners comforted, hungry filled, enemies forgiven, lights under baskets. None of it made a lick of sense to him—and he found that oddly reassuring. To be able to understand the mind of God was a daunting notion.

Then he came to the passage Sara had spoken about regarding the birds and flowers. It was toward the end of the sermon, so he almost missed it. He read it over and over again.

Therefore I say unto you, Take no thought for your life, what ye shall eat, or what ye shall drink; nor yet for your body, what ye shall put on. Is not the life more than meat, and the body than raiment?

Behold the fowls of the air: for they sow not, neither do they reap, nor gather into barns; yet your heavenly Father feedeth them. Are ye not much better than they?

Which of you by taking thought can add one cubit unto his stature?

And why take ye thought for raiment? Consider the lilies of the field, how they grow; they toil not, neither do they spin:

And yet I say unto you, That even Solomon in all his glory was not arrayed like one of these.

Wherefore, if God so clothe the grass of the field, which today is, and tomorrow is cast into the oven, shall he not much more clothe you, O ye of little faith?

Therefore take no thought, saying, What shall we eat? or, What shall we drink? or, Wherewithal shall we be clothed?

(For after all these things do the Gentiles seek:) for your heavenly Father knoweth that ye have need of all these things.

But seek ye first the kingdom of God, and his righteousness; and all these things shall be added unto you.

Take therefore no thought for the morrow: for the morrow shall take thought for the things of itself. Sufficient unto the day is the evil thereof.

Take no thought for tomorrow? Don't worry about what you will eat or drink or wear? How was he supposed to do that? God had always used the farm and harvest to provide for all those things. Until now. God had taken that away as well. How was Donal supposed to not worry about any of that? He shook his head, staring at the page. Finally, he puffed out the lantern in frustration and slunk to his room, leaving the book where it was.

17

A few days later, Donal awoke to footsteps outside his window. Cocking an ear, he waited, breath stuck in his chest in case it was merely a stray dog or a crow pecking at its breakfast. But there it came again. Clear, distinct footsteps. Two sets of them at least . . . and voices. Throwing the covers off, Donal ran to the kitchen, jammed his feet into his wellies, and stumbled out the back door.

"Oy!" He ground at an eye with his fist, trying to clear the blur of heavy sleep from his view. "Who's there?"

Hushed voices drifted from around the front corner of the house, and he hurried to follow them. Two tall gentlemen stood on his front walk. Both wore long, high-quality slicker jackets and wide-brimmed leather hats pulled low over their heads to shield them from the rain that Donal only now realized was coming down in thin streams.

The taller man was gesturing and pointing off in the distance while the other nodded and murmured something in agreement. The second one looked at a tablet in his hand and studied it for a long beat before tucking it back in his pocket and nodding again. Maybe it was the way their faces were covered in shadow from the morning mist and the darkness from their hats. Maybe it was the pretentious way they held themselves or seemed to be making plans for Donal's land as if he wasn't any part of the equation. Whatever it was, their presence stirred an unease in Donal's gut heavier than his mother's old fruitcake.

Donal assumed his most official-looking stance—whatever that meant—and called out, "Can I help ye, lads?"

Their heads spun toward him in unison. Still unable to make out the features of their faces clearly, Donal closed the distance between them.

"Mister Bunratty, glad to find you at home." The taller and, now Donal could see, younger man stepped forward, hand out-stretched. Andrew Osborne.

"Where else might you find me at this early hour?" Donal eyed Andrew's hand for a long beat before reluctantly shaking it.

Andrew breathed out a haughty laugh. "Quite right." He then cleared his throat and gestured to the gentleman with him. "Bunratty, you remember my father, Lord Clement Osborne."

Donal shook the elder Osborne's hand. "Sir."

"Pleasure," the lord replied, his accent tight and thin.

"What can I do for yas?" Donal asked, unable to keep suspicion from lacing his voice.

Andrew flipped his collar up to cover his neck. "I actually thought we might be of some help to one another," he said as he crossed his arms tightly, then eyed the door. "Might we impose upon your hospitality?"

Donal turned and stared at his house. Sara still slumbered inside and likely would another hour or so. "Mightn't we chat in the barn? My daughter's still asleep inside."

The two Osbornes passed a look between them, and the elder finally answered, "That would be fine."

The three lumbered through the wet grass around the other

side of the house and back to the barn. Donal wrestled with the latch and finally, with more trouble than he would've preferred, got it unsecured and swung the door open just wide enough for the men to walk through. Once all were inside, he tugged it closed again. Not so much to keep what modicum of warmth the barn held inside but rather to keep the Osbornes' keen eyes from studying even more of his land than they already had. He felt violated by their brazen confidence in simply traipsing around his property without his knowledge or consent. *That's the problem with the gentry*, he thought to himself. *Think they own everything, even if it belongs to someone else.*

"Right," Donal said, slipping his hands into his pockets. "What brings ye all the way out to Ferry Hill?"

Andrew walked a slow circle around the interior of the barn, seemingly studying every nook and cranny. Bó a Do and Pete—his cattle that ate like pigs—began lowing incessantly at their presence. Donal shushed them and grabbed their morning feed from his grain pile and began filling their troughs, taking comfort in the earthy aroma that wafted up in a dusty cloud as he dumped it in. Just when he was beginning to think he would never hear their reasons for coming, Andrew stepped over to the stall Donal was at and stared at Pete, a strange expression setting onto his face. A peculiar mixture of disgust and confusion.

At last, Andrew spoke. "My man really speaks highly of your stock."

Donal straightened and brushed his palms together a few times. "I'm as glad to hear it as I was that day in town. Did you come all this way for that?"

Andrew scoffed. "Oh, goodness, no." He bobbled his head from side to side. "But also . . . yes. You see, our herd has fallen on hard times during our absence. We lost one heifer to thieves and two other cows to an illness."

Donal's brows pulled together. "Hard luck. I'm sorry to hear that."

"As was I," Lord Osborne mumbled, along with a few choice words for whoever had stolen his property.

Andrew watched his father, annoyance flashing in his eyes before turning his attention back to Donal. "Yes, well. My man insists that any new stock we acquire come from your breeding."

Donal blinked hard and craned his neck to peek at his ever-shrinking herd. "I'm flattered, sir, but I'm afraid that's not possible."

"But of course it is!" Lord Osborne blurted. Then he gestured to Andrew, his expression making it clear he wished to expedite the explanation of the matter. Donal couldn't help but agree.

Andrew shifted his weight and continued, "I know you've fallen on hard times."

Donal blanched slightly. "You do?"

Andrew's gaze drifted around the perimeter of the barn. "Well, 'tisn't a state secret, man. Your barn is a shambles—it looks ready to collapse if one of your cows has a hearty sneeze."

Donal's jaw clenched at the insult, but he swallowed a retort. The steady stream of drips from several spots on the roof and the muted light seeping in from between many of the slats on the walls belied the truth.

"We had originally come out here to propose a contract with you for the next six calves to come from your stock. But once we got here, it was clear you were in no position to feed and care for an expectant heifer six seasons in a row." He waved his arm in an arc. "And judging from the look of those fields, your harvest this year was . . ."

"Abysmal," Lord Osborne interjected.

Donal curled his fingers into a ball and released them, using every ounce of his self-control not to lash out at the old man.

"I was going to say . . . meager," Andrew added. "Either way, your harvest did not meet your needs, and you were left with a fallow field that requires extensive care in order to be of any use at all in the next growing season. Is that about the size of it?"

Donal's gaze dropped to his feet, and he drew a long, slow breath before releasing it in a quick puff from his lips.

"And is that your plow out there? The one you use in your labors?"

"Aye?" Donal's eyes narrowed. "And what's wrong with it?" he asked, knowing full well it had seen too many summers.

Andrew's mouth bobbed open and closed a few times. "Well," he said at length, "it appears to have been repaired . . . several times. And I'm not sure it will last another season."

Donal sighed. "My apologies, but I need to get going about my duties. Did you have something else you wanted to discuss?"

Lord Osborne stepped forward. "My son's point in all of that is if you're going to be of any benefit to us at all—"

Andrew held up a hand, silencing his father. "This is how I think an agreement can be mutually beneficial for all of us, Bunratty. I will pay to repair your barn, purchase feed for your cattle until our contracted six calves have all been safely delivered to our estate, as well as pay for your fields to be restored and recovered so they can be useful in the next sowing cycle, rather than having to sit fallow for two or more cycles to recover on their own."

"Muise." Donal raked his fingers through his hair and squeezed the base of his neck. "That's quite an offer, sir."

"We'll pay you ten percent over the fair market price for each calf, which should ensure a reliable income for you and your daughter for the next several years."

Donal wagged his head slowly, counting how many months it would take for him to be able to provide that many calves. He was down to only one heifer, so she could only calf once every twelve to fourteen months at the fastest. "Six calves, ya say?"

Andrew nodded.

Donal puffed through his lips. "I just want to make sure ye're aware—six calves will take six years at the least. Possibly longer."

"Of course we're aware, man." Lord Osborne growled, as if he hated the very idea that Donal might ever know something he didn't. "The Osbornes have been keeping cattle for four generations."

Andrew arched his brows and took a step closer to Donal. "So, that's ten percent above fair market for the next six of your calves, plus paying to repair your barn and fields and feeding all your livestock for the entirety of the time it takes for the calves to be born and weaned."

Donal's eyes drifted to the ceiling as he let the magnitude of their offer settle in. It made no sense. Yes, it was a fair deal for the cows, but what about the rest of it? The repairs and feed? The breadth of their offer was overwhelming. Finally, Donal looked Andrew fully in the eye for the first time. "Why would you do all that for me? For us?"

Andrew removed his hat and shook it slightly at his side. "It's no charity, I assure you." He replaced his hat. "We need these cows. And there's no way to get them without ensuring the heifer's survival until she can bear them all. Can't have Osborne cattle starting their lives off weak and sickly, can we?"

Donal pursed his lips. *Never mind the fact that the cows ya got from me last time were reared in such "deplorable" conditions.* He resisted the urge to roll his eyes. Andrew's smugness aside, the man had a point. The conditions weren't *exactly* the same as they'd been when they'd brokered their previous deal, and the truth was, this was the first spot of hope Donal had seen in a long, long time. However, he couldn't help the niggling pit in his stomach. It seemed a wee bit too good to be true.

"You make a very generous offer," Donal said after a long beat. "Beggin' yer pardon, sir, but"—he scratched the back of his neck and his lips tugged into a thin line—"what's the catch?"

The elder Osborne scoffed, and Donal wondered—not for the first time—if he was even in full agreement with this whole thing. "*Psh!*" Lord Osborne said, flapping a hand. "There's no catch. It's a business deal, plain and simple."

Andrew patted the air in his father's direction. "My father's right. It's just a business deal." He slid his hands into the pockets of his slicker. "And as I said a moment ago, this is not a charity donation. The money we pay you for the calves is your money. We are paying you for the goods of your calves. The rest of it is a loan."

Donal quickly ran the sums in his head, adding up the totals for the barn repairs, ample feed for the current animals, plus the ones to come—six calves meant they'd be in this deal a good six years or so, the field renewal . . . the ground swayed slightly, and Donal stepped back and leaned against the railing of one of the stalls. The number he totaled was mind-boggling. Even with the leg-up such a loan would provide, Donal wasn't sure he'd be able to make that amount in order to pay it back. But without this deal, if things stayed as they were now, they were looking at having to give up the farm and leave the area, perhaps even sail to America—a thought that nauseated him even further. He splayed his hand across his chin and rubbed at the stubble he'd not yet had a chance to clear that morning.

"When . . . ah . . . when would the loan need to be repaid?" His voice failed to hold the confident, businesslike tone Donal tried to infuse into the question.

Andrew shrugged, and his eyes rolled upward as he thought. "I think year's end should give you ample time."

All pretenses vanished and Donal coughed as though Andrew had pummeled him with the shovel leaning on the wall next to him.

Lord Osborne simply stared at him as a single brow snaked upward before he flashed a look to his son that spoke his doubts about Donal's ability to agree to this deal.

"Year's end isn't much time," Donal said. "We're already halfway through September. Even if I bred her now, she wouldn't calve for at least nine months. So, we're lookin' at June or so before the first calf could be here—which is a fine time to calf, but I won't have the income by year's end. Especially since there's no harvest to sell in the winter months."

Andrew studied Donal, impatience flashing briefly behind his eyes. "That's our offer."

Donal scratched his chin again. "And what happens if I'm unable to make the payment?"

"Then we take over your land and you'll be on your merry way." Andrew sniffed. "I mean no offense, but by the looks of things, that's where you're headed anyway. At least this way you have a chance to stay."

Donal hung his head, hating how right the pompous lad was, and hating even more his inability to not let it affect him. "Can I think about it?"

Andrew's shoulders rose and fell. "Of course. It's the fourteenth today. I must know by the end of the festival. Does that sound reasonable?"

Donal nodded. "Aye."

"Right," Andrew said, clapping his hands together. "Thanks for your time, Bunratty. We'll speak soon."

Donal kept his gaze trained on the ground, barely hearing any of the man's words. His mind was already full and swirling with all the considerations he must give ample attention to before truly making a decision. He managed to mumble an assent.

"We'll see ourselves out," Andrew said as he and his father turned and tromped out of the barn.

Donal flinched at the blast of cold air that shot in when they slid the barn door open, jolting him out of his reverie. He waited a few moments so as not to be right on the Osbornes' heels, then he trudged back to the house, this latest development weighing him down like a millstone.

18

Saturday morning, as Sara made her way toward town, she reached into the pocket on the front of her apron and clutched the slip of paper hiding inside. She peeked down just to make sure the list her father had written for her hadn't magically transformed into some nonsensical piece of newsprint or some other paper since the last time she checked it. She'd seen the two men leaving their house the other day, and she'd seen the way her father had been lost in thought the rest of that morning. The strange tugging in her belly that she usually got when she knew she'd done something wrong had shown up at some point since they'd left. Not because she'd done anything wrong, but because she was so worried about her father.

So, when her da had asked if she'd be up for running some errands in town while he handled some things around the farm, she'd jumped at the chance. Anything to help take some of the pressure off of him. He'd given her very specific instructions about what to say and do at each place. He'd sent her with money for the grocer and told her exactly how much turf or butter to offer to the hardware man. She played his words over and over in her mind, determined not to make any mistakes.

As she came to the crest of the hill, she glanced around. No sign of Margot or her little minions. They'd all kept their word to Catríona and had left Sara alone since that day. Sara's spotty attendance of late probably helped as well. But even when she was at school, they pretty much ignored her, which was fine by Sara. Being ignored was far better than the sort of attention she'd been getting before Catríona had come to her rescue. She and the two girls she got along with at school had played blissfully during recess in the last couple of weeks, which had made the confusing and concerning things she'd been seeing her father dealing with on the farm much easier to handle.

As she approached the town limits of Lisdoonvarna, her mouth fell open. The streets were packed with people milling about. Their voices in conversation grew louder and louder until the din bounced around and echoed through the narrow Main Street. Sara could almost imagine their laughter and shouts springing around like a lamb gamboling on the clouds overhead. Down the road a bit, one man's voice carried above everyone else's. He was shouting about the price of cattle, pigs, horses, and sheep. Ah, a market day.

Sara ducked into the grocer's shop just as a fistfight broke out across the street. She hurried inside and leaned against the window to catch her breath for a moment, eyes wide. She'd hoped it would be a little quieter in here, but it was just as crowded, if not more so. People filled every nook and cranny of the cramped store. She recognized some of them, but many she didn't. Her father had told her that market days were busier because people who lived even farther out of town than they did came to buy or sell livestock and restock on their usual messages—flour, sugar, and the like—because they only came into town a few times a year. Now she understood why he never liked to come on market weekends. He must've forgotten it was this weekend or he wouldn't have sent her on her own.

Pushing herself off the window, she wound through the aisles, skirting around people here and there as she gathered everything from her list. The last things she needed were the flour and sugar, which she had to get from the man behind the counter, because he had to measure them for her. She stepped up to the counter, which came to her chin.

"Excuse me?" she said to the man whose back was to her.

He turned around, but his eyes fell on the woman next to Sara. "Can I help ya, miss?"

Sara opened her mouth to speak, but the woman cut in, asking the man for several pounds of oats.

Sara waited patiently as he measured out the woman's order, bagged it up, and took her payment. When they were finished, Sara said, "Excuse me, sir—"

A man stepped around her, pressed his palms onto the counter, and spouted off his long list of required items and their measurements.

She pressed her lips together and swallowed the frustration that burned in her chest. Finally, she tugged on the man's coat hem. "Beggin' yer pardon, sir, but I think I was next in the queue."

The man looked down at her and chuckled. "I'll just be a wee sec." And that was that.

Once he was finished, another woman patted Sara on the shoulder. "My order is just quick. You don't mind, do you? There's a good gairl." And she nudged Sara out of the way with her hip before Sara could even reply.

"Sara?"

Sara spun and her face split into a grin as she saw Catríona behind her, a basket slung over her arm.

"Are ya alright?" Catríona asked.

She nodded.

Catríona looked from Sara to the counter and back. "Have ya been waitin' long?"

Sara glanced up at the woman who'd bumped her out of the way and was now pretending she had no idea Sara was there. "Well," she said, "I've had a bit of a hard time getting the man to hear me."

"I see," Catríona replied and gestured for Sara to stand next to her. "We'll make sure ye're next, alright?"

Sara smiled up at her and nodded. "T'anks."

Finally, the woman in front of them left with her goods, and Catríona stepped up to the counter with Sara by her side. "Mickey," she said. "How are yas?"

The giant of a man with a shock of black hair and a thick mustache turned and smiled at them. "Catríona! *Conas atá tú?*"

"*Go maith, go maith!*" she replied. "And yerself?"

"Happy out, so I am. What can I get ye?"

"Actually, I believe my friend here was first," Catríona said, smiling down at Sara.

Mickey's mouth rounded, and his eyes grew wide. "I'm so sorry there, pet. I didna realize ye were waitin' to make an order." His cheeks pinkened. "I just thought one them others was yer mammy or daddy."

Sara smiled, but she wasn't sure she believed him. "It's okay."

"Now," he said, leaning onto his elbows on the counter. "What can I get ye?"

Sara pulled the list from her apron pocket and read off the items she needed and the weights of each.

"Verra good, comin' right up." He turned and busied himself gathering up her order.

"So, ye and yer dad came to town today, eh?" Catríona asked.

Sara shook her head. "Just me today. I'm helpin' out gettin' the messages while Da works on things at the farm."

A look Sara couldn't place flashed across Catríona's face before she smiled again. "Well, aren't you quite the lady of the house? Yer dad's a lucky fella to have such a grand helper for a daughter."

Sara's chest warmed at Catríona's praise, and she straightened her posture a little.

"Do you have other errands before ya head home?"

"Aye." Sara nodded again. She held the list up to Catríona, who slid it from her fingers and studied it with a scowl.

"Yer dad's writin's awful," she said finally.

Sara erupted into laughter. "I tell him the same thing!" She wiped at her eyes. "He says he doesn't need to write pretty when the only ones who ever see it are the cows."

Catríona rolled her eyes and laughed. "Well, there's more than cows lookin' at it today, isn't there?"

Sara laughed again as she took the paper back.

"Wouldja like some company on yer rounds?"

Sara peered up at her. "Really? You'd come around with me?"

Catríona nodded. "Oh, aye! I wouldn't pass up a chance to spend time with the famous Sara Bunratty. Not for a million pounds."

Grinning, Sara bounced on her toes. She was so excited at the idea of spending the afternoon with Catríona that she almost forgot to pay for her groceries. After making sure Mickey asked her for the same amount her father had said she'd owe, she placed the money on the counter and slid the items into the satchel she had slung over her back. She looped her thumbs under the straps as she and Catríona left the shop and headed for her other destinations.

Catríona and Sara walked along in comfortable silence as they left the Lisdoonvarna town limits. They'd chatted almost nonstop as they went from shop to shop and place to place all afternoon. Sara had finished collecting all the things on her list, astonishing Catríona with her bartering skills along the way. The child was fearless! It had taken Catríona a lifetime to be able to withstand the back and forth banter a good barter entails without taking rejections of her offered items or prices personally. Even now, it was uncomfortable for her. But not for Sara. She held her own like it was just another day in the market for the nine-year-old. The girl seemed wise beyond her years and still remained a child at heart—something that wasn't easy to do, especially having grown up without a mother. Catríona knew that firsthand.

She glanced down at the girl walking next to her, back laden with the satchel she insisted she carry on her own. She smiled and wagged her head before letting her gaze drift to the world around them. Now that they'd left the incessant noise of the city behind, the silence along the Bog Road was almost deafening, setting a high-pitched ringing in her ears. Gray clouds hung low in the sky, making it seem like the whole world was wrapped in lambswool. Along either side of the road, gorse bushes mixed with ash and windswept hawthorn trees created an emerald barrier to the patchwork fields beyond. Though it couldn't be seen, the air held the salty dampness of the sea as it kissed their cheeks.

While Catríona didn't remember much about living in their farmhouse, she did remember hating how removed from society it had felt. She could still hear the wind howling through the thatched roof as her parents argued in the other room when they thought she was asleep. Her mother had never acclimated to life on the farm after they married and claimed Jimmy had romanticized the life during their courtship. When she left them when Catríona was five, and Dad sold the farm and moved them into town, Catríona had sworn off country living for good. She longed for the excitement and throngs of the big city. She wanted comfort and warmth and the ease of running to the grocer on the corner rather than having to trek an hour or more into town for one forgotten item. As she grew older, even Lisdoonvarna had grown suffocating, with the things that once seemed exciting now feeling commonplace and dull.

But walking down the road with Sara, the peaceful air still and refreshing, with only the sound of the odd birdsong and their footsteps on the packed dirt road, Catríona had to admit she could almost see the appeal of it now.

A small hand slipped into hers, shaking her from her thoughts. And Catríona was grateful. It would be a cold day, indeed, if she ever actually wanted to live out in the countryside.

"Catríona?" Sara asked, looking up at her with wide eyes. Catríona suddenly wondered what Sara had been ruminating on while they walked.

"Mm?"

"Have ya found her yet?" Sara's voice, which had been assertive and sure in town, now sounded small. Timid. Worried.

Catríona stopped walking and turned toward the girl. "Have I found who, luhv?"

"My dad's wife."

Catríona's hand pressed to her chest, and she chuckled. "Oh, sweetie, not yet." Sara's gaze bored into hers, so she hurried to add, "But I'm tryin'! We both are."

"He's stubborn, ya know." The surety had returned, as had her assertive posture.

A full laugh escaped Catríona's lips before she clamped them together. "Aye, that he is."

Sara squeezed her hand. "But he's a good man."

Catríona stooped and met the girl's gaze. "Aye, that he is as well." She stood, Sara still gripping her hand. "And that good man's probably wonderin' what on earth's happened to ye. Let's get ye home."

Sara studied her for a long moment before the customary light returned to her eyes, and she nodded with a smile.

The pair continued on in relative silence, save for the odd remark or two about a tree, cloud shape, or bird that crossed their path. About ten minutes later, they approached the small gate in front of the Bunrattys' house.

Donal was out front on a short ladder, tying off the ends of a thatch repair. Despite the chilled air, he was down to his shirt-sleeves, and Catríona couldn't help noticing the way his shoulder muscles rounded and flexed and his back rippled through the thin shirt as he pulled and tugged at the twine and straw.

"A dhadí!" Sara called but held fast to Catríona's hand as she broke into a swift run.

The satchel bounced and bobbed on the girl's back, and Catríona struggled to keep up, her gait uneven from being pulled by one hand.

Donal turned and wiped his forehead with the back of his leather-gloved hand. A smile spread across his face as Donal turned and wiped his forehead with the back of his hand. A smile spread across his face as his gaze fell upon his daughter. "There's m' girl!" Catríona's heart warmed at the evident love between father and daughter and tried to ignore the flutter in her stomach at his dimpled grin.

He carefully stepped from the ladder and bit the fingertip of one of his gloves and yanked his hand free. He froze, glove dangling at his chin, when his eyes fell on Catríona. He snatched the leather from between his teeth, tugged the glove from his other hand, and set both on one of the rungs of the ladder. "Evenin'." He took a few steps in their direction as he tugged his woolen jumper on. "Did I miss an appointment?"

Catríona swallowed against the butterflies that had awakened in her belly when his eyes met hers. She cleared her throat. "No, not at all. I was just—"

"Catríona did the errands with me!" Sara announced proudly.

Donal looked at his daughter and then to Catríona and back. "Sara, you didna . . ." He turned to Catríona. "I'm terribly sorry. You didn't have to do that."

She waved her hand.

"Sara's fully capable of doing those few tasks on her own," he said as he pinned his daughter with a reproving look.

Catríona stepped forward. "It's grand, so. I offered."

Donal shot her a skeptical look.

"Truly!" she said, laughing. "I saw Sara while I was waiting in line at the grocer. The other patrons weren't lettin' her step up and place her order, so I helped her out, then I offered to go with her on her other tasks."

Next to her, Sara nodded heartily.

"And we were havin' such a delightful time together, we were halfway here before I realized I was walking her home."

"*Dáiríre?*" Sara's mouth was agape, then she burst into laughter. "Ya silly billy, ya!"

Catríona gave a sheepish shrug, warmth creeping up her neck and cheeks. "What can I say? Time—and distance—flies when ye're havin' fun." She dared a glance at Donal's face and found an amused sort of confusion there.

"Well," he finally said. "Thanks fer lookin' after her. And gettin' her home safe."

"'Twas my pleasure."

"Catríona can stay fer tea, right, Da?" Sara asked, already dragging Catríona toward the door.

Catríona bobbed her mouth open and closed, unsure how to respond. Donal seemed equally as flummoxed—or at least equally as uncomfortable.

He followed behind them. "Eh . . . I suppose so. That is, if she has time."

The three entered the house and Sara headed straight for the kitchen and began putting the groceries away and set the kettle on to boil.

"So . . . eh . . . would ya' like to stay fer tea?" Donal asked, stepping up next to her. "We're just havin' beans on toast."

Catríona looked at him, and her heart sank at the sadness that filled his eyes. It was almost as if he was embarrassed about what they were having for dinner. Catríona's gaze drifted around the cozy home. Everything was neat, tidy, and in its place. But if she looked closer, she noticed that everything, while clean, was aged and worn. The curtains were thinning, the fabric on the sofa was beginning to thread. And she wondered for the first time if they had food to spare in order to feed her.

She smiled. "I'm actually scheduled to meet wi' Andrew and his parents for dinner this evening to discuss the progress of his matching."

A mixture of relief and disappointment washed over Donal's face as he nodded. "Right. Next time, then."

"But," she hurried to add, "I'd love a cuppa tea, if it's alright?"

Sara grinned and a small smile tilted the corners of Donal's mouth, his full lips barely moving yet somehow still smiling. Why was she watching his mouth?

"That's grand," he said and slid a third cup off of the shelf.

As Sara busied herself putting the last of the messages away, and Donal prepared the tea, she chatted away to him about all she'd seen and done, including her shrewd bartering skills, freeing Catríona to discreetly look around the house some more.

She stood in the doorway between the kitchen and sitting room. A roaring turf fire crackled in the grate, filling the room with its earthy, musky aroma. Catríona inhaled, her eyes drifting closed, savoring the familiar scent that was almost as comforting as a cuppa. Continuing her scan of the room, she took in the delicate doilies gracing small tables on either end of the sofa. The tables, while not fancy by any means, looked to be handmade and of good quality. She absently wondered if Donal had made them or perhaps bartered for them. In the center of the room, a large trunk served as a tea table of sorts, but on top, a large Bible was splayed open.

She glanced in the kitchen. Donal and Sara were still busy, so she crept over to take a closer look at the Bible. She gingerly ran her finger across the top of the yellowing page. *The book of Matthew. Does Donal read the Bíobla often?*

"Da and I have been talking about the Serp—er—Sermon on the Mount," Sara said, startling Catríona.

"Oh?"

"Aye! It's one of Íosa's most famous speeches."

"Sermons, luhv." Donal flitted an amused grin in Catríona's direction. Then he added, "Tea's ready."

A knock at the door stopped them, and Donal's face filled with questions.

"Who is it, Da?" Sara asked.

He shrugged. "Only one way to find out."

Catríona stepped aside, and Donal brushed past her to open the door.

"Sister Margaret," Catríona heard him say. "Do come in."

The older woman stepped inside and nodded a greeting to Catríona and smiled at Sara. "Hallo, a stoir."

Sara stared at her teacher as if she'd never considered the idea that the woman ever left the schoolhouse. Donal cleared his throat and Sara blinked. "Good evenin', Sister," she said at length.

Donal scratched his jaw. "Eh, we were just about to sit down to a cuppa tea. Would you like to join us?"

"No, no, I won't stay long." She stepped closer to Donal. "I just had a wee question for yas."

"Of course." Donal shifted his weight.

"I haven't seen Sara at school in a while, and I wanted to see if ya had any plans for her to return?"

"Yes, Sister, I'm very sorry 'bout that. Things have just been a mite busy around the farm."

The teacher seemed annoyed as she sucked in a deep breath. "I understand the farm is important, but so is a good education."

"I know, Sister—"

"If you've any hope," she interrupted him, "of Sara having a future beyond farm life, she needs to be in school."

The look of defeat in Donal's eyes was like a punch to Catríona's gut. While she understood a quality education was important, it was clear the Bunrattys were in a rough season, and Donal had no one else to help him. He opened his mouth to reply, but before he could eke out a word, the woman continued on with her lecture. For a Sister, she wasn't showing much compassion, and the more she berated Donal, his parenting, and their situation, the hotter the coals burned in Catríona's chest.

Sister Margaret continued, "If you care for your daughter at all—"

"Och! For Pete's sake!" Catríona blurted out.

Donal, Sara, and Sister Margaret all turned wide eyes on her. Catríona, tempted to shrink back after her outburst, chose instead to simply shrug. "Beggin' yer pardon, Sister, but I'd think it's clear why wee Sara's not been at school." She flitted a glance to the girl, then continued, "Clearly Mister Bunratty needs help, and perhaps if the folk leadin' the community made an attempt to serve rather than scold, he might be able to spare her hands so the girl can get the education."

Sister Margaret blinked hard as though Catríona had rapped her knuckles with a ruler rather than challenged her behavior. "I see," she finally sputtered.

Donal stepped over and laid a hand on Catríona's shoulder. Something akin to admiration shone in his eyes even as his facial expression registered sheepish unease.

He cleared his throat. "I appreciate your concern, Sister, but I'm afraid Miss Daly's right. I want nothing more than for Sara to get a good education and be able to make more for her own life." He looked to his daughter and back to the teacher. "But right now, I'm afraid I need her at home. I promise to get her to school as soon as possible."

Sister Margaret huffed. "Very well. Then I'll leave ye to it." She turned to the door, then stopped and turned back. "I'm just doin' my job, y'know."

The knot in Catríona's gut tightened. She didn't doubt the woman had Sara's best interests at heart, but could she not have a gentler bedside manner?

"I appreciate it, Sister." Donal's words interrupted Catríona's internal monologue. "Thanks for makin' the trip out to check on us."

Her countenance softened, but only some, then she nodded and drifted out the front door.

Awkward silence filled the room until Sara spoke up. "So . . . how 'bout that tea?"

The three burst into laughter and shuffled into the kitchen. Donal pulled out a chair opposite Sara and gestured for Catríona to sit.

She thanked him and lowered herself into the seat while Sara poured the steaming liquid into each of their cups in turn.

"Sara tells me she did some bartering today," Donal said after taking a sip of his tea, wincing at the heat. Clearly he did not wish to discuss the Sister's visit, which suited Catríona just fine.

She set her cup down. "Oh my goodness, you should've seen her, Donal!" She went on to describe how Sara had gotten two of the burliest men in Lisdoonvarna to acquiesce and agree to her terms. "She wasn't takin' no fer an answer!"

"Atta girl." Donal squeezed his daughter's shoulder affectionally. Sara beamed under his praise. For the next while, the three chatted like old friends sharing about their day, telling jokes, and just enjoying the craic in general.

At last, Sara stood and collected their cups. "I'll go feed na ba," she said.

"Aw, peata, ya don't have to do that."

"I've not visited them in three days, Da. They'll think I don't like them anymore!" She scurried to the back door and tugged her wellies on.

"Alright then," Donal said as his chest rumbled with an amused chuckle, reminding Catríona of his humming.

She pressed her hands to her cheeks, hoping to hide the heat that flushed them at the memory of their intimate dance.

"She's a remarkable gairl," Catríona said after Sara had exploded outside.

"That she is," Donal said, still watching the door she'd run out of before getting up and lumbering over to close it after her. "But she's rubbish at remembering to shut the door."

They both laughed. Then the church bells shattered the air in the distance. Catríona shot to her feet. "Goodness, is that the time? Is it six already?"

Donal peeked out the window and winced. "Aye, 'tis."

Catríona bit back an oath, then they both paused and were silent and still, as was the custom when the angelus rang. It was meant to be a call to prayer. Catríona's was a desperate plea that God would allow her to get back to town in time to change and meet the Osbornes without being too terribly late.

"I'm sorry to sip and run, but I'm ridiculously behind." She pushed her chair in. "I'm afraid I must dash."

Donal nodded and followed her to the door. As she hurried down the front walk, she felt his stare burning a hole in her back.

"I could run you up in the jaunting cart," Donal blurted out just as she reached the small gate at the front of his property. She froze, weighing the offer. While she hated for him to go to the trouble of going back into town after working all day, she couldn't deny that getting home as fast as possible would make things much easier for her. Between her foolish mismatch with Andrew and Hester and the ridiculous scene he'd witnessed between her and Donal with the paint, she already felt as though Andrew was slipping away from her. Showing up late for this dinner could very well be the nail in the coffin of her chances to win his heart.

She turned on her heel. "Are you sure it wouldn't be too much trouble?"

The corners of his mouth tugged downward as he shook his head. "No trouble at all."

"Then, if you're sure, it would really help me out." She grimaced. How did she manage to keep getting herself in these ridiculous situations?

A few minutes later, Donal came rumbling up the path along the north side of the house. He still wore his woolen jumper but had put his tweed flatcap on and pulled it low to stave off the chill quickly settling in off the ocean now that the sun had sunk below the horizon.

Catríona stepped over to the opposite side of the cart, but before she could step up and pull herself in, Donal hopped down and hurried around to her side. He grasped her hand and gripped her elbow with his other. His fingers were strong, his grip secure, and his skin masculine and toughened from years of hard labor. She tried to ignore how much she enjoyed the feel of his skin on hers as he helped her step up into the cart.

They were silent as they raced down the road, the horse's hoofbeats and breathing the only sounds to be heard. They hit a bump, sending Catríona slamming into Donal's shoulder, which immediately sent an image of his flexed and rippling muscles hurtling into her mind's eye. She squeezed her eyes shut, desperate to rid her mind of the memory, but it only brought an image of Donal tying the thatch more sharply into focus.

"I really appreciate this," she said, hoping some conversation would distract her mind from its traitorous thoughts.

"Not a problem at all." His gaze was trained forward as the lights of the town came into view. "Ye're heading to your place?"

She nodded in the darkness, and he steered the rig to a stop in front of the Imperial. "Thanks again," she said.

He hopped down and gestured for her to wait as he rounded the backside of the cart. "This step can be a bit wonky," he said, his cheeks pink. "Can't have ya hurtin' yerself." He held out his hand.

She eyed it for a moment before slipping her hand into his. Their eyes locked for a split second that felt like an eternity,

Catríona's heart thrumming inside her chest. As she stepped down onto the rung, it cracked, and she stumbled forward—right into Donal's arms.

He tightened his embrace around her waist and lifted so he could swing her feet free from the cart before setting her gently to stand, his cheek accidentally brushing hers as he did. She pressed her palms to his chest as she struggled to regain her balance, her head spinning at his nearness.

"Steady?"

Catríona wasn't entirely sure if it was a question or advice. She nodded and stepped back. "Thank—" Her voice came out in a squeak. She cleared her throat and tried again. "Thanks again, for the lift."

A playful smile lit his face.

She hurried to add, "The lift in the cart, I mean. For helping me get to town faster." She shook her head and took a step toward the front door of the Imperial. "At least come in and have a drink. I'll tell Peadar it's on me. It's the least I can do."

Before Donal could respond, and before Catríona could do anything else to embarrass herself, she spun on her heel and hurried for the door, almost running right into her father.

"Hi, Da," she said, brushing past him. "I'm late for a client dinner," she called over her shoulder as she scurried up the stairs, willing the burning in her face and fluttering in her stomach to subside.

19

So, how's about that pint?" Jimmy asked, a funny sort of smile on his face.

A pint had never sounded better. Donal nodded and Jimmy offered him a hearty slap on the back as they entered the pub. "I won't stay long," Donal told him. "Sara's at home."

Jimmy's head bobbed knowingly. "'Tis a sacred thing raising a gairl," he said as Peadar slid two dark pints in front of them.

"Hmm." Donal nodded.

"Sacred," Jimmy muttered again before taking a long draw of his drink. He then turned to Donal and added, "And exhausting!"

Donal almost spit out his mouthful of stout as he laughed. "Good gracious me, that's the truth."

"Caty!" The crowd in the pub shouted in unison.

Donal twisted on his stool and followed the lifted glasses of the crowd until he saw Catríona descending the stairs in the fanciest dress he'd ever seen someone wear to a dinner. He wondered where she'd gotten it from, as he didn't imagine there was too much call for such a frock the rest of the year. His glance flitted to Jimmy, who looked just as bemused as Donal, and back to Catríona.

"Alright, alright," she said to the crowd, patting the air. "*Oíche mhaith, gach duine!*"

"Oíche mhaith!" the crowd replied before returning to their drinks and conversations.

Catríona waved at her father, then her gaze met Donal's. She offered a tight smile before turning to go.

Donal watched until she disappeared into the darkness outside before returning to his drink. He felt Jimmy studying him, but when he looked at the man, his attention was fully on his glass—as if the glass was in the middle of the most riveting story he'd ever heard.

"So," Jimmy said after a long silence. "How's the matchin'?"

Donal drew in a long inhale.

"That good, eh?" Jimmy said with a wheezy laugh. "Some years're like that."

Now it was Donal's turn to study his glass. He reviewed the past couple weeks in his mind. He'd been on several outings over the course of the festival so far—most of which were unbearable, starting with that horrendous picnic. Deirdre had been nice enough, but she never seemed to stick around and chat very long, forever rushing off to find her mysterious friend. If it was a ploy to see if Donal would chase after her, the joke was on her. That was exactly the kind of game he refused to play. There were far too many more pressing matters in life than to be messing with silly lovers' games. The truth was only one woman had evoked any sort of real interest or reaction. And the attraction and desires she evoked in him were entirely foreign. He had grown to love Connie over time, and he'd always enjoyed her company. They shared a good life together. But she never inspired passion from—or within—him. Meanwhile this one woman seemed to conjure little else. Passion for life. Passion to be a better man. A better father. Passion to be a husband.

And passion for her ridiculously magnetic lips. And it was the one woman he was fairly certain he'd lost before he even had a chance to win her. Catríona was clearly besotted with Andrew Osborne—for reasons completely unknown to Donal. And this was exactly what he'd been afraid of to begin with.

He snatched his pint glass and drained the rest in one long gulp, then he wiped his mouth with his hand and thanked Peadar for the drink. He bid Jimmy good night without fully looking at him and hurried out into the cold September evening.

—◦◦—

Catríona fidgeted with the fingertips of her gloves as she paced the foyer of the Queens Hotel. She stole a peek around the room to ensure she was alone before examining her reflection more closely in a mirror. She tugged the bodice of Maeve's dress in place. Catríona had begged to borrow it, even though she knew it wouldn't be a perfect fit. She needed a nicer frock than her mother's old one she'd used when she first met the Osbornes.

Curse her thick waist and full bust. She leaned in closer and studied her face, then pinched her cheeks and bit at her lips to add some color to both. Just as she finished her preening, the Osbornes appeared on the landing of the stairs.

She smiled up at Andrew, who seemed to be looking straight through her. "Good evening, Lord Osborne, Lady Osborne, Andrew." She greeted each as they reached the bottom level. Lord Osborne offered a stately nod and Lady Osborne smiled politely. Andrew mumbled a stiff hello without meeting her eyes.

Catríona's brows pressed together, and her lips pursed. What could he possibly be upset with her about? She forced a cordial expression on her face. Perhaps he was only tired or he'd had a row with his parents before coming down.

The quartet were greeted immediately, led through the dining room, and presented with the best table in the hotel. The Osbornes sat without acknowledging the host other than Lord Osborne gesturing for a whiskey. Catríona murmured her thanks as she lowered into her seat as gracefully as she could, given how tightly she'd had Maeve lace her stays.

"Ya won't be able to breathe, let alone swallow a bit o' food," Maeve had said as she had hurriedly helped Catríona dress.

"I'm . . . not . . . there . . . to . . . eat," Catríona had said between the tugs that pulled the laces ever tighter and tighter until Maeve refused to pull anymore.

Now, sitting as straight and tall as she could, a dull ache already burning in her low back, she almost wished she'd listened to Maeve. Almost. But the fact remained, she didn't care if she went hungry for the rest of the week. She had to get back in Andrew's good graces and find a way to convince him she was the one for him. She'd do whatever it took. She'd even spent every spare moment when she wasn't with a client reading the latest papers from Dublin so that she'd have at least a basic grasp on what was going on there. If she was going to convince the Osbornes she belonged in their world, she had to prove she knew what was going on in it, as well as prove that she knew how to behave within it.

She mirrored Lady Osborne's every move as much as she could without seeming like she was poking fun or completely socially inept. Once the drinks had been served—whiskey for the lord and Andrew and port wine for the ladies—the conversation began in earnest.

"Tell me, Miss Daly, what is the latest on the search for Andrew's bride?" Lord Osborne leaned forward and rested his elbows on the table. At a look from Lady Osborne, he sighed and removed them.

Catríona took a sip of her wine and tried not to grimace. Not one to drink often, she longed for a steaming cup of tea or a ladies' pint of stout. "Well," she said as she swallowed, ignoring the pinching under her ribs, "I've found a few ladies that I thought might be a good fit."

Next to her, Andrew snorted.

"But none of them were really the right one." She shifted in her seat and crossed one ankle over the other. "However, not to worry. We typically have one or two duds before we can really narrow down what our client truly wants and needs in a mate."

Lord Osborne pursed his lips and eyed his son, who was waving at the barkeep for another dram. "It's normal, you say?"

"Oh, ay—oh, yes, it is." Goodness, it was exhausting remembering to water down her accent to match the posh, round speech of the Dublin gentry. "Matchmaking and romance aren't an exact science, sir. There's a fair bit of trial and error that takes place."

A young waitress who looked about as sure of herself as a newborn fawn brought over Andrew's new drink. He eyed her as if she were a slab of decadent cake and he hadn't eaten in weeks. Catríona tried not to notice how the girl tensed up as she set his drink on the table. And did he whisper something to her as she did so? The girl's eyes had grown wide, and her cheeks flushed before she turned on her heel and hurried back whence she'd come.

"You see," Catríona continued, keeping her gaze pinned on Andrew, "sometimes a client has a hard time expressing what exactly it is they are looking for. Of course, every once in a while, Cupid's arrow strikes without warning and there's an instant match, but that's the exception rather than the rule."

"I see," Lady Osborne said. "And clearly our son is no exception."

Catríona fought to hide her grimace at the woman's obvious dig at her son. Andrew slowly turned his head and stared at his mother.

Lord Osborne, brows arched, cleared his throat. "I believe what my wife is trying to say is that we've obviously had some trouble finding that best match for Andrew. And, for us, our main concern is not necessarily love."

Andrew scoffed and tossed back his fresh whiskey in one gulp.

"We need a woman who can fit into Dublin society." Lord Osborne took a sip of his own drink. "You see, trouble is brewing down there. I believe we are headed for a long, difficult political battle. We need someone who can weather the coming storm with aplomb and decorum."

"Who won't crumble at the first sign of trouble," Lady Osborne added.

"Oh, Father. Don't be so melodramatic," Andrew said.

"If you'd paid attention to the political climate the way I'd asked you to, you'd know full well I'm not being overly dramatic or cautious. The winds of change are stirring."

Andrew yawned.

Suddenly, Catríona remembered something she'd read in one of the Dublin papers. She decided to test the waters. "Do you think Mister Griffith will have much luck with his agenda?"

Lord Osborne floated a look to his wife. She met his gaze, and the corner of her mouth twitched up. She gave the slightest nod. "You know, I'm afraid he just might. I've heard he wants to create a new party that will carry the so-called moral authority of the nation."

"I can't imagine that would help matters between landlords and the Crown?"

Lord Osborne gestured in her direction. "See, Andrew, Miss

Daly here takes an interest in her nation's most important issues. You should too."

Andrew was too busy whispering to the waitress to respond to his father. Lady Osborne elbowed her son. "It would behoove you to pay heed to this conversation, Andrew."

When he turned to respond to his mother, the waitress scurried off. Catríona couldn't be sure, but it looked as though the poor girl's eyes had filled with tears.

"If Griffith and his ilk have their way, Ireland would cease to be under the Crown at all, which would be the end of estates such as ours," Lord Osborne replied to Catríona. "Which is why it's of vital importance that we stay current on all such matters." This comment was directed toward Andrew.

"And that we find Andrew a wife who understands not only the political climate but the sheer necessity for our family to navigate the coming political storm with wisdom and grace," added Lady Osborne, who, Catríona noticed, had grown suddenly pale.

"I completely understand," Catríona said. "And this is very helpful information as I seek to match Andrew with the best woman possible."

Lord Osborne rose and rounded the table to his wife. "I believe you will." He hooked an arm under his wife's elbow and helped her to stand. "I'm afraid her ladyship is tired and must go on through to bed."

Catríona sat straighter. "Is she alright?"

"She'll be fine," Lord Osborne replied absently. "She's just tired."

At first, Catríona wondered if the woman was drunk, but a quick glance at her glass quelled that concern. She'd barely touched her wine.

Andrew leaned forward, brows pulled tightly together. "But you've not had your dinner, Mother."

"You both go ahead and eat." Her voice sounded thin. "I just need a good night's sleep." With that, Lord Osborne whisked her out of the dining room.

Catríona and Andrew sat in awkward silence for a long while, with Andrew eyeing his empty glass. Catríona had counted three whiskeys so far, but there could have been more while she was talking with his parents.

Then Andrew looked up to the ceiling as if he could see through it up to his parents' suite. "She's never done that before. She lives for dinner—for the fashion, food, wine, all of it."

"I'm sure she's fine." Catríona shifted in her seat to face him more fully.

He met her gaze for a brief moment before he hung his head and shrugged.

"Really," she said. "She just looked tired. I'm sure she's fine." She reached out and squeezed the hand that rested around his empty glass.

He looked up at her again, his eyes red and glassy. "You think so?"

She nodded, though she truly had no idea. "I really do."

He placed his other hand over hers and traced lazy circles on her skin. She shivered at his touch, though not necessarily because it was a delicious sensation.

"Can I ask you a question?" He slipped his hands out from hers and leaned back in his chair.

"Of course."

"What's with that farmer?"

Catríona frowned. "Farmer?"

He tilted his head and pinned her with a look. "The. Farmer."

She stared at him blankly.

"With the paint."

Realization dawned. "Oh! Mister Bunratty."

Andrew snorted. "Yes, Mister Bunratty," he replied, making his accent even more posh, apparently teasing Catríona's formality.

She shrugged. "Nothing's 'with' him. He's a client my father tasked me with matching."

"I've seen you two, you know?"

"Seen us?" Catríona's brows pulled together. "Seen us where?"

Andrew held up his hand and counted on his fingers. "Well, there was the paint, then the afternoon dance—if you dance with all your clients like that, there must be a lot of confused blokes at the festival. And then tonight."

Catríona blinked. "Tonight?"

"Yes," he said, leaning forward, an intensity swimming in his eyes that unsettled Catríona. "Father sent me to collect a parcel for Mother, and I saw you practically throw yourself into his arms."

"Oh, that?" She laughed. "I'd found his daughter in town, and she needed some help, so I walked her home. And I didn't want to be late for our dinner, so Mister Bunratty kindly offered to bring me back to town in his jaunting cart."

The look on Andrew's face filled Catríona with an urgency to convince him to believe her. He had to. It was the truth, after all. He lifted his brows, and she took it as a sign to continue.

"When I went to step out of the cart, the rung broke and I fell." She shrugged. "He caught me, but really quite by accident."

"That's all it was?" Andrew scooted closer. "Truly?"

"That's all." She ignored the nagging in her gut. While that was factually what happened, she knew very well the split second that passed between them when he held her was more than happenstance. But she refused to let herself dwell on that and chose, instead, to dwell on the fact that Andrew's cantankerous mood had been because he was jealous. Of her. Nae, of her relationship with another man. Perhaps her plan had more of a chance of coming to fruition than she realized. She smiled and scooted closer to Andrew.

He reached out and took her hand once more. "You're certain?"

She swallowed. "Certain." In the corner a string quartet began to play a slow air.

Andrew stood and tugged her hand. "May I have this dance?"

A shy smile tickled the corners of her lips. "I thought you hated dancing?"

He urged her closer and wrapped one arm around her waist. "Only if it's not with the right girl."

Catríona bit her bottom lip as a wide smile spread across her face. "I'd be delighted, good sir." She giggled and headed toward the dance floor.

He pulled on her hand until she stopped. She turned back to look at him and he shook his head. "Uh-uh. I know a better place." He drew her to his side and laced his fingers through hers as he led her through the lobby and out a back door behind the front desk.

The night air was cold and damp, but the stars shone in the sky. He led them near a window to the dining room that was cracked open and then settled them in a spot in the shadows next to the orange glow of lantern light that spilled out and pooled on the ground.

He took both her hands, and they began to sway. Catríona shivered and he pulled her closer. Both hands snaked around her waist and tugged until she was flat up against him, then he tightened his hold. "Better?" he whispered, his voice thick with longing.

She tried to respond, but her voice was gone. She nodded against his chest. Except it wasn't better. Their steps were awkward and stilted. He held her so tight that, between his grip and her stays, she struggled to take a full breath.

He pressed his lips against her ear as one of his hands began to slide below her waist. "Andr—" Catríona's voice caught, and she cleared her throat. "Mister Osborne?"

"Mister Osborne?" he murmured against her hair. "Why so formal, Catríona?"

She managed to lean back to look into his face. "You . . . your hand."

His face registered a look of surprise, and he returned his hand to her waist. "Sorry about that." His breath was hot and sour on her face. "I didn't realize."

She offered him a tight smile. "Maybe we should go back inside?"

"You finally convince me to dance, and you want me to go back inside already?" He grinned and his dimples made her smile.

She closed her eyes and shook her head. *Get it together, woman. This is what you've wanted for over a year. Enjoy it!*

"You're right. Let's just dance."

"Good girl," he said and brushed a shock of hair from her face. He then traced a finger slowly down her cheek.

Catríona squeezed her eyes tight again and tried to relax as he pressed his lips to her forehead. She wanted to drift into his kiss, to let it melt her into his arms. But it didn't. It made her insides twist up in nervous knots, and suddenly she was filled with an overwhelming sense of dread that he was going to try to actually kiss her. But she couldn't bring herself to break away as he moved his lips to her ear, then her neck.

How could she convince him to marry her if she couldn't

stand the thought of him kissing her? What kind of wife didn't want to kiss her husband?

You're just nervous, she told herself. It had been a long time since she'd been kissed by anyone.

He finally straightened, and she dropped her gaze.

"Hey," he whispered, his voice even heavier as the whiskey continued to settle into his veins. "It's okay." He hooked a finger under her chin and lifted her face to meet his.

His eyes, red and watery, searched hers for a moment before he tugged her chin closer and brushed a quick peck on her lips. When she didn't protest, he brushed another. Then another. Then, finally, he kissed her with a deep ferocity and forceful longing that scared her. He tasted like stale whiskey and smoke, and she stepped backward. He matched with a step forward until they were pressed up against the outer wall of the dining room. He kissed her like a desperate man searching for a meal, and when he finally pulled away, he swayed a little.

Catríona wiped her chin and took a shuddering breath.

"Right?" His eyes danced with delight. And drink. Clearly he'd not experienced the same kiss she had.

"It's getting late," she said.

He nodded and leaned in as if he was going to kiss her again. She held up her hand, palm facing him. "Andrew."

He nodded. "Right. We need to pace ourselves." Then he leaned close to her ear and whispered, "But don't you worry, there's more where that came from." Then he stepped back, winked at her, and stumbled inside.

A sarcastic laugh tumbled from her mouth while she rounded the outside of the building, making her way toward an tSráid Mhór. As she wound her way back home, she ran her fingers over her lips. She could still taste Andrew's whiskey, and it reminded her why she hated that drink.

Confusion clouded her mind and rattled her heart's cadence as she replayed the evening's events in her mind. On one hand, she found it strangely flattering that Andrew would be jealous to the point of anger at Catríona's relationship with Donal—or any man, for that matter. She'd never in her life dreamed that someone the stature of Andrew Osborne would give her the time of day, let alone be jealous of her attention. On the other hand, his sudden change in demeanor and intensity had been unnerving. She had dreamed about kissing him for over a year . . . but none of her daydreams ever went the way things had tonight.

Admittedly, she likely should have refused his advances until he was sober and less emotional from his jealousy and his concern over his mother's sudden fatigue. But at the same time, she didn't feel like he had truly forced himself on her—she hadn't asked him *not* to kiss her, after all. Then again, none of that explained whatever was transpiring between him and the waitress at dinner. Most ale wenches didn't get teary-eyed serving drinks.

Catríona glanced over her shoulder. The streets, while not empty, were fairly quiet for a September evening. Catríona chalked that up to many merrymakers having been matched up already, now preferring quiet evenings in for conversation and planning. Catríona took the opportunity to tug at her stay laces through the bodice of her dress and wiggle her torso, hoping to loosen them just a mite until she could take the whole wretched thing off when she got home.

Out of nowhere, memories from dinner tonight and tea at the Bunratty's floated into her mind like side-by-side photographs. The easy laughter and comfortable conversation with Donal and Sara versus the stuffy, tight, and unfortunately slobbery experience with the Osbornes. Would she really be able to keep up the airs she'd put on tonight . . . for the rest of her life? Granted, Andrew hadn't proposed—and she had no idea if he even intended to. But that had been her goal from the get-go. She'd created this whole other persona for herself around Andrew and his parents. He didn't even really know the real Catríona. In fact, he barely even knew the putting-on-airs Catríona. But if he did propose, he wouldn't really be asking to marry Catríona Daly. Then again, that's what his family wanted. They were looking for exactly what Catríona had presented them in herself, because she knew that's exactly who they wanted her to be. Or they wanted Andrew's wife to be, anyway.

She tried to imagine discussing politics—which she hated—over breakfast for the next thirty years of her life. As she passed the temporary pen set up near the square for the market weekend, the acrid scent of manure and livestock hide assaulted her senses. She squeezed her eyes shut. "This is why," she whispered to herself. "You deserve better than this."

The only problem was, as the image of Andrew's face floated into her mind, she suspected she was right.

20

Donal paced back and forth in front of the Imperial, the midday light muted under the blanket of dark gray clouds stretching across the sky. The covering tamped down all the sounds and smells of the day, somehow both magnifying and dampening each. The air was eerily still, allowing smoke to curl lazily from the stacks of chimneys lining the tops of the buildings all along an tStráid Mhór. It was also more difficult to suss out the time on days like this, but experience told him it was just now one o'clock. Perhaps a minute or two on either side of the hour.

Behind him, the door to the Imperial Pub swung open. He instinctively turned at the sound to see Catríona scurrying out of the building. She glanced over, and when their eyes met, she froze for a beat before stepping over to him.

"Good afternoon, Donal," she said, her smile genuine but tight.

"Hiya." He tried to ignore the way her hair took on a silvery glow in the gray light. The scent of some sort of earthy flower wafted over and enveloped him like a down duvet.

Suddenly her face fell and worry clouded her eyes. "Oh,

muise." She pressed a hand to his forearm. "We didn't have an appointment, did we?"

His gaze was fixed on her hand on his arm, and he cursed the layers of wool separating them. He shook the thought free and scolded himself for allowing such a brazen idea into his mind. "No, no," he finally said, forcing himself to look her in the eye. "You'd said I had a match meetup for lunch here today at one o'clock."

Catríona clapped her hand on her forehead. "Och! That's right. Deirdre'll be here in a sec. She's delightful." A strange emotion Donal couldn't place flashed across her face as she added, "You'll love her."

He offered a polite smile, still hating this whole cockamamie rigmarole, but then blinked as he registered what Catríona had said. "Did you say Deirdre?"

Catríona nodded.

"Wee sprite of a girl, dark hair?"

She smiled. "Aye! Do ya know her already?"

Donal shrugged. "We've met a couple of times. At the walking tour and the dance in the square."

"What a small world," she said on a laugh. "Are ya still okay to meet with her? Or have ye already decided it wasn't a good fit?"

"No, no, it's grand." But Donal couldn't keep a nagging question from tapping at his mind like a bird on clear glass, and he was trying to decide if he was going to ask it.

"But?" She drew the word out long. Apparently Donal's face registered more than he realized.

He opened his mouth to ask but couldn't figure out how to word it without offending the woman, so he clamped it shut and shook his head. "Nothin'," he said. "Never mind."

Catríona waved a hand in front of her. "Ah no, ya don't get off that easy. What's on yer mind?"

A woman and her son walked past them on the sidewalk, and Donal and Catríona shifted closer to the building to allow them a wider berth. Donal watched them walk away while he formulated his question.

"Beggin' yer pardon," he said, hesitant. "It's just . . . would you not have already checked that before makin' the match? I mean, wouldn't ya need to know if we'd already met—especially if we agreed to part ways instead of carryin' on? I mean . . . you talked with both of us together at the dance."

Catríona's cheeks turned a deep shade of pink, and her gaze fell to the ground.

"I don't mean to presume to tell ya how to do yer job," Donal hurried to add. "I've no idea what bein' a matchmaker actually entails." He squeezed the back of his neck. "It's just . . . when I agreed to work with one, I thought I'd be working . . . y'know . . . *with* one instead of just getting messages on where to be when."

Catríona drew in a deep breath and released it in a long, slow sigh. She then glanced around them before taking him by the elbow and leading him to a wrought iron table on the patio around the side of the building.

"You're right," she said as they both sank into the frigid chairs. She wrapped her cloak around her more tightly and shivered. "This is not the way I typically manage a matchmaking client."

"Alright." He didn't know how else to respond.

She shifted again in her seat. "I am typically much more present in the process. We keep in much closer contact, and I am usually at every meetup to make the introductions."

Donal blinked, taking in the information. He wondered if he should ask the next question that her response conjured and finally decided to. He had no time for games. "So . . . if ya don't mind my askin'—what's different this time?"

Catríona laughed—a bitter-sounding puff of air—and shook her head. "What isn't different?" she muttered as she traced the scrolled design on the tabletop.

Donal's lips pursed and his brows tugged together as he shifted forward in his seat. "Is everything alright?"

She looked past him for a long moment as though weighing exactly how much to say. "It's not any one thing. It's a million different little things that are all stacking up." She shrugged. "Perhaps I'm strugglin' under the weight of it."

His heart clenched at the sadness swimming in her eyes, and he was overwhelmed with a burning desire to fix it for her. "Anythin' I can help with?"

She shook her head. "Da's in the middle of this massively important matching—for Earl Wyndham."

Donal puffed out a breath, nodding. "Oh, right. Lots of pressure, eh?"

"Exactly," she said. "And this whole business with Andrew is proving to be far more difficult than I anticipated."

"Finding him a match, you mean?"

"Aye." Something Donal couldn't read flashed in her eyes. "I didn't know he was coming this year, and normally my father would've been in charge of matching someone of Andrew's pedigree, but with the earl . . ." Her voice fell away.

Donal nodded. "The day after I met yer dad, he told me he had some highfalutin client this year." He shifted in his seat, the corner of his lips curling up slightly. "And that's when he said you'd be matchin' me."

She laughed. "Yeah, that one surprised us both, I think." She wagged her head. "I thought my client roster was full, and then he shoved you through the door."

"That's about how it went on my end too." Donal chuckled. "I was . . . less than eager . . . to work with a matchmaker."

186

"Ya don't say?" she retorted, the playful light having returned to her eyes.

He held her gaze for a long beat, seriousness falling over both of their expressions. "I wouldn't change a thing though," he finally said, his voice barely above a whisper. He kicked himself for the thickness in it. Without even thinking, he reached across the table and squeezed her hand. "It'll all work out. It always does."

She looked at his hand over hers and then met his gaze again, her eyes glassy. "What choice do we have?" Her fingers wrapped around his and gripped.

They sat that way for what felt like an eternity, though likely it was just a second or two, when Catríona's attention snapped to something over Donal's shoulder. "He's all ready for ya'!" she called.

Donal twisted to see who she was talking to. Deirdre was leaning against the corner of the building. She offered a small wave, a strange sort of smile on her face.

Catríona stood and waved Deirdre over. "I was goin' to make the introductions, but Donal reminded me ye've already met." She smiled as she looked from Deirdre to Donal and back.

Donal stood, and he and Deirdre bussed each other's cheeks briefly. "Good to see ya again."

"Likewise," Deirdre replied, smiling up at him.

"Right," Catríona said. "I'm afraid I'm late for another appointment. It seems ye both have things well in hand here, so if ye'll excuse me."

"Of course." Donal resisted the urge to ask her to stay.

"Grand, so," Deirdre replied. "Thanks, Catríona."

They both watched Catríona disappear around the corner, then turned their attentions back to one another. "Shall we sit?" Donal asked, gesturing to the table.

Deirdre smiled, nodded, and lowered into the chair Catríona had been sitting in a moment ago. "How've ya been?"

"Can't complain. Ye?"

"Same."

Uncomfortable silence settled over them. Both looked anywhere but at the other.

Blessedly, Peadar arrived and took their orders. They each ordered the vegetable soup with brown bread and tea.

The food arrived quickly, and Donal relished the earthy, salty soup as it trailed down his throat. He smiled at the healthy smear of butter Deirdre added to her slice of brown bread. When she took a bite, it left a glob on her cheek, and he couldn't help the laughter that bubbled up out of him.

Her cheeks flushed and she shrank back. "I'm sorry. I really love butter."

He laughed again. "Nothin' to apologize for. I eat my bread the same way." He chose not to add "when I can spare the butter."

With that, the ice seemed to have been broken, and they chatted away like old friends, finishing their meal and leisurely sipping their tea. Donal was surprised at how much he enjoyed her company and at how easily their conversation had flowed— once they both relaxed a little bit.

But after one of the bar maids cleared their dishes, Deirdre grew somewhat nervous again. She picked at her thumbnail and studied her lap for a long moment before shooting her gaze up to meet his.

"Donal?"

"Aye?"

"This was really lovely," she said after a brief pause.

He nodded. "Indeed, it was."

She shifted in her seat. "In fact, I've truly enjoyed all our encounters over the last couple of weeks." A sly smile curved her mouth. "Especially our dance."

Donal laughed and rocked back in his chair. "Ah, yes. That was . . . somethin' else."

She matched his laughter before growing quiet again. "That's why what I have to say is so difficult."

Donal frowned. "Alright. Go on."

"When we first met, I really thought that perhaps . . . well . . ." She blushed.

He nodded, a knowing smile lifting his mouth. "I know what you mean. I'd had a similar thought." He rested his elbows on the table. "But . . ."

She sighed. "But I'm afraid I've met a gentleman, and . . . I *know*."

"That's wonderful, Deirdre. *Comhghairdeas*." He leaned across and bussed her cheek, only now noticing the thin gold band on her left hand. "What's his name?"

The grin that split her face was as bright as the sun in July. "Timmy. Timmy O'Hanlon. Weddin's set for next month in Kilkenny."

Donal couldn't help but return her smile at the joy radiating from her, but he also couldn't help the sinking sadness setting in the pit of his stomach.

"I hope you don't think I was leading you on by agreeing to meet you for lunch today. I just really wanted to let you know in person because you'd been so kind to me and treated me so well." Her gaze drifted off somewhere else. "I can't say the same for all the men at the festival."

Donal sighed. "That's very kind of you to say. But truly, I'm very happy that you found someone."

She smiled, the true picture of the ultimate blushing bride. "Thank you." She leaned forward and gave his forearm a friendly squeeze. "And if ya don't mind my sayin' so, I think you have too."

She must've read the confusion on his face because she leaned even closer and flicked her head in the direction Catríona had walked. "I've seen the pair o' ye together several times now, and it's clear to me that she's the one."

Donal scoffed. "That's sweet of you to say." He shook his head. "I don't deny I find her company very enjoyable. But I'm afraid she's not the one for me."

Deirdre sat back and cupped her hands around her empty teacup, brow furrowed. "Why do ya say that?"

He shrugged. "I think she prefers the company of someone else."

"*Tsk*." She shook her head. "Then you need to make her see."

Donal blinked. "See what?"

She smiled. "That ya love her." Then she bobbled her head side to side. "Or at least ye're well on yer way to lovin' her, and whether she sees it or not, she's on her way to lovin' ye too."

―――――◦◦◦◦――――――

For the rest of the afternoon, Donal couldn't shake what Deirdre had said, though he desperately wanted to. He fiercely wanted to think about something—anything—else. Like what he was going to do about the Osbornes' offer, though that vexed him almost as much as the notion that people thought he was falling in love with Catríona Daly. Almost.

All those worries vanished like morning mist in the midday heat when the bell clanged and Sara erupted out of the doors of the school along with most of the other children in the parish. He hardly ever had the chance to meet her as school released anymore, so when he'd agreed to his lunch date with Deirdre, he'd planned to stay around town until the school day finished.

The grin on his little girl's face when she saw him waiting for her made it all worth it.

"Hiya, peata," he said as he scooped her up and twirled her around.

She squealed and pecked his cheek. "Are we walkin' home together?"

"Aye," he said and tossed her over his side to ride piggyback. Sara yelped and then settled in to her place on his back. When had she gotten so big? And when had he stopped giving her piggyback rides so often?

The first leg of the journey home, Sara filled him in on all the drama going on with the other girls in class. "But it's the most amazing thing, Da, they leave me out of it!"

"Do they now?" he said, huffing as they made their way up the first rise along the Bog Road.

He felt her nod. "Yep. Ever since Catríona gave out to Margot and her pals on the road that day, they don't say boo to me."

Donal's heart clenched with gratitude at how Catríona had cared for his girl even before she really knew either of them. "Well, thank God for Catríona."

"Go cinnte!"

Once all the excitement of the day had been shared, they continued on, Donal's huffing and the occasional caw of a raven the only sounds. The air was cool but comfortable, and platinum clouds still hung low in the air. Though Donal couldn't help but notice how they darkened to a heavy pewter, then slate, then black the closer to the horizon they stretched. He studied them for several paces but there was no way of telling if they were heading out to the Atlantic or coming in toward land from it. He prayed it was the former.

After a few long moments of silence, Donal stopped, crouched down, and Sara slid off his back. They were only a few minutes from home, and the closer they got, the heavier the decision he had to make weighed on him. While he didn't want to place undue responsibility on the girl's shoulders, he also felt it only fair that she be aware of what was at stake.

"A gentleman came and saw me the other day," he began. "Two, actually."

"The men with the hats?" she said as she kicked a rock down the path.

He glanced at her from the side of his eye. "The hats?"

She nodded. "I saw two men in long coats and big hats leaving last week. I just woke up and looked out the window because I heard voices. I saw them leaving."

"Oh." Donal swallowed, unsure why it bothered him that she'd seen them. Almost like he needed to protect her from them, though they posed no real threat. "Yes, those men."

"What did they want?" She slipped her hand into his.

He smiled at the gesture. "Well . . . they want some of our cows."

Sara stopped and yanked his hand. "No! Not our *ba*!"

He chuckled and tweaked her cheek with his free hand, and they continued walking. "No, darlin', they want the baby cows that our cows will have."

"Oh, right. That's okay, then."

"They also want to pay to repair our barn and get the field ready for the next sowing season so we don't have to wait for it to repair itself."

She stopped again and turned to face him fully, eyes and mouth wide with delight. "It's just like the flowers!"

He crouched down and rested his rump on his heels to be eye-to-eye with her. "The flowers?"

She nodded, a wide grin stretching from ear to ear. "Just like Íosa said in the Sermon on the Mount!" She cupped her wee hands on his cheeks. "He said not to worry about it, and He was right!"

Another verse drifted into his mind like the faint smoke when a candle is snuffed. Something about having faith like a child. "Well, I suppose ye're right. I hadn't thought of it that way."

She rolled her eyes playfully. "How else are ya supposed to think about it, ya silly billy!" She dropped her hands and began skipping toward home.

Donal followed her. "Well, ya see, peata, it's not so much like a gift. We have to pay back the bulk of it. By the new year."

"Okay," she said, still skipping.

"If we don't . . ." He paused and watched her, the epitome of childhood innocence. He couldn't bring himself to weigh her down with the cares of the adult world, so he simply said, "It's risky if I can't pay it back."

She started hopping along on one foot, her arms swinging to keep her balance. "Is it risky if you don't accept it at all?" Her voice was light and carefree, as if this wasn't the biggest decision Donal had ever had to make.

"Well . . . yes, I suppose it is."

"But if you do agree, things for sure get better?" She switched to the other foot as their house came into view. "At least for a little bit?"

"Yes," he answered slowly.

She stopped and turned to face him, breathless from her jumping, and shrugged as if to say, "So what's there to think about?"

"I'll put the kettle on," she called as she spun on one foot and sprinted for the front door.

He watched her disappear into the house and wagged his head. Was it really that simple? He entered their sitting room, slid the door closed, and leaned against it. His gaze fell on the giant Bible still sitting open to the book of Matthew.

He rounded the trunk and sank onto the sofa, letting his eyes drift over the page. "Is this really how You work?" Though it seemed silly now, he never thought about God using other people to provide for their needs. When he read passages like the Sermon on the Mount, he always envisioned the food or money or whatever just sort of . . . appearing . . . without any explanation. Taking anything else from other people had always felt somehow . . . shameful. Like accepting help from others was an indictment on his ability to provide for his family and care for his property. He supposed that was one of the reasons he'd never worked too terribly hard to cultivate the relationships Connie'd had in the community. As though in order to prove he was a real man, or a quality farmer, he had to do it all on his own. But Sara's simple view of God's provision had shaken him to his core and now made him question everything he'd been holding on to.

Yes, it was one of the simplest notions of all. And yet, simple did not mean easy.

"Da, tea," Sara called from the kitchen.

"I'll take mine in a bit," he said as he hurried to the small table in his room to scribble out his intent to accept the Osbornes' offer. He'd run it over to them the next time he was in town.

21

Catríona rested her elbows on the table in the dining area of the modest family home. She'd been so caught up with the festival and everything going on with Andrew that she'd almost forgotten the other aspects of her job. Donal had reminded her of that the other day. Now, with another successful plucking of the gander completed, she sat with the happy families, sipped tea, and waited for the appropriate time to take her leave.

In truth, she was ready to go home before she'd even arrived, but to refuse the celebratory tea and cakes or biscuits would not only be unheard of but also incredibly rude. So, she sat at the table nursing her cuppa and watching the joyous party unfold. The bride and groom stood in one corner in hushed conversation, completely enamored with each other. Meanwhile, the parents, aunts, and uncles were scattered around the room in various states of sobriety.

"I canna believe yer man is comin' here, like!" the groom-to-be's father was saying to the future bride's uncle.

"Can ya not? I say it's high time!" the uncle replied.

"Why's that? He's a Meath man who served the commonwealth well in the Boer Wars. Why should he hafta come all the way out this way?"

"He'll be an earl one of these days," the other man said. "'Tis only a matter of time."

"So?"

Catríona's ears perked up at the mention of a future earl. "I beg yer pardon, lads, but who're ya speakin' about?"

The groom's father looked at her like she had three heads. "Yer man Reginald Brabazon, o' course."

Catríona's brows soared. "Lord Ardee is coming here?" She stood and stepped closer to them.

Both men nodded.

"Is he comin' for the festival?"

The uncle scoffed. "Hardly," he said. "He's lookin' at a parcel o' land down the Kilfenora Road."

The wheels in her mind were turning a mile a minute. "I see."

The bride's grandfather stepped up, shook Catríona's hand, and thanked her for a job well done, then he smashed his hat onto his head and shuffled out into the night. *Brilliant!* His going paved the way for Catríona to leave as well. But not before she got a bit more information.

"When does he arrive?"

"On the morrow," they answered in unison.

"Do ye know where he's stayin'?"

They both leveled a look at her and all three said together, "The Queens Hotel." Of course. It was where all the titled folk stayed. Catríona thanked them for their time, then made the rounds of goodbyes, which took far longer than it should have. The goodbyes always did. There was the initial goodbye in the kitchen, then another offer for just one more cuppa tea. "To warm ya for the journey home. It's freezin' out," the bride's mother had said.

After the tea, there were the farewells and side conversations all the way down the hall to the front door. Once at the door, another round of well-wishes and good lucks, and another offer of tea. The first offer could never be refused, but the second was up to the visitor. Catríona politely declined.

When she turned the handle of the front door, a gust of wind nearly ripped it from her hand.

"Good gracious me," the bride's mother screeched. "It's ragin' out there. Will ya not take one more cuppa afore ya go?"

"Thank you, no," Catríona called over the gale. "I must get home and see to my father." The parent card always worked like a charm, and the woman nodded and waved her off. Catríona couldn't hear her over the roar of the wind, but she knew the woman still stood in the doorway, waving and calling "*Slán! Slán leat!*" and "*Slán abhaile!*" just for good measure.

Catríona wrapped her cloak tightly around herself and ducked her head against the violent wind. Her hair whipped all around, stinging her face. Thankfully this house was much closer to town than her last plucking of the gander, so she was back at the Imperial fairly quickly. As she entered, it took all her weight to close the door, and her cheeks burned at the sudden and intense heat inside.

"Ya alright there, Caty?" Peadar asked, polishing a glass in his hand.

"Where's Da?"

Peadar poked the glass in the direction of their office. Catríona thanked him and hurried in.

She burst into the office. "Da! Are ya still lookin' fer someone for the Wyndham girl?"

Her father looked up at her, and his eyes grew wide as he slowly rose. "Caty, are ya alright?"

She flapped a dismissive hand. "I'm fine, Da. Did ya hear what I asked?" It was only then she noticed a young man as

197

thin as a rail in the seat across from her father, looking at her, his mouth agape.

"Oh, beggin' yer pardon. I didn't see ya there. I'm terribly sorry."

Her dad scanned her from head to toe before lowering himself to sit again. "Go upstairs, get yerself cleaned up, and meet me back at the bar. I'll be done in a wee while."

She nodded and turned to go.

"And Caty?"

She stopped and turned back to him. He made a wild gesture to his head, then pointed to her. She frowned, unsure what he could possibly mean, and headed upstairs to hang up her cloak.

Once in her room, she caught a glimpse of herself in the mirror and let out a cackle. Her hair jutted out in all directions, some of it matted to her face. If her hair had been white, she'd have looked exactly like her father. At that thought, the smile slipped from her face. Her poor husband—if she ever landed one, that is— he'd have to wake up to this mug every day for the rest of his life.

Taming her locks took far longer than she would have appreciated, and Catríona was fairly certain there was now just as much of her hair stuck in her brush as there was growing out of her head. But half an hour later, she reappeared downstairs and sidled up to the bar just as Peadar slid a steaming pot of tea and a fresh cup in front of her.

"Saint Peadar," she said, inhaling the deep, comforting aroma and relishing the warmth radiating from the porcelain pot.

Peadar chuckled and offered a friendly wink before heading to the other end of the bar to serve another patron.

Moments later, Catríona's father appeared on the stool next to her. He bussed her cheek. "Ah, there's my daughter."

She glanced at him from the corner of her eye and smiled. "Hi, Da."

"Rough one out there, eh?"

She nodded. "The pluckin' went fine. But the weather's gettin' wild."

He reached over and poured some of the tea from her pot into the cup he'd brought over with him. He never washed that cup. Said it was seasoned exactly how he liked it and to wash it would ruin the flavor of the tea. He was cut from a different sort of cloth, that man.

"They're sayin' it's gonna be a real corker out there for a few days."

"Mm?" she said around a sip of tea.

His head bobbed next to her. "Hurricane force if the pains in m' knees have anythin' to say about it." Then he shifted to face her more fully. "But I suspect ya didn't bust in and interrupt a client meeting to chat about *an aimsir*?"

Hang the weather, she'd almost forgotten! She snapped her fingers and spun to face her father. "Wait'll I tell ya! Guess who's comin' to town tomorrow, God willin'?"

"Santy? I don't know!"

She laughed. "No, not Father Christmas, but almost as good." She paused until she thought her dad might actually crawl out of his skin. "Lord Ardee, future earl of Meath."

"*Mar dhea*." He scoffed.

She shook her head. "I'm serious! The lads back at the plucking said he's comin' to look at a parcel of land out the Kilfenora Road, and he's stayin' at the Queens."

Her father's eyes lit up like a child in front of a bowl of sweets.

"I was thinking," Catríona continued, "that if you invited Miss Wyndham and her father to have drinks or tea at the Queens, and be there to make the introduction . . ."

His face brightened slowly, along with hers, already taking her idea and hatching it into his own plan. "Brilliant girl." He pressed a kiss to her cheek and scrambled off his stool and back to his office.

———————⊶∞⊷———————

The storm had raged all night and all through the day Friday, and Donal could do nothing but hunker down with Sara inside their house. It had been far too dangerous to venture into town, but as morning dawned on Saturday, Donal couldn't keep the anxious thoughts at bay. The Osbornes were shrewd businessmen—they didn't get to their position without being so. But he worried that they would not consider a mere storm reason enough to miss the deadline for accepting their very generous offer. The delay in acceptance had also given Donal ample time to think, rethink, and overthink his decision. It was a generous offer, yes, but that's what vexed him about it. It almost felt too generous, even with the caveat that he pay back the inordinate sum by year's end. But after all was said and done, Donal wound up in the same place he'd landed after he'd told Sara about the deal.

The plain truth of it was, without this deal, they would most certainly have to sell the farm and leave—even if Donal miraculously found a wife before the festival ended next week. Unless the woman was royalty herself, she likely wouldn't bring the resources necessary to get them back on their feet and to where things were before Connie passed six years ago. Had it really been six years?

Memories of the past half decade flashed in his mind's eye in a blur. So many years, so much time had passed. A realization dawned slowly like a turf fire on a cold day, hesitant to catch. He and Sara had been living without Connie for twice as long as they had lived with her—yet he'd been acting like it was only a wee while ago that she left this earth. He'd allowed the grief and hardships and unknowns to tug at him like a wayward cow on the plow, digging him into a rut that was almost impossible to get out of. How stubborn he'd been all this time. How foolish. Now, though, a lifeline had been offered. And instead of seeing it for what it was, he eyed it warily from the bottom of the pit he'd put himself in. Well, no longer. He stood from the table so fast he almost knocked his chair over. He tromped to his room and snatched his written intent to accept from his desk, then trudged back to the kitchen where Sara sat playing with her rag doll.

"I have to run into town really quickly, but I'm only going to the Queens Hotel, so it shouldn't be too long."

Sara nodded, not interrupting the song she was humming.

"Stay inside and keep the doors closed. I'll stoke the fire before I go."

She looked up, smiled at him, and said, "Okay, a dhadí."

He bent down and pressed a kiss to her forehead, then grabbed his slicker, tucked the paper in the inner breast pocket, and tugged his wide-brimmed leather hat onto his head.

---∞---

Twenty minutes later, Donal wedged his way into the lobby of the Queens Hotel. Everyone and their brother milled about inside. A young lady approached and offered to take his slicker.

"Looks like everyone else had the same idea I did," he said as he handed her his coat after removing the paper from the inner pocket.

"Ye're tellin' me," she said. "Not a soul ventured onto the street yesterday 'cause of the weather. Apparently, they couldn't wait another day to let it pass over before getting back to business." She shrugged and disappeared into the crowd.

He was already regretting coming out. He'd barely been able to see five feet down the road on the way in, thanks to the lashing rain and gale-force winds. He'd almost been blown into the verge several times. He determined to make quick work of things and get back home to Sara. He craned his neck to look over the sea of heads and spotted Andrew and his parents at a table in the far corner of the dining room.

Weaving through the throng of people, Donal made his way to the small family. When he approached them, he greeted each by name. Andrew and Lord Osborne didn't notice Donal at first. Lady Osborne appeared very pale and weak, and she stared far off, as though her mind was a million miles away.

Perhaps the weather has her unsettled, he thought to himself. And who could blame her?

"Bunratty!" Andrew called upon finally making eye contact with Donal. He drained his glass, then stood and extended his hand.

"Mister Osborne. Lord Osborne. Lady Osborne," Donal greeted them each in turn again, now that he had their attention, shaking the men's hands and nodding at the lady.

"I presume you've ventured out in this hellacious deluge because you've come to your senses and decided to accept our offer?" Andrew said as he plopped down in his seat, causing his mother to flinch.

Suddenly, the windows rattled and the air around them stilled and almost crackled. Pressure filled Donal's ears, and he winced at the compression pulling against his eardrums. It was as if the air in the building had been sucked out of the room, and every voice fell silent in the eerie vacuum. The pressure built to an almost unbearable state. Then, just as Donal was certain his ears would burst, it vanished. For a brief moment the wind was silent. Someone unfamiliar with the area would've thought the storm was dying out. Everyone else knew better.

From some odd corner of the room, a voice croaked out, "God save us."

As if on cue, the storm picked back up with more vengeance than ever. Rain and hail pounded the windows with such force, Donal feared it might actually break the glass. The wind slung the elements all about like a giant chasing its prey, before swirling this way and that, seemingly unable to decide which way to direct its wrath.

Donal nodded in response to the question he'd almost forgotten Andrew had asked. "Aye," he said, though he wouldn't have agreed to the way Andrew had put it. But Sara was at home, and Donal needed to get back as quickly as possible. He was foolish to have come out in such conditions. Surely, if this was God's way of providing, He would've worked things so that the deal was still available once the weather was safer to venture out. But none of that mattered now that he was here. "If you please, I'd like to move fairly quickly to sign the agreement. Sara's home alone." Donal set his written intent to accept on the table and slid it toward Andrew.

Andrew waved a dismissive hand. "Of course, of course," he said, waggling his empty glass in the direction of the waitress. "We'll just have our barrister bring the papers down."

When the waitress arrived with a fresh dram of whiskey, Andrew said, "Be a dear and send word to Mitchum that we're ready for the papers."

She dipped a curtsy. "Yes, Mister Osborne."

"There's a good girl," he replied, a sickeningly sweet smile on his face as he winked at her.

She hurried off and rounded the corner.

Donal bit the inside of his cheek as the minutes ticked by. Finally, he set his elbows on the table and leaned forward. "Might we agree that my written intent is enough for now and sign the papers when it's more . . . agreeable conditions outside?" He ground his palms onto the tabletop and pressed himself to stand.

Andrew motioned for him to sit back down. "Nonsense, you're here now, might as well get it settled right."

Meanwhile, Donal sent up silent pleas for Sara's safety over and over as ten minutes dragged on. Then twenty. Finally, thirty minutes later, a tall man wearing a dark suit, with a full mustache and greasy black hair slicked back, entered the dining room. Just behind him, Donal noticed Catríona and her father enter the foyer with the fancy man Donal had seen that first night or so of the festival.

He turned his attention back to the Osbornes. Mitchum arrived at the table and took his time greeting each member of the Osborne family. He barely paid Donal any mind at all. He then produced a thick stack of papers and handed them to the younger Osborne.

Donal bit back an oath as Andrew took his time reading over every page. Or feigning to do so. Meanwhile, outside the wind quieted a mite, and the rain seemed to slow in its lashing, though the storm still held plenty of power. Finally, after what Donal was certain was at least five times as long as was truly needed, Andrew flipped the papers open to a page near the back and signed near the bottom. He then spun the stack around toward Donal and handed him his fountain pen.

Donal scanned the page, and when Andrew said, "It's all in good order, I assure you," it was all Donal could do not to jump across the table and throttle the man where he sat. But that would do neither of them any good, though Donal suspected he might enjoy it very much. Ignoring the man's remark, he finished reading. The terms still gave him pause—he could literally lose everything.

Ye'll lose it all fer sure if ya don't sign. Donal shook the thought free, took the pen, and scribbled his signature at the bottom of the page.

"Brilliant," Mitchum said, snatching up the documents. "I've had a tentative order for the supplies on hold until I knew for sure you were going to agree to the terms. I'll tell the man to go ahead and get them coming. If we're going to have a June calf, there's no time to waste."

Donal nodded, then stood, thanked the father and son, and excused himself. Just as he reached the entry from the dining hall into the foyer, a man, soaking wet and splattered with mud, burst into the hotel.

"There's been a collapse!" he shouted. "Every able-bodied man is needed."

"Whose place?" someone called.

The man's eyes drifted to the ceiling as he tried to recall the name. "Eh . . . McDougal's, Bolger's . . . and . . ." With each name, a fresh spate of gasps filtered up from the crowd, only to be shushed again as everyone waited with bated breath to see who was next. ". . . And Bunratty's."

Instinctively, Donal's eyes found Catríona's—which registered the same horror threatening to suffocate him. "Sara," they both mouthed in unison and bolted for the door. Along with almost every other person in the building. The harder Donal tried to reach the exit, the more bodies seemed to jam in between him and the route of egress. Finally, a weathered hand shoved the person in front of Donal aside, and then another, and a clear path emerged. At the end of it stood Jimmy Daly, concern swimming in his eyes.

"I'm of no use to anyone out there." Jimmy inclined his head toward the street. "But the least I could do is make sure ya can get to yer wee gairl."

Donal squeezed Jimmy's shoulder, unable to voice his thanks. Jimmy nodded and then shooed him out the door.

Donal set off at a sprint, wishing he could've brought the cart, but for the debris littering the road. He paid no mind to the puddles blocking the path, turning the dirt road into a muddy lake. Three times Donal's wellies were almost sucked off his feet by the muck. Blessedly, the wind had died down to a dull roar, and the rain had slowed to almost a drizzle. But that didn't matter a lick if anything had happened to Sara. He never should have left her. He knew he took her independence for granted and that one day it would come back to haunt him—he just never figured the reckoning would come so soon. He bit back an oath as the road seemed to stretch longer, pulling the usual journey to twice or three times the distance. No matter how fast he ran, he never seemed to make any ground, while it seemed other men flew past him, their feet barely skimming the surface of the water. For Donal, however, the puddles practically pulled him under like a siren, bogging him down and slowing his speed.

At last, the orange glow in the windows of his house came into view as he crested the final rise. He released a sob of relief to see the structure still standing. Though it was too dark to make out any details, he presumed the roof had likely sustained sizable damage, but at least it hadn't come down on top of his daughter.

"Sara!" he called, his pace quickening despite the burning in his legs. Bursting through the front door, he stopped short at the puddle sprawling across the living room floor. "Sara!" he called again, sloshing his way into the kitchen. But she wasn't there either. Surely she hadn't slept through the whole thing?

He hurried to her room only to find it empty, as was his own room. A gnawing dread clawed at his gut as he screamed her name. Where else could she be? Would she have gotten frightened and tried to run to a neighbor's place?

Then, through the small window in his bedroom, he saw torches crisscrossing back and forth in front of the barn.

Donal's heart sank. "No, no, no, no, no," he muttered over and over as he hurried back through the house and out the door. As he approached the barn, clouded darkness filled the void where the black silhouette of the two-story barn should've been. Donal's gaze floated down until, in the brief light as someone with a torch passed by, he could just make out the crumbled rubble that used to house his cattle. A guttural cry ripped from his throat.

Owen approached him. "It's alright, it's alright, Donal." He pointed to the field behind them. "I think all yer stock're out. The door must've blown open before she fell. It'll cost a bit to rebuild, but ye've still got yer animals."

Donal's gaze followed Owen's pointed finger and counted. One, two, three. Only three. Donal's stomach roiled, but he refused to completely fall apart until he found Sara and made sure she was safe. He turned wide eyes to Owen, all warmth draining from his face.

It was then that Owen's gaze dipped to Donal's side and back to his face. "Sara's in the house, aye?"

Donal wagged his head from side to side, watching as realization dawned, and the same fear that gripped him now took hold of Owen.

"Sara!" Donal screeched as the rain began again in earnest, this time without the howling wind. He broke into a sprint toward what remained of the barn. "Sara!" he called again, reaching where the door should have been. He began clawing at the splintered planks of wood, yanking sections up and throwing them over his shoulder.

Behind him, Owen shouted instructions to the men, who dispersed to each corner of the large barn and began digging through the remains. Every once in a while, a man would whistle or whoop or holler and everyone would still, straining to hear any signs of life beneath the ruins of the old structure. But again and again, it turned out to be nothing, and with each pause in the search, Donal lost a little more hope of finding his little girl alive.

22

Time stretched on slow like cold molasses, distorting Donal's judgment of how long they'd been searching for Sara. Had it been two hours? Only one? Or had it been only half an hour? It was impossible to tell. Lungs burning from the effort, fingers numb and raw, splinters covering his arms, Donal sank to his knees under the weight of the reality that the likelihood Sara would be found alive was waning.

They'd been digging for what seemed like ages, and the rubble pile had hardly diminished. They'd never get through it all in time. Hopelessness pressed down on him like a millstone, pulling him deeper and deeper into the suffocating depths of despair.

"Oy!" a man called, and the work stilled. In the torchlight, Donal could see the man hunch over closer to the mound of splintered wood. He paused, then dropped to his knees and pressed his ear against the wreckage. Suddenly, he shot to his feet. "*Anseo! Anseo!*" he screamed, pointing at the pile beneath him.

Donal gasped and scrambled to his feet, unable to quell the flood of tears pouring down his face. Stumbling over planks of wood, not caring if his legs got jabbed by an odd nail or splinter, he made his way as quickly as he could to where Willie stood. The rest of the search party joined them.

"I heard what sounded like lowing," he said. "And I canna be sure, but I thought I heard . . . a voice."

"Where?" Donal asked, desperation lacing his voice. He dropped to his knees where Willie gestured and cupped his hands against the debris. "Sara! Sara!" he called. All was silent, save for the rain, as they all strained to hear if any reply came.

A long moment passed, and Donal's lungs burned as he held his breath, not wanting to risk missing a single sound. Just when he thought his chest would burst, a muffled cry rose from deep within the pile of mangled wood, hay, and mud.

A collective cheer erupted from the men, and then all at once, they sprang into action. Boards and pieces of walls were flung off and then they'd wait while Owen inspected to see what to move next to ensure the whole thing didn't collapse beneath them.

"We're comin', Sara!" Donal called. "Hang on!"

The men worked and moved together in a well-choreographed dance, and after a few moments, tiny fingers emerged through a small opening in the debris. Donal flopped to his stomach and gripped her fingers, letting his baby girl know he was coming to get her. As he kissed her fingertips and whispered a prayer of thanks, a cacophony of voices filled the air.

"Hang in there, Sara!"

"We're comin', Sara!"

"Good girl! A clever girl!"

Donal swiped at his eyes and spoke softly, praying she could hear him. He told her what they were doing and explained what the banging noises were. She must've been so afraid, and he didn't want her to be frightened anymore if he could help it. He shimmied around to the opposite side of the pile so the men could clear the pieces beneath him, and at long last, Sara's whole body could be seen.

Her dress was tattered and soaked through with rain and caked with mud. A large gash left a red streak across her forehead. Donal called out for a rag, and one presented itself from over his shoulder. He yanked it out of the provider's hand and wrapped it around Sara's wound.

"Dadaí?" Her voice was hoarse and weak.

"I'm here, darlin'. Dadaí's here. You're safe now." He scrambled into the empty space where Sara lay curled up next to Pete. Slipping one arm beneath her shoulders and the other under her knees, he scooped her up and cradled her close. "You're safe now. I've got you. Shh," he crooned in her ear despite the lump blocking his throat.

He stood and ambled up and out of the debris and managed to make it back down to solid ground before collapsing onto the mud and sobbing into Sara's hair. Behind him, someone said something about the heifer, but all his attention was pinned on his little girl.

Slowly, she slipped her arms around his neck and gave a faint squeeze he would've missed had he not been so desperately relieved to have his daughter in his arms, alive.

"I'm tired, a dhadí," she whispered.

"I know, peata, I know." He kissed the top of her head. "But I need ya to stay awake a wee while longer, alright? Can ya do that fer me?"

She nodded against his chest, but she grew more limp in his arms with each passing moment. Stumbling to his feet, he headed back to the house. Once inside, he walked circles around the kitchen and sitting room. Water pooled on the floor in places, and rain still dripped from a few spots on the ceiling. Donal startled when Owen spoke.

"Ye can't stay here tonight, Donal."

Donal looked at Owen, knowing the man was trying to tell him something, but for the life of him, he wasn't able to make sense of what was being said.

"C'mon." Owen wrapped his arm around Donal's shoulders. "Let's go."

Owen led him out the front door and to the road. "Yer horses seem fine, if a bit spooked. But I'm afraid yer cart's destroyed."

Donal looked at him.

"So we'll hafta walk to town," Owen continued.

Nodding, Donal placed one foot in front of the other as he murmured promises in Sara's ear that she was going to be okay and that he was going to take her somewhere warm and dry.

The closer they got to Lisdoonvarna, the more people lined the road. Some were handing out blankets, others cups of tea. Donal kept his eyes fixed on the horizon, determined not to stop or talk to anyone until he made it to town and had Sara checked by the doctor.

"We need to take her to a hotel," Owen said quietly.

Donal bobbed his head in agreement. The first one they approached was the Queens Hotel, but the foyer was chockablock, as it seemed to have become a staging area of sorts for people to find loved ones, organize help parties, and the like. Donal just needed a warm, dry bed for Sara.

Jimmy scurried down the front steps as they passed by the Queens. "Take 'er to the Imperial." He pointed up an tStráid Mhór. "Catríona's got rooms, beds, and baths ready."

Tears pooled in Donal's eyes, and his thanks refused to slip around the knot in his throat, so he merely nodded. Jimmy nodded back, and as Donal passed, he could hear Jimmy telling Owen they needed to hurry. That Sara looked in a bad way.

Donal quickened his steps and as he burst through the door, Doctor Forster met him and led them to a guest room that

Donal had never realized existed on the ground floor just beyond the stairwell. Despite its proximity to the pub, inside the room was quiet, and a warm fire crackled in the small hearth along the western wall.

The doctor gestured for Donal to lay Sara on one of the two single beds. Donal hesitated, not wanting to let her go after such a harrowing ordeal.

Doctor Forster laid a gentle hand on Donal's shoulder. "I'll take good care o' her, Donal," he said. "Ye can stay the entire time. But the girl must be checked over. Let's set her on the bed, aye?"

Donal studied the doctor for a beat before shuffling to the bed nearest the fireplace and gingerly laying Sara on it, taking care not to jostle her head too much. She whimpered and reached for his hand. "I'm here, luhv, I'm here. I'm not goin' anywhere." He took her hand and sank onto a low stool next to the bed.

———————∞———————

The door to Donal and Sara's room was opened a crack, and Catríona peeked inside. Sara lay on the bed, asleep or unconscious, Catríona didn't know. A white bandage had been wound around her head, and a deep red stain had seeped through. The blankets were pulled up over her chest, and her arms rested flat on top of them. She looked so small and pale. So young. For all her insights and astounding capabilities, she was still just a wee child.

Next to Sara, Donal sat on a low stool with his elbows perched on the side of the bed, his hands folded as though in prayer. He stared at his little girl. Tears stung Catríona's eyes at the sight. She couldn't imagine what he must be feeling. When the man announced there'd been a collapse on Bunratty property, her heart was immediately seized with worry—nae, terror—for Sara. She couldn't fathom how much more so it had been for Donal.

She tapped quietly on the door, but Donal didn't move.

The jug and basin in her hands grew heavy, so she pushed the door open, stepped inside, and placed the steaming set on the dresser. "How is she?"

Donal looked at her, his eyes streaked with red, tears making clean tracks down his mud-laden cheeks. The sadness swimming in them nearly undid her. "She's resting," he said, his voice thick and rough with emotion.

"That's good. Rest is good."

Donal turned his gaze back to his daughter, his hands folded, lips pressed against his thumbs.

"Doctor Forster said he got Sara nice and clean but that you were still a mess." Catríona gestured to the basin. "So I brought you some hot water and a towel."

When Donal didn't move, Catríona took the basin and silently stepped to his side. Still, he stared at Sara.

Catríona crouched down, set the washbowl on the floor, and rested her hand on his shoulder. He flinched at her touch.

"Donal," she whispered.

Slowly, he turned and met her gaze. The pain contorting his face, clouding his eyes, gripped her heart and wouldn't let go.

"I-I . . ." he stammered. "I almost lost her."

Her vision blurred as she nodded. "I know."

They both moved at the same time and in a flash, they were swallowed in each other's arms. "I know," Catríona whispered again as she tightened her embrace.

Donal's head fell onto her shoulder, and he wept. Horrible, mournful sobs full of the guilt a parent felt when trauma befell their child and full of the pain of everything that almost was. And everything that would never be after the devastation of his home and land.

She held him as he cried, ignoring the tears streaming down

her own cheeks, moving her hand to grasp the hair on the back of his head, then rubbing comforting circles around his back.

Eventually his sobs slowed, his breaths came more easily, and he was quiet for a moment. "I almost lost her," he whispered again, his voice cracking.

"I know." She sniffed and pulled back so he could look at his little girl. "But ya didn't. She's here, and she's strong. And she's going to be okay."

He took a deep, shuddering breath and nodded, as if seeing for the first time that his little girl really was going to be okay. That she was bumped and bruised but otherwise healthy and fine, sleeping soundly next to him. He nodded again.

His eyes flitted from Sara to Catríona and back.

"Let's get you cleaned up, aye? We can't have ye catching a cold when Sara needs ya strong and healthy by her side." Catríona smiled and held the warm, damp towel aloft before slowly bringing it to his forehead. Gently, she wiped the mud away before dipping it back in the water and wringing out the excess. "Look at you," she said with a chuckle.

Donal turned his hands over, looking at the mud and splinters covering them. She took the towel and carefully wiped the palm of one of his hands. He winced when she brushed one of the splinters.

Catríona sucked in a sharp breath. "Sorry," she said, keeping her gaze fixed on his hands. Working slowly and tenderly, she pulled the shards of wood from his skin and wiped it clean with the cloth. She set the towel back in the basin and ran her fingers softly over the sore, raw places creasing his skin. Taking his hands, she turned them over and cleaned the back of each one. Then she slowly slid her fingers between his, pressing their palms together. Donal froze, then closed his fingers around her hand and pulled them close to his face. He brushed feather-soft kisses against the back of each of her hands.

Catríona's breath stilled in her chest, and she resisted the urge to let her eyes drift closed at the sensation of his lips against her skin. Forcing herself, instead, to trace the contours of his face with her gaze, drinking in every last feature as though she'd crossed the desert without water. When his gaze lifted from her hands to her face, she looked away and picked up the cloth again.

"There's mud all over here," Catríona said as she dabbed at his cheeks while avoiding his gaze, making soft, gentle strokes. She bent down to refresh the towel, and when she straightened again, their eyes locked. Her breath caught in her chest as they spoke volumes between them with just a look. Donal's eyes held such intensity and longing that it rattled Catríona in the most deliciously terrifying way. It both invited her in and set butterflies loose in her stomach.

Slowly, almost as if in a trance, she let go of the cloth and lifted her hand to his face once again. She traced her finger across his forehead, moving a shock of hair aside, then trailed her hand down his cheek and over his jawline when he reached up and took hold of it, pressing it fully on his cheek. Then, with his other hand, he cupped her face.

When their lips met, it was like the first warm rays of summer, when the clouds parted and one's skin instantly warmed at the sun's gentle but fervent touch. Their kiss was slow. Sweet. Tender. But as Donal slid his hand around to the back of her head and gently pulled her closer, they melted into a far deeper, more intimate kiss. The kind that left both breathless, knowing the other in a way they'd never know another.

Catríona slipped her arms around his neck and Donal slid off the low stool onto his knees as she sank fully into the moment. Then they broke apart and he held her gaze fast. Both held their breath, and Donal searched her eyes as the world around them seemed to still. Suddenly they both reached for the other and collided again in a passionate embrace, trying to make up for lost years and express in a single impassioned, lasting kiss all that was in their hearts before they couldn't anymore. When they finally separated, breathless and spent, Donal pressed his forehead against hers.

"Sorry," he murmured before a soft laugh rumbled in his chest.

Catríona rolled her eyes, pulled back, and once more framed his face in her hands, wagging her head. She opened her mouth to reply when Sara stirred next to them.

"It's about time," she said, her voice still groggy with sleep, then she rolled over and began snoring softly as Donal and Catríona looked at each other, eyes wide, and tried to stifle their laughter.

Donal found his way out to the pub for a cup of tea after cleaning himself up and changing into a fresh set of clothing that had been sitting on the chair in his room. Doctor Forster had said they were for Donal. He had no idea where they came from, and they weren't a perfect fit, but they were dry, warm, and clean. The ivory linen shirt had a deeply plunging neckline that laced with a cord. And the trousers came complete with a pair of *braces*, which Donal very much appreciated since they were a little too big in the waist. He tugged the second brace strap up over his shoulder as he approached the bar.

Catríona and Jimmy sat in hushed conversation. They both looked exhausted.

"Thanks again, for the hospitality," Donal said as he slid onto the stool next to Catríona. "Keep a tab and I'll settle up once we're back on our feet."

"*Wheesht!*" Jimmy flapped his hand while shaking his head

adamantly. "All the management's in agreement. We aren't makin' a penny off this. No way."

Donal raked his hand through his damp hair and down the back of his neck, too tired to argue. He'd find a way to repay their generosity one way or another.

"How's Sara?" Catríona asked, her cheeks blushing prettily when she met Donal's gaze.

"Still sleepin', thanks be to God," he said. "But the gash on her forehead looks nasty. Doc said something about how I should care for it, but I can't remember a word of it, I was so wound up."

"Don't blame ye one bit," Jimmy said, nursing a pint.

Donal twisted to look around the strangely empty pub room. He'd hoped to ask the doctor for a refresher on Sara's care, but he didn't see him.

"Do ya know where Doctor Forster's gone?" Donal asked.

Catríona gulped her mouthful of tea and nodded. "Aye, he was called out to the Queens Hotel."

Donal instinctively shot a glance outside. "More storm victims, I'd wager."

Catríona shook her head as Donal tried to ignore the way she licked her lips. "Sounded like somethin' else. Some kind o' medical issue with a guest."

"Busy man. Busy night," Donal said.

Jimmy murmured his agreement. "I'll bet he's really missin' auld Doc Westropp, God rest his soul."

"Don't we all?" Catríona added.

The trio sat in silence for a long time. With each passing moment, Donal's eyelids grew heavier and heavier. The clock over the bar struck three in the morning and Donal yawned. "Right," he said, slipping off the stool. "Thank ye both again, for . . . well . . . for everything. Sara and I would be sunk without ye."

"Don't give it another thought," Jimmy said as he scratched

at the white stubble lining his jaw. "Happy to do it. If ya need anything in the night, just holler."

"I will."

As Donal shuffled toward his and Sara's room, he sensed Catríona behind him. When they were shadowed near the stairwell, he turned.

She reached out quietly and took his hand. He squeezed her fingers and searched her eyes, willing her to read in his all he couldn't bring himself to say.

"Ye'll be alright?" Catríona asked.

With his free hand, Donal brushed his fingers through her fringe and tucked a stray piece behind her ear, reveling in the way her eyes fluttered closed at his touch. "I will be," he whispered.

When she met his gaze again, her eyes reflected the same tender longing that swelled in his own heart. A longing that reached beyond physical lust or outward attraction. A deep, burning desire to abide in and to traverse the joys and sorrows of this world together. To know and be known, mind, body, and spirit. He stepped closer, his mouth tipping up at the sound of her breath hitching.

He leaned down, pausing just before their lips met, reading her eyes, her face, making sure she was in agreement. She released a nearly inaudible shuddered sigh and nodded ever so slightly. He shifted the hand he was holding until their fingers laced together, then he slowly, tenderly, pressed his lips against hers. She tightened her grip on his hand and melted into his kiss.

Though it pained him, he pulled back, gave her fingers one final squeeze, and slipped his hand from hers. "Good night."

Her gaze dropped to the floor, then she smiled up at him through her lashes. "Oíche mhaith."

23

Sunday morning dawned bright and still, feeling more like a summer's day than the end of September. The sheer magnitude in the difference of Mother Nature's attitude reminded Donal of a woman who'd decided the argument with her husband was over and moved on as if nothing had happened, leaving everyone else in the house dazed and confused. Donal stepped outside the Imperial, tugged the unfamiliar tweed coat over his shoulders, and joined the steady stream of people drifting out to the countryside to survey the damage—either to their own property, to their family's property, or to a stranger's out of sheer, morbid curiosity.

Sara was in the capable and watchful hands of Catríona for the next few hours, so Donal headed out to learn the extent of the destruction and make a plan.

A slow smile slid onto his face at the thought of Catríona, and his lips tingled at the memory of her kiss. He'd never experienced anything quite like it before. Was this what passionate love felt like? What he felt for Catríona—both physical attraction and emotional connection—was unlike anything he'd ever encountered before. He'd never understood the big fuss everyone made over love and romance. It all seemed a big ado about nothing. Or, at least, nothing that lasted. After all, physical beauty eventually faded, life experiences could dull one's body, relationships grew and evolved beyond the need for what always seemed a trivial piece of the marriage pie.

Now, however, he was rethinking his entire worldview on the matter. The way Catríona evoked dreams and passions within Donal both moved and motivated him more than anything else had before in his life, save for providing for and protecting Sara.

In fact, the things he was feeling and thinking regarding Catríona were—in some ways—very much the same way he thought toward his relationship with Sara. The desire to provide and protect—and be willing to do whatever it took to ensure that she was cared for, even placing himself in harm's way if need be. The drive to succeed and make her proud. The immense pride at seeing her live into the potential God created within her. Then again, his thoughts surrounding Catríona were also very, very different in many ways as well. The memory of their first embrace washed over him again, setting his heart racing, filling him with an ache to be near her.

He was so consumed with his thoughts that he very nearly walked along without noticing how drastically the landscape had changed in the wake of the storm. The verge tracing either side of the road outside of town was almost unrecognizable. Trees had fallen, brush had been ripped apart, and the typically pristine emerald patchwork of fields and rock walls was littered with all manner of debris.

Conversation among those on the road was at a minimum, as every soul along the path understood—and felt in their bones— the gravity of the situation. Miraculously, no one had been killed in the melee, but plenty of property and livestock had been lost—which was almost as devastating.

The majority of the crowd split off and headed down the

Kilfenora Road, leaving Donal to traverse the final half mile in solitude. As he scanned the horizon, the gentle slope of Cork- screw Hill rose softly from the north and fell to the south, bring- ing to Donal's mind once again, the Sermon on the Mount and the mystery of Providence. All the events from the past week or so tumbled around his mind like the rubble in the storm. From realizing he was likely going to lose the farm no matter what he did, to Andrew Osborne seemingly coming to his rescue with an astounding and entirely unexpected offer, to almost losing Sara, then her life being spared. The dramatic highs and lows of it all left Donal feeling like he'd ridden out the hurricane in a hooker boat out on the Atlantic.

But his thoughts were halted midstream as his property came into view in broad daylight. His steps slowed, and his mouth fell open. The top layers of thatching on the roof of their house were almost completely gone, and the white paint on the walls was now chipped and peeling in places. The little fence sur- rounding the property leaned sadly, almost lying flat on the ground. He scrubbed his hands down his face and took a long, deep breath. Thankfully, all the windows appeared to be intact, and the house had stood solid and strong.

He stepped toward it, but instead of heading inside, his feet led him around the north end, toward the barn. Or where the barn had been. Tears stung his eyes at the sight. Seeing it now in the bright light of day, it seemed even more miraculous that Sara ever made it out of the tangled mass of wood, mud, and other debris. He swiped at his cheeks and moved closer when something clanged at his feet.

Stooping down, he picked up the twisted piece of metal and brushed the mud and muck from it. The clasp he'd bartered with Willie for. He tossed it back down and shook his head, standing again. Fat lot of good it would do him now.

Familiar lowing filled his ears, and he turned, his jaw once again falling slack. Someone had built a makeshift corral and managed to harangue his wayward cattle and horses inside it.

"Well, whatta we have here?" As he neared, the lazy tail swishes sped up and *Bándearg*, his favorite horse, trotted over to greet him.

Donal took stock of Bó, Bó a Dó, Bó a Trí, and Pete. *Oh, Pete.* The heifer had one hoof totally bandaged and immobilized, and a black tarlike substance was scrawled in a zigzag along her left rump. "What happened, lass? Eh?"

He slid his hand up the bridge of her nose and scratched between her ears, just where he knew she liked best. The low, guttural, almost growling sound let Donal know he'd hit just the right spot. "Are ya alright, Pete?"

"Yer bó is gonna be alright, we think."

Donal spun on his heel at the familiar voice. "Willie, was this you?" He hitched a thumb toward the corral.

Willie shook his head as he approached, hand extended. "Not just me. 'Twas a whole lot of us."

Just then, Andrew pulled up on his horse and slid out of the saddle. His dark eyes were filled with something akin to fear or anger as he scanned the perimeter of Donal's property.

"Andrew." Donal greeted him with a nod. Andrew nodded but didn't look at him. Donal turned back to Willie. "So, ya really think she'll be alright? Pete, I mean."

Willie let out a puff of air, his lips flapping together. "I reckon she will." He stepped closer and pointed at various parts of the cow as he spoke. "We aren't sure if her leg is broken er not. Owen was able to brace it pretty well. She won't plow for ya anytime soon, but she'll be alright afore long."

"And here?" Donal gestured to her rump.

"She had a right good gash there. We think from when the

barn come down, but we don't know for certain." He scratched at the back of his head. "'Twasn't near as deep a cut as it first looked. Superficial, really."

"But will she be okay to calf?" Andrew asked, his tone biting and irritated.

Willie waggled his head, the corners of his mouth tugged downward. "I don't see why not."

"Good." Andrew crossed his arms.

"I wouldn't plan on puttin' her with the stud right away."

Andrew turned and paced a few steps toward the house, muttered a curse, and paced back toward Willie and Donal.

Willie floated a look at the man's back. "Better to be conservative now so she'll be fit fer the long haul than rush it and risk losin' her altogether."

Andrew scoffed. "Stupid cow."

Donal resisted the urge to snap a rebuttal at Andrew and instead studied Pete's side and then rubbed the cow's nose again. "What were ya up to, young lady? Huh?"

Willie glanced at Donal out of the corner of his eye. "Ye're not gonna believe it," he said.

Donal folded his arms across his chest and angled toward the man.

"Best we can figure, the latch busted off in the storm. That or the doors just blew open. Anyway, we think Sara ran out there to try and close it so the cattle wouldn't escape. But, of course, they did."

"Of course."

"All of 'em except Pete here. We think she refused to leave Sara, lay down, and sorta wrapped herself around the girl like a shield of sorts." He shrugged. "And then it all came down."

Donal stared at him blankly. Was he saying what it sounded like he was saying?

As if reading the question from Donal's mind, Willie added, "Yer cow saved Sara's life."

"Oh, for Pete's sake," Andrew blurted out.

Willie and Donal burst out laughing.

Andrew looked at them like they had three heads each, clearly unaware of his unintentional joke.

He growled. "Get your laughter out now, lads, because you won't be laughing when you hear what I have to say."

Donal and Willie turned their full attention to the young man. "What is it, Osborne?" Donal asked, working to keep annoyance from his voice.

Andrew swung his arm in an arc. "Look around, man. Your assets are destroyed!" When Donal said nothing, he continued, speaking as though Donal was a child. "When property is damaged, it costs money to repair it. Your barn ceases to exist. Don't you see? It's going to cost far more than our original agreed-upon price to repair—nae—rebuild it."

A pit sank in Donal's stomach like a boulder in a lake. He had completely forgotten about the deal with the Osbornes. No, that wasn't true. He was so relieved that Sara was alright, and so worried about how he was going to scrape together a livelihood when his property was in shambles, that he didn't even consider how the damage could affect the terms of their agreement. Surely it wouldn't negate all of it.

"So . . . what . . ." Donal couldn't even formulate a coherent question. He wasn't sure he knew what exactly he wanted to ask. The prospective answers to all the questions swirling in his mind were terrifying.

Andrew sighed heavily and squeezed the bridge of his nose. He might as well have said, "Must I spell everything out for you, man?"

Instead, he drew in another long breath, as though this

conversation was requiring every ounce of patience he could muster. "I'm going to have to talk to my man again." His voice was low and measured, and Donal wasn't sure he'd heard the man correctly.

"I'm sorry, could you repeat that?"

"We're going to have to calculate this all over again!" His shout caused the cattle to jump. Pete mooed her annoyance. "I must talk with Mitchum. Meet us at the dining room of the Queens tomorrow at four o'clock."

Before Donal could reply, Andrew stormed off through the muck.

<hr />

Catríona stood and held the string out at arm's length and let the horse chestnut dangle down in front of Sara. Playing conkers worked better when both players were standing. And in truth, even better played outside. However, Doctor Forster had given strict instructions that Sara was to stay in bed for at least one more day after today, and the list of activities to occupy the girl was growing thin. They'd already drawn more pictures than they could count, told every joke they knew, and grown tired of making up stories. Catríona flinched and let out a screech as Sara's conker came cracking down directly onto Catríona's, which broke in two, ending the game.

Sara chuckled in victory, her eyes dancing with delight.

"Well done, you," Catríona crooned, secretly glad to reclaim her seat on the chair next to the bed. Her father had replaced the short creepie stool with one of the chairs from the bar, making her role as caretaker for the day far more comfortable. She retrieved her teacup and Sara's glass of milk from the bedside table. She handed Sara her glass and then took a long, hearty sip of her tea.

"So, when are ye and my dad gonna get married?"

Catríona spewed her mouthful of tea all over the floor, then clapped a hand over her mouth, her eyes wide. She looked at Sara from the side of her eye. The girl sipped her milk and stared at Catríona as if she'd asked the most natural question in the world. Taking a moment to compose herself, Catríona took the towel from the tea tray and wiped her mouth and then the floor. As she cleaned up the fine misted spots from the ground, she racked her brain for how to answer.

"Well . . ." Catríona began slowly. "Why do you think we're gettin' married?"

Sara inclined her head, her face painted with incredulity.

"Sara"—she shifted in her seat, cleared her throat, and tried again—"I know you saw yer dad and me . . ."

Sara pressed the tips of her pointer fingers together and made kissing noises before erupting into a fit of giggles.

Fire spread across Catríona's cheeks, and she rolled her lips into a thin line. "We've not really talked about . . . what I mean is, sometimes a man kisses a woman, but . . ." Catríona rubbed circles on her temples, hoping to quell the dull ache that was quickly taking up residence in her head.

"Don't ya love him?" All hint of joking was gone, and only sincerity and curiosity shone in the little girl's eyes. And far too much hope than Catríona could bear to extinguish.

Someone needed to teach the child about appropriate topics of conversation and how not to put their conversation partner on the spot. Nevertheless, Catríona had been asking herself the same nagging question since their embrace. Longer than that, really, if she was honest with herself. What, exactly, did it mean to love someone? If it meant finding someone handsome or beautiful, then half the world could say they were in love with the other half. If it meant enjoying someone's company, well, too many people could say they were in love as well—

and one person could theoretically be in love with multiple people. But what was it that qualified someone to forsake all others and commit themselves body, mind, and spirit to one person, for better or worse, richer or poorer, in sickness and in health, until death parted them? All of these things flashed through her mind in a split second, and she hadn't an answer for any of it.

"I care about your father very much," she said at length. But as she thought over her time with Donal the last few weeks—at the way he spoke to her, treated her, the ways he taught her to think differently simply by challenging what she'd already believed, she had to admit she did more than care for him. When she recalled the taste of his kiss, the warmth of his embrace, the connection they'd shared once they knew Sara would be alright, she knew that there was no one else she'd rather experience those things with. And when she thought of Donal having to walk through the loss of his home, his farm, and even his daughter, a deep, burning, intense desire to do anything she could to prevent that from happening made her realize she'd sacrifice just about anything to keep him from having to do that. Her eyes welled with tears, and her mouth fell open.

There was no doubt in her mind—or her heart. She loved Donal Bunratty. A single tear slid down her cheek as she turned to look at Sara, whose face split into a wide grin.

"Ya do love 'im. I knew it."

Catríona winced. "Aye, I think I do."

"That's okay. I think he loves you too."

Catríona laughed.

"And Catríona?" Sara asked, suddenly growing very serious.

Catríona scooted to the edge of her chair and took hold of the girl's hand, worried she might be in pain or getting sick. "Yes, luhv?"

"I kinda love ya too." Her shoulder rose and fell, then her eyes widened, and she added quickly, "But not in the same way my da does." Then she doubled over with laughter.

Catríona couldn't help but join in the laughter, and she leaned over and pressed a tender kiss to Sara's head. "And I love you."

24

That evening, festivalgoers itching to get back to the craic filled the Imperial, the Ritz, and every other pub lining an tStráid Mhór. They spilled out onto the streets weaving throughout the not-so-sleepy village. A cacophony of music littered the air of Lisdoonvarna, each window in the town pouring out its own jig, reel, or hornpipe.

As Donal strolled up to the Imperial, he spotted Catríona standing in the doorway, leaning on the jamb. She appeared to be a million miles away in thought. He watched her for a moment, his chest warming at the sight of her, wondering what on earth the future held for them. As if she felt his gaze on her, she blinked suddenly and turned to him, a warm smile spreading across her face when their eyes met.

Donal moved closer. "Evenin'."

"Good evenin' yerself." Her gaze dipped briefly from Donal's eyes to his lips and back. "Sara's doin' great. She's asleep."

Donal nodded. "Thanks for lookin' after her today. I know you had other things ya could've been doin'."

She shook her head, eyes locked with his. "Wild horses couldn't have kept me away." She reached over and set her hand on his shoulder and gave a squeeze while she inclined her head in the direction of the Bog Road. "How'd it go?"

Donal scratched at his jaw, the shock of seeing the ruins of the barn in the light still fresh in his mind. "The house is still standin', thanks be to God. But the barn . . ." His voice trailed off, and he shook his head.

"I'm so sorry."

"Ye should see it." He looked over his shoulder as though he could see his property from the doorstep. "It's a miracle Sara made it out 'tall."

"*Tsk.* 'Magine," Catríona murmured.

"Does Peadar have any tea ready?" Donal asked as he started to step around her and into the pub.

"Donal." When she met his gaze again, the uncertainty in her eyes made him pause, and his pulse kicked up a notch. "I think we need to talk."

Donal stifled a groan. He was no expert in the matters of love and the heart, but he did know that nothing good ever came from a woman uttering those words. He swallowed hard. "Alright."

"Walk with me?"

Donal backed off the front step and swung his hand in a low arc toward the street. "Of course."

They walked in silence for several minutes, strolling along as if Donal wasn't slowly dying inside wondering what she had on her mind. Meanwhile, everyone else on the streets seemed to whirl around them in double time, almost in a blur as Donal tried to give Catríona time to decide how she wanted to start.

"Sara's an amazing kid," she said at last.

Donal nodded slowly, unsure where this might be headed.

He was staring at the ground ahead of them while they walked, but he could hear the smile in her voice as she said, "We had so much fun today. That girl and her jokes."

Laughter rumbled in Donal's chest. "Oh, yes, we've had many a family joke night in which neither of us can breathe and not a single eye is dry by the end of it."

"I believe it."

More silence yawned between them as the sounds of revelry swirled in their midst.

"She's also very . . . observant."

From the corner of his eye, Donal caught Catríona stealing some glances in his direction. When he didn't say anything, she took a deep breath and continued. "She thinks . . . that is, she asked me . . ."

They'd arrived at the edge of town, and the dark reaches of County Clare lay ahead of them. Behind them, the ever-livening party of Lisdoonvarna nearing the end of the matchmaking festival grew to a near frenetic celebration, as if each visitor was attempting to make up for the time lost due to the storm. Without words, they both turned and began walking back toward the center of town.

"She asked you?" He drew the last word out, hoping she'd pick up where she left off.

She nervously glanced at him, then dropped her gaze to the ground. "She asked if . . . we're in love."

Heat flashed up Donal's neck and face and he blinked hard. "Oh, she did, did she?"

"Mm-hmm."

A flurry of dancing, laughter, and merrymaking surrounded them in the streets. As they passed the Imperial, Donal saw couples swaying to the music in the golden lantern glow. Other couples sat along the square, and groups of friends shouted and squealed. And in the quiet moment between him and Catríona, he reached over and laced his fingers between hers. At the touch of her skin, his whole world stood still though his heart raced forward. No one else even seemed to notice the two of them existed. Each man and woman were in their own little world, while Donal and Catríona had wandered into what felt like a dream. He peeked over at Catríona, and a sly grin played at her lips. He almost asked her what she told Sara, but in all honesty, it didn't matter.

The truth was, Donal was falling madly in love with this woman standing next to him. And while he wasn't sure he was ready for the rest of the world to know, it felt a little bit perfect that Sara could already tell. After all, if things continued the way they seemed to be, this was a development that would greatly affect her life as well.

"Are you angry?" she asked, her voice quiet and timid. A side he'd yet to see from Catríona.

He stopped walking and tugged her hand so that she faced him fully. "Why would I be?" He stepped closer and stroked the back of his finger down her cheek.

"Sara's your daughter. And while I love her to death, I don't want to overstep my bounds."

When he laughed, her eyes widened.

"I didn't tell her we were in love or that we were gettin' married or anything." She shrugged. "But I also . . . didn't tell her we weren't in love."

Donal smiled. A scant handbreadth separated them, and he hardly wanted to breathe, lest he break the spell that was building between them. "Ye're a good woman, Catríona Daly."

She blushed and looked away.

"And," he said as he cupped a hand on her cheek, "I do believe I'm fallin' in love with ya."

Her gaze swung back to his, eyes even wider. He brushed a tender kiss to her lips.

She pulled him closer and kissed him twice more. "Me too."

Later that evening, after an entirely satisfying dinner of lamb stew and brown bread, Catríona had made her rounds to check in on her other clients. Her father's meeting with the Lords Ardee and Wyndham had gone fairly well. While no official agreement was struck, Catríona had seen Ardee and Wyndham's daughter riding out to the countryside in a carriage in the early afternoon, and she hoped that was a good sign. Those who lived within the court in England often operated one of two ways. Either they were in a mad rush to sign on the dotted line and get things going or they moved as slow as a slug after a snowstorm. And while Wyndham certainly must hold some urgency, having lost two of his three daughters far too young, he didn't strike Catríona as the type to rush into something that would affect his family for generations to come. Coupling that with the fact that Lord Ardee was already in his early thirties and had yet to wed, Catríona's instinct was leaning strongly to the long-road side of the spectrum.

All of Catríona's other clients seemed happy enough—a few were so shocked and overwhelmed by all that had transpired in the last several days, they felt the need to rush home to check on their own properties. Others seemed to have taken the storm as a sign that there wasn't a moment to waste, and she'd scheduled two more plucking of the ganders tonight. Once a couple decided to proceed with an engagement, after the plucking of the gander, the wedding could be scheduled as soon as the following day or as far out as another year. Now, though, as she made her way back home, fatigue began to settle on her shoulders like a yoke. The final week of the festival was often the most exciting, with lots of decisions being made, but that also meant lots of hurried agreements, dowries, and the like. Plus, the pressures of nearly a month straight of all-night revelries began to take a toll. Catríona wasn't as young as she used to be—and she had no idea how her father managed to continue with his vim and vigor year after year. Jimmy Daly was just a different breed of man entirely, she'd decided.

Music spilled out from the wide-open door to the Imperial Pub as the silhouettes inside bounced and bobbed to the lively beat. Catríona stepped inside but she didn't even make it to the bar before she stopped in her tracks. There in the center of all the action, Donal danced with Sara. Well, more like Sara sat on one of the tall barstools and Donal danced around her, keeping hold of one of her hands. The top of the stool swiveled from side to side as Donal jigged and reeled, his legs flailing about in a merry blur. Sara's belly laughter carried over the tunes, and Catríona's cheeks ached from the smile that stretched across her face as she watched the scene unfold.

When the song ended, Donal bowed to his dance partner, and Sara carefully bowed her head in return. The crowd erupted into applause, and Donal gave a funny little wave to honor their recognition. She'd never seen him so . . . silly. She instantly adored this side of him and wished she could replay this moment anytime she wished to relive all the emotions the sight of father and daughter conjured in her.

As the musicians started a more subdued but still upbeat tune, Donal scooped Sara up off the stool and situated her on his hip. She laid her head on his shoulder, her finger tracing lazy shapes in his stubble as if trying to connect the hairs into an image. She smiled as he whispered something in her ear before they both caught sight of Catríona.

The grins they offered her filled her with warmth from the inside out, and she made her way to them.

"That was quite the show," Catríona said.

"Bah. 'Twas nothin'. Just a bit o' nonsense."

Sara picked up her head. "It was fun, a dhadí." Her face had turned paler in the last few moments, and her eyelids looked heavier than a bag of wet sand.

"It was, wasn't it?" He kissed her cheek. "Now, though, I think it's time we got you back to bed."

Sara started to protest, but then yawned and nodded. "Good night, Catríona," she said, her voice matching the weight of her eyes.

"Oíche mhaith, peata." Catríona blew her a kiss. "Sweet dreams."

Donal mouthed, "I'll be back in a few."

Catríona nodded and settled onto a stool at the bar, thinking she might be heading off to sleep soon as well.

Twenty minutes later, Donal shuffled back through the main room of the pub and over to Catríona, dark circles hanging below his eyes.

"Ya look wrecked," she said as he sat next to her.

"Gee, t'anks a million." He offered her a playful, sarcastic smile and rested his elbow on the bar top.

"It's been . . . an excitin' few days."

Donal shook his head. "That's one way to put it."

"Why don't ya head off to sleep?" She bumped his shoulder with hers. "I won't tell anyone ye were in bed before midnight on a festival night."

Donal chuckled and fidgeted with his thumbnail. "Speakin' of the festival . . ." His voice trailed off.

Catríona's brows pulled together. "Aye?"

"I've changed my mind." He kept his gaze fixed on his hands.

Catríona's heart lurched, and she chewed the inside of her cheek, afraid of what he could mean but knowing she had to ask. "Cha—" The word got stuck in her throat. She swallowed hard and tried again. "Changed yer mind?"

He scraped the corner of his bottom lip with his teeth. "I have."

"All . . . alright. About what?"

"I don't think I need a matchmaker anymore." He looked at her fully, his face as solemn as a funeral. But then he broke, and a grin split across his face.

"Och, ya scallywag." She swatted his arm. "You scared me to death."

"Is that alright wit' ye?" The jest faded from his eyes, a hopeful seriousness taking its place. "I've truly no interest in pursuing anyone else."

Catríona's cheeks burned, and her heart pounded out a beat like the bodhrán in the corner. "Else?"

He nodded then reached over, took hold of her hand, and pulled it to him. He pressed a kiss to the back of it and met her gaze. "No sense in lookin' any further when you've found what yer heart desires."

She searched his gaze for any sign of joking and found none. "Have you really? Found what yer heart desires?"

He drew in a shaky breath. "I have." His voice was thick with emotion. He leaned in closer and dropped his voice to a whisper. "That is, if she'll have me."

She let her eyes drink in the sight of him. The rugged features of his face, the deep hazelnut sea of his eyes, the full, rounding of his lips. Her pulse quickened the more she truly weighed the thought of sharing her life with Donal Bunratty. She suddenly realized what she'd been running from all these years had been a lie.

She hadn't been running from the life of a rural Irish farmer's wife or the stench of the livestock or even the hardship of country living. No, what she'd been running from was the betrayal her mother had left in her wake. What Catríona truly wanted to escape was a life devoid of love, purpose, and belonging. And her life would be exactly that without Donal and Sara in it. They were everything she never knew she wanted, and what stood before her now was so much better than she could've imagined or ever planned for herself. She bit her lip and pressed her forehead to his. "Aye. I think she will."

25

Four o'clock couldn't come fast enough. After getting a good report from Doctor Forster that morning, and seeing some color return to Sara's cheeks, Donal couldn't wait to get to his meeting with Andrew and Mitchum. He was equal parts excited to find out the plan so he could start putting it into motion and dreading whatever amendments needed to be made, for fear that he'd never be able to pay it off. But he'd rather know than spend endless hours and days guessing and concocting the ultimate worst-case scenario.

As he rounded the corner to the Queens Hotel, Doctor Forster was coming out, his face lined with concern. When he saw Donal, the doctor rushed over.

"What is it? Is Sara alright?"

"Oh, she's grand. Happy out. I'm just here to meet . . . uh, a business partner." He stumbled over the last words, but he couldn't think of a better way to describe why he was meeting Andrew Osborne. And it wasn't entirely untrue. Though, it felt a bit more like an indentured servant arrangement than a true partnership.

The doctor deflated with a sigh of relief. "Thanks be to God. She looked so great this morning, I couldn't imagine she'd have taken a turn so suddenly." He turned and looked up at the windows lining the length of the hotel. "But after this week, ya never know."

Donal had no idea what the doctor meant by that, but he realized for the first time that the man must see some pretty heartbreaking things in his line of work. Donal shoved the thought aside before his mind could wander too far down the what-if path in regard to his own daughter's harrowing experience. "Thanks to yer good care, she's right as rain. Or is well on her way to bein' so."

Doctor Forster nodded and patted Donal's shoulder. "*Iontach*." Then he pressed his hat onto his head. "Excellent," he repeated, then bid Donal farewell.

Donal steadied himself with a deep breath before climbing the steps to the entrance. The foyer was all but empty, and Donal made his way to the dining room. Andrew was sitting at a table in the far corner, his father and Mitchum flanking either side of him. Andrew lifted his hand in Donal's direction. Donal removed his hat and nodded before making his way to the table.

The four men exchanged greetings, though Lord Osborne looked particularly solemn, and Donal lowered himself into his seat and asked for some tea when the waitress came by.

Andrew scratched at the side of his nose and shifted in his seat. Donal had never seen the man look so uncomfortable—nae, sheepish.

"I'm afraid I must start by offering my apologies," Andrew said.

Donal frowned. "Apologies? For what?"

"I'm afraid I was a bit . . . irritable . . . when we spoke yesterday."

Donal swallowed a laugh. Irritable? The man had been as pleasant as a thorn in a shoe in just about every encounter

Donal had had with him. But he tried his best to keep his countenance neutral.

Next to Andrew, Mitchum snorted.

"Alright," Andrew said, rolling his eyes. "I was a bit short with you yesterday, and I needn't have been. I was bothered by all the damage from the storm . . ." He paused for a breath. "Not only that, but I'd just learned some rather distressing news right before heading out to your place, and I took it out on you."

"I'm terribly sorry to hear that," Donal said. "Anythin' I can help with?"

"Afraid not, chap." He shrugged. "Anyhow, let's get down to business."

Donal nodded and straightened in his seat.

Andrew turned his attention to Mitchum, who was studying a ledger of some kind and seemed to be taking great lengths to prevent Donal from seeing it. Mitchum wasn't an incredibly tall man, but he carried himself as though he was. The dark, bushy mustache under his nose reminded Donal of a fuzzy caterpillar, and the haughtiness that shone in the man's eyes irked Donal deeply.

"Right," Mitchum said with a sniff. "We've gone over things several different ways, but the unfortunate fact of the matter is that any way you slice it, that was one of the most expensive storms I've ever seen."

Donal blinked. "Okay . . ."

"At first we thought we might be able to use some of the existing structures from the barn, but after looking at it yesterday, it's clear that it must be rebuilt from the ground up."

Donal knew that much already. *Just get to the numbers, man.* He clenched his teeth, sending an ache snaking along his jaw and around the back of his neck.

"So, after calculating all new materials, foundation, and the like, this is the additional amount we believe it will take to bring everything on the property up to standard." He slipped a square of paper from his ledger and slid it slowly across the table with one finger until it stopped in front of Donal. Then he added, "That figure is on top of the sum in the original agreement— which, as you know, has already been spent on supplies."

Donal looked from the paper to each man and back. "Ye're jokin', right? We can't just talk about it?"

Mitchum stared at Donal through narrow eyes, judgment oozing from every pore on his slender face. He nodded once toward the paper.

Donal sighed and picked up the slip, bracing himself for whatever number might be scrawled on the other side. Upon seeing the amount, he coughed as though Pete had kicked him in the shin. "Twent—" he shouted, then paused and flashed a glance around the room. He lowered his voice. "Twenty thousand pounds?" He winced at the crack in his voice.

Mitchum shrugged. "That's what it will take to bring things to the level needed in order for our agreement to continue."

Donal fell back against the chair, defeat covering him like a shroud. He braved a glance at Andrew, who studied him, his face registering no emotion whatsoever. His gaze flitted to Lord Osborne, who seemed a million miles away, lost in thought.

"I . . . that's quite the tidy sum," Donal managed to say at last. "Will the repayment deadline be extended as well, to account for the extra costs?"

Andrew shook his head. "I'm afraid not."

"But that's not fair!" Donal shot forward and pressed his forearms onto the table. "You can't possibly expect me to repay the original debt plus an additional twenty thousand in just three months' time?"

Andrew shrugged. "I'm sorry, but I'm afraid the timeline is strict."

Why? It made no sense. Donal doubted very much that Andrew was sorry about any of this. "Then I'm afraid I must back out of the agreement altogether."

Mitchum grimaced. "Hard luck, ole boy. You already signed the original deal. If you back out now, the property is ours."

Donal stood, hands fisted at his sides as he tried to recall all the fine print on the original contract. Had it really said he forfeited his land if he backed out after signing? "That can't be right. You can't do this!" He didn't care that people were beginning to stare. He wasn't going to let these crooks steal his land and livelihood right out from under his nose.

"Come now, Bunratty. Do you really want to walk away from this?" Andrew rested his elbows on the table, and Donal wanted to smack the patronizing look off of his face. "Sit down and let's talk. If you walk away now, you and Sara have nothing. But sign the new agreement and you at least have a chance at paying back the loan."

"This can't be right," Donal repeated. "How can you get it all? You said yourself the original deal was off."

Andrew held up his index finger. "I said the original deal needed to be revisited and adjusted. I never said it was off. All of the details are there in black and white. We can have a different barrister look at the contract if you like."

Before Donal could agree to that, Andrew added, "But that will cost even more."

Donal ground his teeth and squeezed the back of his neck. Hang it all, he should've listened to his gut from the beginning. He always suspected Andrew was a snake in the grass. Now, he wasn't sure which was worse, Andrew orchestrating this whole thing, his father for just sitting there like a puppet letting it all happen, or Mitchum for his smug enjoyment of the whole fiasco.

What was he going to do now? If he backed out of the deal altogether, where would he and Sara go? If they stayed, how on earth would he save up enough money to pay this exorbitant amount back, let alone have enough to feed his daughter?

"Do not worry about what you will eat, or where you will sleep, or what you will wear."

The nearly audible thought arrested him, and he almost looked around to see if anyone else had heard it. He couldn't decide if the thought was comforting or infuriating. He was almost getting sick and tired of having that blasted Sermon on the Mount invading his mind at all hours of the day and night, only to leave him with more questions than answers. And just when he felt he had a handle on God's provision, something else cropped up, causing him to question everything he thought he knew.

"What say you, man?" Lord Osborne grumbled. "We haven't got all day."

Donal sucked in a long breath and released it. He saw absolutely no way that he'd be able to repay such an outrageous amount. But the thought of the Osbornes getting their hands on Donal's property if he walked away now turned Donal's stomach. He felt trapped in the middle of an impossible situation. Both of his choices—walk away and hand the keys to his veritable kingdom over to Andrew or sign this new agreement and be indebted to the man for even more—seemed equally horrific. But the slightest hope of keeping his property and home—a fool's hope though it may be—was better than just handing it over straight away.

Donal scratched the back of his head and set the slip of paper on the table. "What do I need to do? Is there a new agreement to sign or what?" Resignation filled his voice, though he tried desperately to keep it from doing so.

"Good man." Lord Osborne slapped his knees and stood. "Mitchum will make sure everything's in order." He then hurried from the room.

I'm sure he will.

On cue, a folder practically materialized in Mitchum's hand. He tugged a thick stack of papers from it and flipped to a page at the end.

"Mister Osborne's already added his signature, so it's just missing yours." Mitchum handed the document to Donal along with his fountain pen. "This document spells out just what we've discussed here—the additional sum for the new repairs, et cetera."

Donal took a seat again and scanned the text. It seemed everything was as Mitchum said. There were no hidden terms or loopholes. At least not that Donal could see. Once again, he was at the precipice of an impossible decision. Ignoring the overwhelming sense of déjà vu, Donal scribbled his name before he had time to change his mind.

"Right, now that's settled, there's just the small matter of the calving to discuss."

Donal, who was already halfway standing, paused, his rump hovering above the seat. Slowly he lowered himself back down.

"I'd like the first one to have a July birth."

Donal coughed. "July? That seems a bit soon, what with Pete's injuries. June is for sure out."

"Hence July." Andrew scoffed. "If you're that worried about it, have the veterinarian check her out first."

"You employ a vet?"

Andrew's forehead creased. "What? Of course not. I presume there's a man around here who does that?"

Donal sighed. "Aye. I'll send for him when we're done here." Suddenly, a wild hair struck him, and he added, "And I'd like half of the calf fee upon confirmation of the pregnancy. The other half when the calf arrives to your estate."

Andrew's lips tugged into a thin line and he shook his head. "I'm afraid not. We've never dealt with our stock that way."

Donal leaned forward, his voice filled with urgency. "C'mon, man. Work with me, will ya? I know it might be a mite unorthodox from the way ye normally do things, but I just need a little leg up to get us goin' again."

Andrew studied Donal's face for a long moment before matching Donal's positioning. "Alright." He leaned close to Donal, his voice a whisper. "I'll try to convince Mitchum. But I wouldn't hold my breath if I were you."

If there was a chance of a bit of money making it into Donal's pocket before July, he'd gladly take it. "Fair enough." He stood and held his hand out to Andrew.

Andrew hesitated briefly, then took Donal's hand and shook it.

26

The next morning, Donal hurried out to his property to meet the veterinarian after a restless night with Sara. They'd spent most of the evening in their room as the festivalgoers had been a bit too lively for Donal's liking, and Catríona had been out visiting clients. The wound on Sara's head was healing nicely but was beginning to itch, which caused her to whine incessantly about anything and everything that came across her mind. The discomfort also kept her awake a large portion of the night, and Donal absently wondered as he lumbered along the Bog Road how he'd ever survived her infancy when she was up several times a night to eat and have her nappy changed.

When he arrived at his property, Doctor Quinn was already there. Donal stifled a yawn as he greeted the man who was treated practically like royalty in the county.

"Thanks for comin' on such short notice," Donal said as he shook the man's hand. "I'm afraid I can't offer you any tea." He grimaced and gestured to the house.

"Ye're grand, now. I was tryin' to make my rounds throughout this area after the storm anyway. Figured there had to be some animals that were in a bad way." He turned toward Pete. "One of which I see ya have here."

"Aye, unfortunately." Donal stepped closer to the beast and explained what had happened in the barn with Sara.

"Muise! Thanks be to God that yer wee girl is alright!"

Donal nodded. "Thanks."

"As fer this fella . . ." Doctor Quinn rounded Pete's side and ran his hand down her flank. "Oh, pardon me. As for this lass, I'd say she's lucky to be alive as well."

Donal folded his arms and chewed his lip, waiting for the doctor to continue.

"Ye've done a right fine job fixin' her up, I must say." He dabbed his finger on the black sludge covering the wound on her side and gave it a quick sniff. "This salve saved her a whopper of an infection, I'd wager."

"Really?"

"Oh, aye. A brilliant move on yer part."

Donal shifted his feet. "I have good neighbors. They fixed her up for me while I was lookin' after Sara."

"Well, thanks be to God for good neighbors then. Because of them, yer heifer'll be right as rain in no time."

Donal released a breath he hadn't realized he'd been holding. "She will? Oh, that's grand, so." He hesitated to ask the pointed question, but he needed to know. "And . . . is she fit to calve?"

Doctor Quinn's head whipped around, his eyes wide. "Well, not right now, she's not." He patted Pete between her ears. "But she will be."

"Do ya think she'd be ready for . . . uh . . ." Donal pressed his eyes shut and squeezed the bridge of his nose with his thumb and forefinger. "For a July birth?"

"July?" The doctor's brows soared. "No, no, not July. Maybe . . . September."

Donal's head fell forward, and he cupped his forehead in his hand.

"She'll be well healed by July, Donal. It's the gettin' her pregnant part that concerns me. Ya'd have to breed her next month, and I'm afraid that whole process will do more damage than a July birth would be worth."

"I see." Donal dropped his hand.

"Just give her a couple months to heal and recover." He tousled the cow's tuft of hair between her ears. "She's been through quite an ordeal."

Yeah, so have I. And it's not over yet, apparently.

Doctor Quinn turned and headed over to his cart. He rustled around for a moment before tugging something out and returning to Donal.

"My fee's ten quid." He adjusted his money pouch in his hand. "I've change if ya need."

The dull ache that had been forming between Donal's eyes spread and wrapped around his whole head. More money he didn't have, just to try and hold onto a home he couldn't currently live in, that he likely would have to leave in a few months anyway. "Gimme just a moment."

"O'course. Take yer time," he called after Donal as he trudged to his house.

Grateful to find the interior of his home in the same state in which he'd left it, he strode over to the press in the kitchen. He pulled his emergency stash of money from inside the teapot he never used. His last ten pounds.

Catríona sat in the sitting room of Lady Osborne's suite and forced her mouth not to fall open.

The lady reclined on a chaise lounge, a heavy blanket over

her lap. Her cheeks had grown gaunt and her skin wan. But her glare had lost none of its intensity.

"Lady Osborne, I'm . . . I'm so terribly sorry."

The lady blinked slowly. "Call me Ruth," she said, her customary staidness returning. "Just while it's only us two."

"Very well." Catríona nodded. "R-Ruth." Her lips hesitated to form the word, for fear that the woman had changed her mind in the split second since she'd uttered the allowance. "And the doctor is certain?"

Ruth pressed a mirthless laugh through her lips. "Look at me, my dear. I'd say he's fairly certain." Her gaze drifted to the window, and she was quiet for a moment. "Even if he wasn't sure, I am. I can feel it in my bones. Literally."

Catríona's heart squeezed. Ruth Osborne had seemed the most formidable woman Catríona had ever met. To see her now, practically growing weaker by the minute, filled Catríona with a sadness she couldn't explain.

Ruth shook her head. "Don't give me your pity, child."

Catríona's mouth did fall open now, and she waved her hands in front of her. "I wasn't meaning—"

"I know." Ruth sighed. "I know what you meant. But that's the whole reason we hadn't said anything to anyone before now. I couldn't bear the thought of all those 'poor Lady Osborne' stares every time we went out."

Catríona blinked a few times. "You've known?"

She nodded. "The diagnosis came just after we returned home from last year's festival."

When Catríona's eyes grew wide, Ruth shrugged a single shoulder.

"When Andrew was matched with that . . . one . . . last year, I was so hopeful that I might perhaps have a grandchild by now that I could at least watch grow up for a little while." She adjusted the blanket on her legs. "No one knew how long I had, but everything felt normal for a long time. So, when we had to return to the festival again this year, I presumed everything would be alright."

"Have you tried—"

Ruth's lifted hand stopped Catríona midsentence. "We've tried it all. I've even visited all the spa wells that supposedly carry so many healing powers. But the pain and weakness hit very suddenly a week or so ago and things have progressed very quickly." She coughed a sarcastic laugh and swung her hands in an arc over herself. "As you can see."

"What can I do for ya, Ruth?" Catríona scooted to the edge of her seat. "I assume ya didn't just summon me here to share yer story? Is there any way I can help?"

A sly grin tilted the woman's lips. "You're a clever girl, Catríona. That's one of the reasons I chose you."

"Well, cleverness is a handy trait to have in matchmaking."

Ruth shook her head. "That's not what I meant. Well, at first, yes. But I've chosen you for a far greater task."

Catríona's brows pulled together. "Oh? What's that?"

Ruth adjusted herself to sit up straighter on the chaise. "As you're well aware, Andrew has struggled a bit in the task of finding the future Missus Andrew Osborne."

Catríona's heart sank. She hoped the Osbornes wouldn't spread a bad word about her skills and tarnish the reputation her dad, and his parents before him, worked so hard to build. "I've been trying my best, really." Ruth lifted her hand again before Catríona could explain herself further.

"'Tisn't your fault, lass. I place the blame for all the mishaps and missteps squarely on the shoulders of my son." She slid the heavy blankets from her legs and set her feet on the floor. Waving off Catríona's offer of help, she rose on shaky limbs and hobbled over to sit in the chair next to Catríona's. Then, to Catríona's utter shock, she reached out and took hold of Catríona's hand.

"You, my dear girl, have been a bright spot in this whole dark journey." She patted Catríona's hand and leaned in closer. "And that's why I've chosen you."

Catríona frowned. "Beggin' yer pardon, Lad—er, Ruth—I'm afraid I still don't understand."

"You've shown yourself a worthy opponent for my son. You're not afraid to challenge him and push him to be better and to grow. You've also proven your ability to hold your own within the tenuous atmosphere that is gentry life in Dublin."

Catríona's eyes darted to their hands and back to Ruth's face, her head spinning. She tried to wrap her mind around what the woman could possibly be talking about. Surely she didn't mean . . .

"And when you showed your vast knowledge and understanding of the political climate over drinks the other night? Well, that's when Lord Osborne and I knew." She leaned closer still and whispered, "You are the woman for our Andrew."

All the air seemed to rush from Catríona's lungs, and the room felt as though it were filled with water instead. "Lady Osborne," Catríona said, pushing herself to stand, letting the woman's hand slip from hers. "I'm . . . I'm flattered."

Donal's face flashed across Catríona's mind, and she turned away. How was this happening? Less than a month ago, Catríona would've likely fainted at such a statement, and she'd have lunged at the chance to marry Andrew. In fact, the words would've hardly left his mother's lips before Catríona would've been packed and ready to head off to start her new life as far away from here as she could've gotten.

"I know you're surprised," Ruth said. "That's why I wanted to let you know first. Before I spoke with Andrew."

Catríona spun around to face Ruth again. "You mean, Andrew doesn't know this is what you want?"

"Well, he didn't. But I'm afraid Lord Osborne let it slip last night." Ruth slowly pushed herself up to stand again. "It took some convincing, to be sure, but that doesn't matter. He'll do what he's told."

The tiny ember of hope in Catríona's chest grew to a flicker. Andrew quite literally had his choice of any woman he wanted. The chances of him actually wanting to spend the rest of his life with her seemed slim. If he made a big enough stink, perhaps he could convince his mother to change her mind.

"Andrew's had plenty of opportunities to choose a wife. The one he chose last year . . . well, she just wasn't a good fit. She was so touchy and sensitive. She got offended at every last thing Andrew said and did." Ruth shook her head, then reached out a hand to steady herself. "No, he's had his chance. Now, he's going to do what his father and I say. I'd like to see him safely married and well on his way to becoming a father before I . . ." Her voice trailed off.

Catríona's gaze drifted to the floor. She couldn't imagine what this woman was going through, knowing her passing from this world to the next was coming at any time. Sure, every human on earth was in the same situation. No one knew when it would be their time to pass on. But she knew it was coming. And soon by the looks of it. It must be a very helpless, lonely feeling. But Catríona couldn't agree to marry Andrew just because his mother was dying. It wasn't fair to either of them.

The image of Donal's face floated into her mind once again, setting her heart thumping. Everything had changed so much in such a short period of time. She couldn't fathom being with anyone else. And the thought of living a life without Donal and Sara in it sent icy shivers down her spine.

Suddenly the door to the room opened, and Lord Osborne strolled inside.

"Ah, good," he said. "Have you told her yet?"

Ruth nodded. "Only just."

"Good show. It's a brilliant plan, eh?"

Catríona stepped back a few paces. "I'm very flattered, Lord and Lady Osborne. Truly, I am." Catríona moved closer to the door. "But I'm afraid I must decline your very kind offer."

Ruth shuddered. "Nonsense. I've just told you you're the woman for Andrew, and that's that."

Lord Osborne scoffed. "They're two peas in a pod, Ruthie."

Lady Osborne turned to face her husband, her posture impeccable. Catríona wondered how much energy that simple task was requiring at this moment.

"Aren't they just?" the lady replied.

"Why," Lord Osborne continued, "she has the same look on her face as the lad did last night. Remember how Andrew's face clouded? He looked like a pouting child."

Catríona could picture Andrew, shoulders slumped, lips protruding. She shuddered as she suddenly realized she had no idea why she'd found Andrew so enticing before. The unwavering confidence she'd so admired now just seemed like immature arrogance. His chiseled features, which had been so irresistible mere weeks ago, elicited no emotions or response from her at all. Watching his parents, imagining their conversation last night, a pathetic pout plastered on his face, she could finally see Andrew for what he truly was. A spoiled, entitled child who didn't care what it took to get what he wanted. A shiver snaked its way up Catríona's spine as she realized that that was all she'd been to him as well. In a flash, she could taste his whiskey-soaked kisses from the night they'd danced together. Her stomach churned. She was a means to an end for him—his end. And there was no telling how many others there had been.

"I remember," Lady Osborne replied to her husband.

Lord Osborne stepped forward and placed his hands on his wife's shoulders in a rare show of affection. "We just want to see him securely wed before . . . while we're all still together. Right?" The catch in his voice took Catríona by surprise.

The lady's posture softened slightly, and she nodded, her muscles shaking just a mite. She seemed so tired. So frail.

Suddenly, Ruth Osborne was no longer an intimidating gate-keeper who had the power to crush Catríona's dreams. Not because of her illness but because Catríona had been blessed with a view few likely saw. They'd invited Catríona behind the curtain of their puppet show, and she'd seen the strings, watched the mouth of the puppet master moving. Now, Catríona could see the woman for what she really was—a master choreographer whose carefully crafted world was in danger of collapsing.

Catríona cleared her throat. "I'm terribly sorry, Lady Osborne, Lord Osborne. But I'm afraid that's not a decision you can make for me." She collected her cloak from the rack by the door and flung it around her shoulders. "I'm flattered, I really am. But it's just not the right fit. For me."

Fire flashed behind Ruth's graying eyes and a muscle popped at her jaw. "Don't walk out that door. You'll regret it."

Catríona swung the door open and hurried into the hallway, the echoes of the woman's screams and threats chasing her all the way into the street.

27

Donal's heart seemed lodged in his throat as he walked back toward town, looking for Catríona. He could hardly form his thoughts with the words he knew he needed to say to her as he cursed, not for the first time, this whole ridiculous experience. What he wouldn't give to turn back time to Sara's birthday. He'd have turned down her birthday wish, and they'd still be happy at home. He'd have been there during the storm to convince Sara not to run outside, and they'd have stayed safe in the house.

Or you'd have run out after the livestock and been killed yourself, leaving Sara an orphan.

He shook the thought free, refusing to entertain any other idea than the one that convinced him things would've been perfectly fine if only he'd never agreed to attend the blasted matchmaking festival. Then he never would have met Catríona and wouldn't be having to do what he knew needed done. He'd opened himself up to the idea of love, and—just as he suspected—all it was going to do was cause him and his little girl endless heartache. He blinked away the stinging in his eyes and swallowed against the burning in his throat as he thought about having to tell Sara. She'd be crushed.

As he passed beside the gardens of the Queens, he heard two men talking. Their voices were familiar, and Donal slowed his steps as he tried to place them.

"You know, it's not a terrible idea," the first voice said. "Quite ingenious, actually."

"I don't know that I'd go that far, Mitchum."

Of course. Andrew Osborne and "his man."

"I mean it," Mitchum said. "I wish I'd been the one to think of it."

"Easy now. My father's not here for you to lick his boots."

"Little Andrew Osborne getting married."

Donal's brows lifted as he feigned tying his shoe to listen more, feeling only slightly guilty. "I never thought I'd see the day you'd settle down," Mitchum continued.

"Who said anything about settling down? Mother wants me married before she dies, and that's exactly what she'll get. I owe her that much."

"Right," Mitchum said, a question lingering in his voice.

"Look, the girl's fine company. And we'll have some fun. But just because I'm married doesn't mean I can't still live my life."

"You dirty dog." Mitchum's statement of condemnation held a tone of awe rather than judgment.

Donal could almost see Andrew shrug as he made the next statement. "And when the old lady's gone, little wifey-poo can go stay in Mother's old quarters, and I'll go on and have some real fun. Now we just have to convince her to agree to it all."

"You're terrible."

"That's what the ladies tell me," Andrew said. "And then they beg for more."

The men's footsteps faded toward the building but Donal just stood there. He wondered what poor soul had been matched to that scoundrel—and he hated that Catríona had to be the one to do it. Wagging his head, Donal continued on his way to town, grateful that the Osbornes would likely be returning to Dublin now that they'd struck their agreement and the young lad was finally matched to some poor, unsuspecting waif.

As he approached the fork in the road near the front entrance to the Queens, Catríona came barreling around the corner.

"Hey, there," Donal called. "Are ya alright?"

She jumped and spun, taking a defensive stance. Her breath came in short puffs, and her eyes were wide and wild.

"Catríona? What is it?"

The sight of who she was looking at must have finally registered because she blinked and then threw her arms around Donal's neck. "Oh, thank God," she whispered, her warm breath tickling the back of his neck.

"What's happened? What's wrong?" He gripped at her waist and tried to push her away from him to look in her face, but she wouldn't budge.

"I just . . . just give me a minute."

At first, Donal hesitated, but as she tightened her hold, he slid his arms around her and held her until her breathing slowed and he could no longer feel the pounding of her heart against his own chest.

Finally, Catríona took a deep, steadying breath and stepped back. "Thank you. And sorry."

"What's all that about? Did someone hurt you?"

She laughed. It came out a nervous, bubbling sort of sound. "No, no. Nothing like that. I just . . ." Her voice faded, and she looked away for a beat. "Just a particularly frustrating client meeting. That's all."

"Are ya sure? Ye're certain ye're okay?"

"Aye." She nodded.

Of course, he thought. *She just had to broker the Osborne match.*

Then she slipped her hand into his. "I'm even better now that I get to walk with ye."

Donal's heart sank. *Don't say that. Please.* He gave her a tight-lipped smile but couldn't bring himself to let go of her hand. Not yet. A bench in front of the hotel caught his eye. "Sit with me?"

They settled themselves, and she snuggled up close to him. His eyes slid shut, and he took a deep breath, trying to bolster the courage needed to do the hardest thing he'd ever had to do.

"We need to talk." The words were sour in his mouth.

"Oh," she said on a laugh. "That doesn't sound good."

He scooted away so that a couple of inches separated them. "I don't remember if I've told ya, but I've had an offer with the farm."

Her brows lifted. "Oh? Is it goin' to help you and Sara?"

He waggled his head. "It is . . . but it's going to change a lot of things."

"Oh?"

Donal took another slow breath. "The Osbornes have offered to purchase the next six calves Pete has."

"That's wonderful! That's going to help so much!"

Donal nodded. "They've also offered to pay to repair the barn and get the fields ready so I don't have to let them fallow."

She suddenly blinked and held up her hand. "Wait, did you say the Osbornes? As in Lord and Lady Osborne. Andrew Osborne, Osbornes?" Her eyebrows had nearly disappeared into her hairline.

"Well, aye. But that was before the storm."

Catríona tossed her hands and scoffed. "The scallywag's reneged on the offer, hasn't he?"

Donal shifted in his seat and stared at his hands. "Well . . . no. But the repairs are a loan. And the storm damage has added . . . an exorbitant amount to the bill." Catríona's face blurred behind the rebellious tears that filled his eyes. "And I'm afraid he's given me a rather short time frame in which to repay the loan."

She reached over and took his hand, her touch instantly soothing his raw nerves and simultaneously pouring salt into the wound of his breaking heart. He pulled his hand from hers. "I have nothin' to offer ye. I can't give ya the life ya deserve. I can't give ya . . . anythin'."

She sighed and took his hand again. "I don't care about that, Donal. I don't. We'd be a team, you and I."

Hot tears streaked down his cheeks. "Ya don't understand. I'll barely be able to provide for m'self and Sara, let alone you. You deserve so much better, to be comfortable and not wonder where yer next meal will come from. I cannot marry ya, Catríona."

Catríona gripped his face in her hands and waited until he met her gaze. Her eyes swam in her own tears. "Donal Bunratty, ye're not getting' rid of me that easily."

"Don't." He shook his head, his eyes drifting downward.

"Don't what?" She bent to force him to look at her again.

"Don't . . . don't make this any harder than it has to be."

She smiled. "Nothin' hard about lovin' you."

His face crumpled and he fell into her embrace. "I'm tryin' to do right by you, Caty. I love ya too much to force you to live a life of poverty."

She held him tight, tears sliding off her cheeks and onto his neck and shoulders. After a long moment, she pushed away. "Look, there was a time not so long ago that I might've agreed with ya."

Donal shifted and slid himself back away from her. She was too close. He couldn't think straight with her so near.

She continued, "The idea of havin' to struggle was one of my biggest fears—and the main reason I couldn't wait to get out of Lisdoonvarna."

"I know that," Donal said. "And that's not the life I want fer you. You deserve to be with someone who can shower ya with pretty dresses and fine food. Not some bloke who can barely feed ya beans on toast." His head fell forward, defeated.

"But now," she continued, unfazed by his statement, "I'd rather live in a hovel with rags for clothes and nary to eat but a blade of grass between us if it meant we'd be together." Catríona gripped Donal's shoulders. When he didn't meet her gaze, she shook them slightly. He looked up, and when their eyes locked, she said, "I'm. Not. Going. Anywhere." Then she pressed her lips to his forehead. He closed his eyes as the last vestige of his resolve crumbled under the freeing weight of her love.

He pulled her close until their lips met. They melted into a tender, passionate kiss, not caring a button that someone might pass by. He'd never felt more at home than when he was with Catríona. And in her arms now, he couldn't help but feel that he could conquer the world.

"Ye're a stubborn woman," he said when they pulled away.

She brushed a kiss to his nose. "Thank you." They laughed and Donal stood, holding his hand out to her.

"Let's go home," he said as he helped her to her feet. As they turned to go, Donal couldn't be sure, but he thought he'd seen someone watching them from the downstairs parlor window. He risked a glance over his shoulder as they walked away. Andrew Osborne's glare could've burned a hole in the glass windowpane.

28

The next morning, a knock on the door to Donal and Sara's room startled Donal as he sat near their small fireplace reading. Sara was still sound asleep even though it was already eight o'clock. Donal cracked the door open and peeked out.

"Jimmy," he said, keeping his voice low. Concern clouded Jimmy's face, and his pinched features sent a pit into Donal's stomach. He stepped out and slid the door closed. "Is everything alright?"

"I was goin' to ask ya the same thing." He held up an envelope with Donal's name in scrolling letters on the back of it. "This just came fer ya by courier."

Donal frowned. He didn't recognize the script—no one he knew used such fancy writing, and the envelope had no postage markings on it. Dread swirled around him, and he shuffled to one of the nearby tables and sank into one of the chairs. Jimmy sat next to him as Donal broke the seal and opened it, taking care not to tear the contents.

As he read the message, all the heat drained from his face, and the paper fluttered onto the tabletop. His head sank into his hands.

"Och, lad." Jimmy set a large hand on Donal's back. "What is it? Can I help?"

Donal groaned and shook his head. He nudged the letter with his elbow, and he heard Jimmy pick it up.

"I don't understand."

Donal dropped his hands into his lap. He explained the agreement he'd made with the Osbornes and about the amendments to that agreement after the storm. "They'd originally said I had until the end of the year to repay the loan to rebuild the barn and fix the fields. Now, they're sayin' I have to repay at least half of it by next month or they'll evict us."

Jimmy muttered an Irish oath under his breath and picked the letter up again. His eyes flitted across the page as he read. "They've moved up the due date because ye're too risky of an investment? Seafóid!"

Donal tossed his hands. "Nonsense or not, they've done it. And now I have no hope of ever paying it off. Sara and I will have to leave." A wave of nausea washed over him as he realized the worst of it. "And I won't even have the benefit of selling the farm. According to the agreement, they own it already." He groaned and dropped his head onto the table. Agitation stirred in his gut. He wrestled between the urge to cower in a hole and sleep to escape the reality he was facing and the desire to find Andrew Osborne and pummel him. Nervous energy coursed through his body and sitting here made him want to crawl out of his skin. He shot to his feet, knocking his chair over, and stormed outside.

⊷◯⊶

Catríona sat in the office with Maeve, comfortable silence filling the room. When Catríona had filled her friend in on the latest, she was rewarded with a blast of righteous indignation and offers for Maeve to take matters into her own hands. Catríona smiled at the fresh memory. While she had no doubt Maeve could hold her own with the Osbornes, or any champion prize fighter for that matter, she'd assured Maeve all that was needed was her support.

Donal entered and greeted both of them along with Catríona's father.

"That's my cue." Maeve stood. "Call me if ya need me." She bent and bussed Catríona's cheek.

"I will," Catríona said on a laugh. "Thanks."

Donal slid onto the bench next to Catríona and took her hand, their fingers intertwined under the table. Her father was on the other side of Donal, who sat straight and proud, but Catríona knew he must have been terribly nervous. She glanced at the mantel clock. Five minutes to one. The Osbornes would be arriving any minute. When Donal received their message moving up the payment due date, he was going to rush down to the Queens to give them a piece of his mind, but he'd run into Catríona, and after getting him to explain what had happened, she convinced him to wait. When he calmed down, Donal had said he was tired of meeting the Osbornes on their turf and summoned them to the Imperial instead.

"Do you think they'll actually come?" Catríona asked him.

"They will if they think they're going to get their money."

Movement out the window caught Catríona's eye. She turned to see Andrew and Mitchum coming up the walk. Donal had been right.

When the men had come into the office and all the greetings said, tea offered, declined, and offered again, Peader came in with a tray of tea and biscuits for them all.

"So," Andrew said, eyes darting between the three, "I presume you received our message."

JENNIFER DEIBEL

Catríona had to bite back a sarcastic retort. *No, we'd just asked you here to play snooker.* She inwardly rolled her eyes.

"I did." Donal's face was stoic and his voice steady.

"And?" Mitchum said, his mustache twitching.

"Are you willing to advance me half the payment for the first calf now as a stud fee?"

Mitchum scoffed. "Absolutely not. Out of the question."

Donal looked from Mitchum to Andrew, his unvoiced question written on his face.

Andrew shrugged. "You heard the man. Afraid it isn't possible."

"Then I'm afraid I won't be able to make the payment. One month—in the autumn—is hardly enough time to garner any sort of notable income for a farmer. Particularly given the circumstances with the hurricane." Donal's eyes narrowed. "But I think you already knew that."

Mitchum slid a skinny folded document from his inner jacket pocket. "Then, according to the stipulations in the agreement, your land and all the buildings and livestock within it now belong to the Osborne estate."

Donal's jaw worked back and forth, but he said nothing.

"And while there are provisions in the contract that allow for us to keep you on to manage the land for us," Andrew said, "we believe it's in our best interests that you and your daughter vacate the premises. We'll find our own manager and caretaker."

"You're evicting them?" Catríona erupted. "Have you no heart? Where are they supposed to go?"

Andrew's shoulders rose and fell. "I'm afraid that's none of my concern. Mister Bunratty should've weighed all the options and consequences before signing the agreement."

"You know I had no choice," Donal ground out the words through gritted teeth. "This was your plan all along."

265

Andrew's face was the portrait of innocence. Except nothing about Andrew Osborne was innocent. "My good man, there's always a choice," he said.

Catríona looked from Donal to her father and back. Her father was being uncharacteristically quiet and calm throughout this whole conversation. Then again, he was not familiar with all the ins and outs of what had transpired. But it was unlike him to be silent in the face of such grave injustice.

"Donal, let's fight this," she said. "Surely there's a loophole. Let's take the contract to a barrister or something."

Donal shook his head. "No, Catríona. It's over."

She stood, ramming her thigh into the table. She bit her cheek and rubbed the spot, then turned to Andrew. "Isn't there something that can be done?"

Mitchum shook his head. "I'm afraid not. What's done is done." Despite his words, his face made it clear he wasn't the least bit sorry about any of it.

Andrew stood. "Well, there is one thing."

Mitchum spun his head to look at Andrew. "What are you doing?"

Andrew waved him off, but Mitchum was soon on his feet and almost nose to nose with Andrew. They engaged in a heated, whispered debate.

"When last I checked, Mitchum," Andrew shouted, "you worked for us. Not the other way 'round."

Mitchum turned, fuming, and lowered himself back into his seat.

"As I was saying," Andrew said, deliberately pacing the room, hands clasped behind his back. "There is one way in which Donal and little Sara can stay on their land. And I will consider the debt repaid, and we will abide by our original agreement of purchasing the next six calves."

Catríona's gaze shot to Donal. Disbelief and suspicion clouded his face. His eyes dark and brows knitted, he slowly stood. "What are you saying, Osborne?"

"I'm saying, there's a way for you to have your cake and eat it too."

"And how's that?" Donal asked.

"Simple." Andrew locked his eyes onto Catríona. It felt as though her heart stopped, and her whole body grew cold. "If Catríona marries me, I'll consider that as payment for your debt."

The room erupted as Catríona, Donal, Jimmy, and Mitchum all shouted their dissent.

"You can't be serious, man," Mitchum was saying. "There's no financial sense in that."

"What?" Catríona's father said. "That's nonsense. Do ya even love the girl?"

"Absolutely not," Donal shouted, shaking his head. "No way."

"Are you jokin'?" Catríona blurted. "You people don't take no for an answer!"

Andrew held his hands up in mock surrender. "Look," he said, his voice sickly sweet. "It's just an option."

"The answer's no," Catríona said. "It's not an option!" She sidled up next to Donal.

"Fine." Andrew shrugged. "You and Sara have until the first of October to pack your things and be gone."

"G'on wit' yerself," her dad said. "Let's talk about this for a minute."

Andrew crossed his arms. "Seems to me there's nothing to talk about. There are two offers on the table. Bunratty can renege on the bargain we struck, vacate the premises, and move on with his life. Or Catríona can marry me, Bunratty's farm will be rebuilt as we agreed, and he can carry on there and have all he's ever wanted, knowing his debt has been paid." A sick gleam danced in Andrew's eye as he looked between Donal and Catríona. "Not a bad price to pay for your dreams, eh, Bunratty?"

Andrew lifted his cup from the table and drained it in one gulp. "I'll give you all a moment to discuss." He spun on his heel and headed for the front door. "Mitchum?" he called over his shoulder.

Like a scolded puppy, Mitchum got up and followed his master out the door.

Once the door closed, Donal turned to Catríona. "Absolutely not."

Catríona searched his face, imagining what life would be like if he and Sara were evicted from their land—from the home that had been in Donal's family for generations. They couldn't live at the Imperial forever. No matter how generous her father wanted to be, the hotel needed that guest room to survive. And what if she and Donal got married? Would the three of them live in her bedroom in the flat she shared with her father? She didn't make enough as a matchmaker to pay for them to have their own place. And neither one of them wanted to emigrate to America. As many wonderful things as they'd heard about it over the years, Ireland was their home. Catríona wanted to raise her family on this island. And she suspected Donal felt the same or he would've left a long time ago.

The thought of marrying Andrew Osborne made Catríona's skin crawl, but she didn't see any other way. How could she condemn Donal and Sara to a life of poverty, wasting away in the poorhouse, when it was in her power to prevent it?

Donal frowned. "You're not actually considering this?"

She took his hand. "There is no one I'd rather spend my life with than you."

Next to Donal, her father coughed.

"I'm sorry I didn't tell ya, Da. I was goin' to." Catríona turned back to Donal. "But what was it you said to me earlier? I love you too much to relegate you to a life of poverty. I couldn't live with myself if you and Sara were barely scraping by in a workhouse somewhere, or on a boat to America, when I knew I had it within my power to stop that."

Donal tucked a piece of hair behind Catríona's ear. "And what was it you said to me? I'm. Not. Going. Anywhere."

Catríona grabbed Donal's face and kissed him hard and good. "I love you, Donal Bunratty, but we need to at least think this through."

Round and round they went, Catríona trying to do the right thing by Donal and Sara, and Donal insisting they'd find another way to make things work. Finally, her dad stepped forward.

"Would the both o' yas just shut yer traps for a wee sec?"

Catríona and Donal turned to look at him. "I've been tryin' to tell ye for ten minutes, but I canna get a word in edgewise with the two o' ye." He shook his head. "Sit. Both o' yas."

They did as he bade, and he settled himself in a chair across from them. "Now, first of all, ye're both nuts if ya think that I—and the rest o' the world, for that matter—couldn't see the two of ye are head over heels fer each other."

Catríona and Donal looked at each other wide-eyed.

Her father nodded. "Aye, it's that obvious."

Catríona blushed and Donal reached over and took her hand.

"Second of all, there's somethin' that I need to tell ye."

"Alright," Donal said, his thumb rubbing arcs on Catríona's hand.

He turned to Catríona. "Ye remember when I sold the farm after . . . well, when I sold the farm."

Catríona nodded slowly. "Aye." The word slipped out long, laden with unspoken questions.

"You were young enough then that I don't know that you ever thought much about it. But I knew that raisin' a girl on m' own wasna going to be easy." He shifted in his seat. "So, I set up a little nest egg."

Catríona blinked. "A nest egg?"

Her father nodded and leaned forward to rest his elbows on his knees. "I took the money from the sale, along with the money my parents left me when they passed, and I used some of it to get us set up here"—he gestured in an arc over their heads—"but I put the rest in the bank. I knew eventually ye'd grow up, and I had no idea then if ye'd be wanting to take on the family business or if ye'd meet a bloke and want to go off an' set up yer own place or what have you."

Catríona's pulse quickened. "What are ya sayin', Da?"

He drew in a deep breath. "I'm sayin', I've been holding it aside, and it's been earnin' interest until I knew the best time and way to use it or pass it along to ya." A knowing smile spread across his face. "And I knew yas were sweet on each other, but to see you willin' to sacrifice and marry that . . . that . . . cad so that Donal and Sara could have a life?" He sniffled and pulled a handkerchief from his pocket and wiped his eyes. "That's true love right there. The Good Book says it best, that there's no greater love than to be willin' to lay down yer life for yer friend.

"And what ye're thinkin' of doin', Caty? Ye're layin' down yer life." He shook his head. "And I love ya, but I don't think you'd have been willin' to do something like that a year ago. Or even a month ago. Ye've grown, Caty. And ye've had a big hand in that, Donal. Ye've loved my girl like I would have—even when ya wouldn't admit it to yerself."

Donal squeezed Catríona's hand, and he shifted in his seat.

Catríona's mind swirled, and the beating of her heart filled her ears, so she wasn't sure she was actually hearing her father correctly.

"I'm gonna pay that debt," he said.

A sob burst from Catríona's mouth, and she clamped her free hand over it. Donal wagged his head. "Jimmy, that's mighty generous of ya, but I can't let ya. This is my debt, not yours."

"And why not? Ya love my daughter, aye?"

"Well, of course, but—"

Her father leaned forward. "And ya were plannin' on askin' her to marry ya, aye?"

A sheepish grin tipped the corners of Donal's lips. "Well . . ." His cheeks flushed. "Aye. With your permission, of course."

Catríona's father turned to her. "And ye were gonna accept, aye?"

She bit her bottom lip but couldn't keep the smile from spreading across her face as she nodded. "I would have, aye."

Her father held his hands up, palms facing the ceiling. "Then ye're practically my son already. And now that we're family, what you carry, I carry, and the other way 'round."

"Oh, a dhadí." Tears streamed down Catríona's cheeks.

Donal rubbed the back of his neck. "I dunno, Jimmy. It's so much money."

He nodded. "Aye, 'tis. But I've been savin' so's I could provide a good start for my Caty. And if it's a choice between her hitchin' her wagon to that bloke or livin' on yer land with ye and Sara, there's no question." He scooted to the edge of his chair and gripped Donal's shoulder with one hand and Catríona's in the other. "I love ya both. And I want to do this fer ye."

When the pair still hesitated, he scoffed. "Och! Think of it as a weddin' gift, alright?" He eyed them, his brows sky high. He craned his neck forward awaiting their answer.

Catríona looked to Donal, who searched her face for a long moment, his hand tightening around hers.

"What d'ya say?" Donal asked, a playful spark lighting his eyes. They also held a hint of something akin to a lost puppy. "Wanna marry me?"

She reached over and took his other hand, her cheeks burning from the wide smile she couldn't wipe from her face. "I though' ya'd never ask."

Donal released a relieved sigh and scooted closer until their knees bumped. He laughed and took her face in his hands. "Say it again. Say ye'll marry me."

Their eyes locked, and she held his gaze for a long moment, her chest warming, her pulse racing. "I'd be honored to marry ya, Donal Bunratty."

He pulled her close and kissed her soundly.

"Alright, alright, there's plenty o' time for that stuff," Catríona's father said. "It's not a done deal yet—the marriage or the debt."

Catríona laid her head on Donal's shoulder and looked at her father, tears blurring her vision. "Thank you," she mouthed.

"'Tis my pleasure, peata."

29

Donal squinted against the afternoon sun as he watched the main street for Andrew and Mitchum to return. When the men had been nowhere to be found in the square, Donal sent word to the Queens that they'd reached a decision. Who knew how long it would take for the pair to come back? Donal wouldn't be surprised if they took their sweet time, if for no other reason than to make Donal squirm. Except he wouldn't. He had his plan now, and he was so close to being free from the Osbornes' oppressive debt he could almost taste it. But he couldn't bring himself to believe it all was real until he had the receipt of payment in his hands. And he wouldn't breathe a word of any of it to Sara, who had met another little girl in the square earlier that morning. The two were now playing happily in Donal and Sara's room.

He could scarcely believe this was actually happening. It was still extremely difficult to let Jimmy pay his debt. It felt like charity he didn't deserve—and he didn't want it hanging over his head the rest of his life, driving a wedge between him and his father-in-law-to-be.

But Jimmy had pulled him aside after he and Catríona had officially agreed to wed.

"I want ya to know that I mean what I said. 'Tis a gift, not a loan." Then he'd clapped his hand on Donal's shoulder. "I love ya like I would a son. But even more than that, I'm glad my Caty's found herself a good man. She's been . . . searching . . . for a long time. And I don't mean for a man. I mean fer herself. I was beginnin' to wonder if she'd ever find her way out of the dark maze she'd lost herself in, but then you came along and brought her to her senses. She was chasin' after that fool of an Osborne, and I'm afraid she almost caught him too."

Donal shook his head.

"What is it, lad?" Jimmy had asked.

"I'm . . . I'm afraid. That I won't be enough for her."

"*Wheesht*!" Jimmy flapped his hand. "Ye're more than she ever hoped to dream for. And ye're exactly the sort o' man I've been prayin' and beggin' God to bring her."

Donal had mulled that conversation over and over in the past hour, and the more he thought it through, the more peace slowly filled up his heart. Then, unbidden, the verses from the Sermon on the Mount echoed in his mind, and the world around him spun slightly. Donal froze. Was this God's provision? Had he orchestrated this whole winding road from the beginning just to end up here?

Before Donal could chase that idea any further, Andrew's golden hair appeared at the end of the road, bobbing alongside Mitchum's oil-slicked coif and bushy mustache.

Donal turned and called over his shoulder, "Here they come."

Catríona sidled up next to him and wound her arm through his. Her smile, though genuine, was also tenuous. At the table next to them, Maeve nodded at Donal and winked at her friend. A fear flickered behind Catríona's eyes that echoed in Donal's own heart. They were both thinking the same thing. There was no reason to believe the Osbornes would accept the payment and relinquish Donal's property. Especially if it meant leaving town with Andrew still unmatched before his mother met her untimely demise.

Donal sighed, bent, and kissed the top of Catríona's hair, which smelled of lavender and was comfortingly warm from the afternoon sun.

When Andrew and Mitchum were several yards away still, Donal and Catríona turned and took their previous places back in the office.

"So," Andrew said as he swept in, arrogance painting his face, "you've reached a decision? I presume you've come to your senses?"

Donal nodded. "I have."

"Good man." Mitchum sniffed. "You have one week to vacate—"

"That's not what I mean," Donal said, lacing his fingers through Catríona's.

"I see." Andrew's eyes flashed. "Then I'm afraid I must insist that you let go of my fiancée's hand. Catríona?" Andrew snapped his fingers and pointed next to him.

Donal glanced at Catríona. Her eyes were as wide as saucers, and she made a move like she was going to stand up—to pummel Andrew, Donal was afraid. As much as he might have liked to witness that, he couldn't have his future bride arrested for disorderly conduct or some such nonsense. He laid a hand on her forearm. Her jaw flexed, and she huffed a long breath out her nose.

"Actually, I won't be marryin' ya, Mister Osborne," she replied, her chin high, brows arched.

"I'm afraid you don't understand the terms of our agreement," Mitchum said.

Donal shifted in his seat. "I understand them all too well.

And I have decided to just end it all here. Now. And pay the debt in full."

Andrew and Mitchum erupted into a spate of condescending laughter. "And just how do you plan to do that? You couldn't afford the price of eggs mere hours ago."

"A lot can change in a few hours," Catríona said.

Jimmy crossed his arms and leveled his gaze on Andrew. "I'll be takin' ye to the bank, where the full amount of Mister Bunratty's debt—plus one month's interest, as a show of good faith—will be paid to you."

Mitchum flashed a look toward Andrew, whose brows were low over his eyes.

"From what Donal has said, the supplies for the barn and other repairs have already been ordered, aye?"

Andrew nodded.

"Then this will settle Mister Bunratty's account for good," Jimmy added. "Donal keeps the ordered supplies, and his land full and outright. Then this matter is never to be spoken of again."

"And the cattle?" Andrew asked through gritted teeth.

"That is up to him," Jimmy said, turning his attention to Donal.

Donal looked to Catríona, hoping she could read the question in his eyes. *Should I continue with that deal? This is going to be your life too.*

She tightened her grip on his hand and drew in a deep breath. The shake of her head was so slight, Donal almost missed it. And yet it was as though she'd screamed it from the top of the Cliffs of Moher.

Donal shifted back to face Andrew. "I'm afraid upon further consideration, I cannot in good conscience sell my livestock to the Osborne estate."

Mitchum shook his head. "Unacceptable. Lord Osborne made it very clear that this whole deal was in order to secure Bunratty cattle for the next several years. We cannot very well—"

Andrew lifted his hand, silencing his man. "The full amount, plus interest, you say?"

Jimmy nodded.

Mitchum turned to Andrew. "Andrew, no," he hissed. "Your father—"

"It's more money than we paid out," Andrew said. Then he glared at Donal. "Besides, there are better places to get cattle than from some culchie in Lisdoonvarna."

Mitchum ran his hand over his pointed nose and bushy mustache. "And what about the girl?" If he was attempting to be discreet, he was failing.

Andrew looked Catríona from her head down to her toes. "I don't want anyone's sloppy seconds," he said, his expression laden with disgust.

Donal's jaw clenched, and his right hand balled into a fist. He was ready to haul off and punch Andrew right in the face, but next to him, Catríona laughed.

"Thanks be to God," she blurted out between guffaws.

"Do we have a deal?" Jimmy asked, hand extended.

Mitchum's mustache twitched, and he shook his head, eyes pleading silently with Andrew.

Andrew looked from Jimmy to Mitchum and back, then he stared at Jimmy's outstretched hand for a long beat. He eyed Catríona briefly, then took Jimmy's hand. "Deal."

<hr/>

Sara sat wide-eyed at the table in Catríona's office. The dish of jelly and ice cream in front of her gleamed in the lantern light. Sara delighted in jiggling the dish and watching the red jelly wiggle and dance. When she scooped up a bite, she did her own little jelly dance—wiggling her rump in the seat and rubbing her tummy.

"Is it good?" her dad asked.

Sara licked her lips and went in for another bite. "*An bhlasta*," she murmured around the mouthful.

He chuckled and Catríona smiled. "I'm glad," Catríona said.

She scooped up another spoonful. "I wish we could have this every day."

Her dad rolled his eyes. "I bet you do." Then he glanced at Catríona with a funny look. "But we can't have it every day. Because not every day is a very special one."

"Well now, that's very true," Catríona added with a playful smile.

Sara stopped eating and thought for a moment. It wasn't her birthday—she'd just had that. And Da's birthday wasn't until December. "Is it yer birthday?" she asked Catríona.

Catríona nibbled the corner of her lip and shook her head. "Nope. Even better than that."

Sara scrunched up her face. The only thing better than a birthday was Christmas, but it was only September. Suddenly, she noticed that her dad's hand was wrapped around Catríona's. Her cheeks were a pretty shade of pink. And they were both grinning like the cat who ate the canary. Sara paused, her spoon midway between the bowl and her mouth, melting ice cream dripping and splashing onto the table.

"Sara," her dad said, clearing his throat. "Catríona and I . . ." He turned to Catríona, grinning like the boy in Sara's class when he snuck sweets into school.

Sara lowered her spoon, her mouth forming a big circle. "Ya are not!" She looked at Catríona, in case her father was joking with her.

Catríona nodded. "Mm-hmm."

Sara jumped out of her seat. "Are ya really?"

"Really," her dad said. "We're gettin' married."

Sara's heart did a jig, and she all but tackled her father in a hug. The joy bubbling up inside her was so great, she couldn't hold it in. A great big belly laugh exploded from her before big, fat sobs shook her whole body.

"Aw, peata, it's okay." Her father smoothed her hair back from her face as she cried into his chest.

"Do ya mean it? Ye're really marrying Catríona?"

"I do. I am." She felt him nod against her head, his whiskers scratching her scalp through her hair.

"Oh, a dhadí!" She threw her arms around his neck and squeezed as hard as she could. When her tears subsided, she pushed away and swiped the back of her hand under her nose and sniffed. "It's about time!"

The three erupted into fresh laughter, and Sara went around and stood between them and they wrapped themselves into a giant hug.

30

"Hiya, Donal," Owen said, entering his shop from the back room, wiping his hands on his apron. "How go the repairs?"

Donal sighed. "Finally makin' some progress, but it's slow goin'." He craned his neck and looked around the shop. "Osborne said a lumber shipment had arrived?"

"Aye." Owen jammed a thumb in the direction of the large doors behind him. "Stacked up out back there." He reached below the countertop and shuffled around before producing a yellowed piece of paper and handing it to Donal. "Here's the receipt. It's all paid fer."

"Grand, so." Donal folded the receipt and slipped it into his pocket. "Listen, Owen, Willie told me that ye were one of the men who helped set up the pen and wrangled my cows after the storm."

Owen nodded matter-of-factly.

"He said you provided the wood for the pen?"

Owen busied himself wiping at a spot on the counter. "I did."

"What do I owe ya?"

Owen looked at Donal like he'd just proposed marriage. "Ya don't owe me an'thing, Donal."

"No, no, I can't accept yer charity. Please, let me pay for the supplies and yer labor."

Owen pursed his lips and pressed his palms flat on the countertop. "I don't know if ya remember, but my wife and Connie were good friends."

Donal's brows furrowed. "Aye, I remember." He shrugged. "Though, for a while there, I had forgotten."

"And do ya remember when my Maggie had our third *babaí*? Connie brought several meals, plus some blankets for the wee thing."

Donal searched his memory, and faint images of those events—and others—materialized in his mind.

"And when Sara was born, and Connie was in a bad way, we did the same," Owen reminded him.

Donal nodded. "Ya did."

Owen bent and leaned his elbows on the counter. "Helpin' one another isn't charity. It's bein' neighborly." He scratched at his ginger beard. "Nae, it's basic human decency. Donal, ye've never had to do any of this alone."

Donal's eyes drifted to the ceiling. Hang it all if he hadn't cried more in the last week than he ever had.

"When Connie passed, we all—me, Willie, even Black-eyed Jack—wanted to rally around ya." He shrugged. "But ya pushed us all away."

Frowning, Donal shook his head. He hadn't pushed them away. He just needed . . . space. Time to sort out what he was going to do. Sara was so little, it was all he could do to make it through each day remembering to get them both fed, let alone to take care of the farm. And as Sara grew, it just was easier to handle it all himself. He was the man of the house, and he should've been able to provide what they needed on his own.

"Ye're a proud man, Donal. Ya always have been. But there's

no shame in lettin' yerself be a part of the community around ya." Owen came around the counter and leaned back against it. "We've missed out too, ya know?"

"Missed out?"

"Ye've kept to yerself for six years. And ya've been sorely missed." He grinned. "Especially at the dances." He winked and mimicked a little jig.

Heat rushed to Donal's face, and he scrubbed his hand down it. "Aw, muise, don't remind me."

They were both quiet for a long moment, then Owen cleared his throat. "So . . . is it true?"

Donal blinked. "True?"

"Are ya gettin' married?" His eyes twinkled.

"Good grief, word travels fast around here."

Owen laughed. "Welcome to Lisdoonvarna—where the only thing waggin' more than the flags in the wind are the tongues. Especially when it comes to love."

Donal shook his head. "I guess so."

"Will ya stay at yer place?"

Nodding, Donal said, "That's the plan." He scratched the back of his neck. "But it'll be a long while before that can happen. So, not sure when we'll actually wed."

"Oh?"

"It's gonna take me ages to get the roof fixed and clean up all the water damage from the storm. And rebuilding the barn will take even longer."

"Is that right?" Owen asked, his voice flat.

"Aye." Donal's lips pulled into a thin line.

Owen leveled a stern look at Donal.

"What?" Donal asked, blanching.

"Och!" Owen tossed his hands and let them slap against his sides. "Have ya not heard a word I've said?"

He must've read the confusion on Donal's face because he stepped closer and placed both his hands on Donal's shoulders. "Let us help ya!"

Instinctively, Donal crossed his arms over his chest and shook his head. "I can't let ye. It's my property, my mess. Ye shouldn't have to take time away from yer families and work just to help me."

Owen sighed. "Hang yer pride, man! Let yer community come alongside ya." He bent to force Donal to look him in the eye. "We want to! We all do! We just didn't want to force it on ya, but it's clear ya weren't goin' to come to yer senses on your own."

It had been so long since Donal had opened himself up to anyone or let them into his world. It felt foreign and strange. And yet, the idea of working alongside a group of men he respected to ensure his family was set up for success was entirely enticing. Slowly, his head bobbed.

"Good man," Owen said, squeezing Donal's shoulders. "When do ya want us out there?"

"Saturday, say nine in the mornin'?"

Owen grinned. "Grand. I'll let the lads know."

Saturday morning, Donal, Catríona, and Sara headed out to the farm while it was still dark. Granted, the sun didn't rise until well after seven o'clock this time of year, but they were all eager to get started on finally fixing up their home. Donal smiled as he swept the dried mud, muck, and leaves from the sitting room while watching Catríona wipe the surfaces of the furniture. *Their home.*

If all went well with the help of the lads, the work might be done in a month or so, and they could finally think about setting a date for the wedding. Donal was almost giddy at the thought of Catríona living here with him and Sara, and he had a hard time being patient. Though he knew it was the best course of action for all of them.

Suddenly she realized he was watching her, and she stilled then turned to look at him.

"What're ya lookin' at, Donal Bunratty?" she asked, her tone playful.

He grinned. "At my future wife."

In the kitchen, Sara giggled. Catríona's cheeks flushed, and she matched his smile. "Alright, g'on then," she said, turning back to her task.

Donal studied her for a minute, then leaned the broom against the wall and snuck over to her and slid his arms around her waist.

She hummed softly and chuckled. "Hey there, mister." She wrapped her arms over his and leaned her head back against him.

He pressed his cheek against hers and then turned and brushed it with a kiss. "Are ya sure you're ready to be Missus Bunratty?"

She craned her neck to look up at him, her face serious, eyes intense. "More than ready, Mister Bunratty."

His mouth slipped up in a sideways grin, then he bent and kissed her lips softly. Just as she melted into his embrace further, a rumbling out front yanked their attention away from each other.

"What in the world?" Donal muttered as he and Catríona made their way to the front door, Sara's footsteps trailing behind them. When Donal opened the door, his mouth fell open.

Catríona gasped and pressed her palms together, fingers against her lips. "*Moladh Dé*," she whispered in awe.

Wagons, supplies, and people were pouring up the Bog Road, with Owen and Willie in the lead. Maggie Madigan and Maeve approached the house together, their arms laden with baskets boasting every kind of food one could imagine. "Where'll I put these?" Maggie asked, breathless.

"Here, let me help with that." Catríona skirted around Donal and slid one of the baskets from her arms. As the women headed into the kitchen, Catríona flashed Donal a look of sheer delight and surprise, her eyes shining with unshed tears.

"Look, a dhadí, there's more comin'!"

Donal nodded and smiled down at Sara. "Aye, luhv," he said around the lump in his throat, "there are."

Owen and Willie approached, and Donal stepped outside. "Why don't ya go see what ya can do to help Catríona and Miss Maggie," he said to Sara, who nodded and scurried back inside with a whoop.

"Right," Willie said. "Owen's organizin' everything for the barn."

"And Black-eyed Jack is workin' on all the smithing materials—clasps, hatches, nails, and the like. Meanwhile, Tommy Tiernan's organizing all the thatching," Owen said. "And Maggie's in charge o' the women and the inside of the house."

Donal's breath puffed out in disbelief. "I . . . I don't know what to say."

Willie grinned. "Say ye'll buy us a pint when it's all done, and then get to work!"

The three burst into laughter. "It's a deal." Donal shook Willie's and Owen's hands.

The day passed in a blur as the flurry of activity reached an almost frenetic pace. When they paused for lunch, Donal couldn't believe what he was seeing. The framing for the barn was already complete and standing, the roof repairs were almost done, and smoke once again curled lazily from the chimney in his house.

As they finished the last of their tea before returning to work, Catríona slid under Donal's arm and wrapped hers around his waist. "We are so very blessed," she said.

"Aye, that we are." Donal nodded. "I'd completely forgotten."

She frowned up at him. "Forgotten what?"

"What it's like to have community. Family."

Sara appeared on his other side, and he took hold of her hand. "Hallo, peata. Are ya bein' a good helper?"

"Uh-huh!" She nodded excitedly.

"The best," Catríona added.

"Here, a dhadí." She held up a small purple flower. It was almost unheard of for flowers to bloom so late into September.

"What's this?" he asked.

"It's a flower of the field." She pushed it toward him. "Just like in the—"

"Sermon on the Mount," he finished with her. "Aye, darlin', it sure is."

———◦∞◦———

By the time the sun sank below the horizon, the entire project was finished. Exhausted men and women reclined on the grass outside, enjoying the last drops of tea before heading to their respective homes.

Donal lowered himself to sit down next to Owen and Willie and their wives. "I . . . I don't know how to thank ye. I'll never be able to repay yer kindness."

Owen pinned him with a look.

"Alright, alright. So I won't try to repay it." He looked up at the stars. "But I'll try to be a blessing like this to someone else."

"By golly, Willie," Owen said, slapping his knee, "I think he's startin' to get it."

The group erupted in laughter, but Donal couldn't get over the fact that the community had done in one day what would've taken him months, if not longer, on his own. Now he, Catríona, and Sara could start their life together as soon as they wished. And they'd have missed out on that opportunity had Donal let his pride keep him from accepting a bit of help from those who cared about him—which, as it turned out, was a far larger group than he would've ever dreamt.

Finally, the last of the tea was spent, and people began to trickle back toward their own farms or back to town.

"Truly," Donal said to Owen and Willie who were now standing and folding the blankets their wives had spread on the ground for them to sit on. "Thank ye both. From the bottom of my heart."

Both men shook Donal's hand in turn. "'Twas our pleasure," Owen said.

"But don't think we've forgotten about that pint!" Willie called over his shoulder as he and his wife headed for the road.

Once they'd bid all their guests goodbye, Sara grabbed his hand and hopped up and down. "Come see what we did!"

It was only then that Donal realized he hadn't been inside the house since everyone had arrived. He'd been so busy helping with the barn, field, and all the other outside tasks, he'd almost forgotten just as much work was going on inside.

Catríona took his other hand, and the three walked to the back door of the house. Soft orange light glowed in the windows, and the tangy aroma of the turf fire in the hearth wafted over them. The night was cool and the weather mild, with hardly a hint of wind—entirely unusual for this time of year, but very much appreciated given the recent events.

Donal tugged the back door open and gestured for the girls

to go ahead of him. As he followed them inside, his breath caught in his chest. You would never know there had been any damage at all. The floor practically sparkled it was so clean. And the musty odor from the moisture sitting so long in the closed-up house was gone.

"You ladies have outdone yerselves," he said, spinning a slow circle to take in every detail. He met Catríona's gaze. "Ya must be exhausted."

She nodded. "Absolutely wrecked." She stepped over and kissed his cheek. "But entirely happy."

Sara led him around, showing him each task she'd helped complete, until at last the tour was finished. Both Catríona and Sara looked almost dead on their feet. "I'm so proud of ya both. Amazin' work."

"I could say the same fer ye, Mister Bunratty." He warmed under Catríona's praise and took her hand.

"I'm tired, a dhadí," Sara said around a yawn.

"Me too, darlin'. Let's head back." Donal stepped into the sitting room and arranged the fire so that the embers would stay warm overnight but not pose a fire risk being unattended.

"Aw, can't we stay here?" Sara whined.

Catríona knelt low to look Sara in the eye. "We didn't bring any of yer things to be able to stay here tonight." She glanced at Donal, gratitude shining in her eyes. "We didn't think it would all get done today, remember?"

Sara nodded.

Catríona stood and scooped Sara up into her arms. "So let's have another wee adventure until we can get you and yer Da back here."

"And you!" Sara protested.

"Aww, luhv." Catríona chuckled. "Don't you worry about that. I'll be here just as soon as yer Da and I can get married."

Sara's lip stuck out in an exhausted pout. "When will that be?"
Catríona looked to Donal.

His lips twisted to the side as he thought. "Well, that's a good question. We'd been planning to wed as soon as the work was done, but we also thought it would take much, much longer to finish the work."

"Get married now!" Sara perked up, her eyes alight with excitement.

Donal laughed. "Oh, peata, I'm afraid we can't have a wedding tonight. We're all too tired, for one."

"I'm not that tired."

Donal gestured for them to head to the front door. "Well, then there's the matter of the priest. I'm afraid he's already in bed."

Sara sighed. "Oh."

The trio slipped out the front door into the night and headed up the Bog Road.

"But," Donal said, drawing out the word, "perhaps tomorrow?"

Catríona and Sara gasped. "D'ya mean it, Da?"

"Donal, are ya sure? So soon?"

"I am if you are." He slipped his arm around Catríona's waist. "I don't know about you, but I don't want to wait a second longer than I have to, to be your husband."

In the moonlight, he could see the smile stretch across Catríona's face. "What d'ya think, Sara?"

"Yay!" Sara shouted and wriggled to be put down, her exhaustion completely forgotten.

Donal stood with Jimmy at the top of the aisle and scanned the crowd who'd arrived for the special ceremony.

"I must admit," Donal said quietly, "I'm a bit surprised all the pieces fell into place so quickly for this weddin'."

Jimmy snorted. "Are ya jokin'? This is Lisdoonvarna at the close of the matchmaking festival. There's been hundreds of weddings this month."

Donal's eyes widened, and he looked at Jimmy. "Dáiríre?"

"Oh, aye." Jimmy nodded. "Everyone just knows ya better be ready for a weddin' at the drop of a hat this time of year. Now, if ye'll excuse me." He patted Donal on the shoulder and scurried off toward the back of the room and out the door.

Donal laughed but stopped when Sara appeared at the end of the aisle, hand in hand with Maeve. Sara's hair had been wound into bouncy curls, and a wreath of delicate flowers adorned her head. Tears stung his eyes as she slowly made her way toward him, her ruffled dress swishing with each step. He winked at her, and she grinned back at him, then the two girls took their places across the aisle from him.

A collective gasp from the crowd pulled his attention away from his daughter. Catríona stood in the sunlight, her arm looped around her father's. She wore a simple but elegant dress the color of fresh cream, and she held a bouquet of flowers and greens. But it wasn't her dress or her flowers that stole his breath. It was the radiant glow on her face and the joy shining from her eyes.

It seemed to take ages for her to reach him at the altar, and when she finally got there, it was all Donal could do not to scoop her up in his arms right then and there.

Jimmy took her hand and gently urged her to go to Donal. She stepped up next to him and slid her hand through the crook of his elbow, and Donal never felt more alive as she smiled up at him, unshed tears glistening in her bright blue eyes.

"Hi," she whispered.

"Hi yourself," he whispered back before the priest began the ceremony.

The exchanging of vows and rings passed in a blur. Donal wasn't sure he'd even said his right. But before he knew it, the priest was pronouncing them husband and wife. Donal softly pressed his lips to Catríona's, and she pulled him closer, melting into a deep embrace—to thunderous applause from the crowd.

She took her bouquet from Sara, and she and Donal made their way back up the aisle and out into the bright autumn sunshine. Once free from the watchful eyes of the congregation, Catríona pulled him into a kiss that stole his breath and curled his toes. A kiss conveying everything they'd been through up to this point and hinting at the promise of all that was to come.

The party that followed rivaled any of the matchmaking festival thus far, with lively music, incredible food, and more joy than Catríona would have ever thought possible. She'd shared dance after dance with both Donal and Sara, as well as one tearful waltz with her father. As she sat and sipped some tea, trying to catch her breath as Donal danced with Sara, Catríona watched all the people who had gathered to celebrate her and Donal. So many people who loved and cared about her and her new little family, it was overwhelming. Her eyes fell upon Maeve who was dancing in the corner with a lad Catríona had never seen before. The way they moved together reminded Catríona of the first dance she'd shared with Donal in the square. A slow smile spread across her face at the memory.

Then her gaze drifted to her left hand, and she spun the gold band—a family heirloom her father had surprised her with— around her finger. How odd it felt . . . and yet, how natural. She thought ahead to her first night in her new home—the farmhouse with the thatched roof and the livestock sleeping in the barn a few yards away. She shook her head. The Lord certainly had a fine sense of humor, leading her to end up with exactly what she didn't want. Except it was everything she could want and more.

The lively reel came to an end, and the leader of the musicians announced, "Right, folks, it's gettin' late, and our happy couple needs to get to their beauty sleep." A round of laughs and good-hearted jeers rumbled through the crowd as men elbowed one another, a knowing gleam in their eyes.

"And for their final dance before they head off into the sunset—though the sun went to bed long ago—the groom has requested a very special song."

Catríona looked to Donal. A special song?

"Would the bride and groom please come out to the dance floor for the final dance of their weddin' celebration."

Catríona made her way to Donal's arms in the center of the floor as the musicians began to play "An Cailín Bán"—the same song they'd danced to in the square. Catríona let herself get lost in his embrace and laid her head on his chest as he hummed the tune to the song that would forever be Catríona's most favorite. They swayed and twirled together, and when the final note struck, Donal hooked his finger under her chin and lifted her face to his, stealing her breath with a kiss. Whoops and hollers exploded around them, followed by a rousing round of three cheers for the couple.

When the din finally quieted, Donal said, "Let's go home."

Epilogue

Bunratty Farm
January 1908

Catríona set the kettle on to boil and smiled at the scene unfolding out the small window over the basin. The weather was unseasonably warm and calm, so Donal was in the pen, training the new colt. Sara stood, bouncing her brother, *Donal Óg*, on her hip and pointing out things they saw.

Catríona rounded the counter and headed to join them outside. "How's he doin'?" she asked her husband when she reached the pen.

Donal steadied the young horse and smiled at her, his breathing heavy from the exertion. "He's a good one."

"And what about this wee fella?" She tweaked her nine-month-old's cheek.

"He's a good one too, Mammy," Sara said, a mischievous smile on her face as she handed her baby brother to Catríona. "But he's also stinky!" Sara cackled and ran off toward the barn.

Catríona gasped playfully at Donal Óg. "Did she say that? She's very bold, isn't she?"

Donal Óg squealed and poked his finger in Catríona's mouth

293

just as she discovered that Sara had, in fact, not been exaggerating. She grimaced and turned back to Donal.

"Luhv, Da will be here any minute. Come on in when ya can."

He nodded as he patted the colt's neck.

"Sara," Catríona called just as the girl reached the door to the barn. "Daideo's on his way. Please come clean up after ya see to the cattle."

"Alright," Sara called and stepped through the barn door. That girl loved her stock. And now that they had a dozen cows and as many horses, she spent whatever time she wasn't at school taking care of them, and she couldn't be any happier about it.

Catríona hurried inside, changed the baby's nappy, and got the tea steeping. By that time, Sara and Donal had come in and were washing up just as her dad arrived.

He poked his head in the front door. "Hallo?"

"Hiya, Da," Catríona said, bussing his cheek. It had been over two years since she'd moved out of the flat they shared in the Imperial, and while she wouldn't change things for the world, she did miss all the time she used to spend with him.

Donal Óg flapped his arms and grinned at his grandpa, a string of drool hanging off his chin.

"Daideo!" Sara cried and ran to give him a hug, taking care not to knock him over. Dad hadn't slowed down a mite since she'd left, but his steps were just a little less steady these days. His back a little more hunched.

He hugged Sara, tousled Donal Óg's hair, and shook Donal's hand, then the five of them settled around the fire in the sitting room. Once they had caught up on the chitchat and daily goings-on, her dad grew serious.

"Donal, Catríona, I've somethin' to tell ye."

A pit sank in Catríona's stomach, and her breath caught. She instinctively reached for Donal's hand.

"What is it, Da?" Donal asked.

"Do ye remember, back in the festival when ye first met, that I was tasked with matching Earl Wyndham's daughter Aileen?"

Catríona blinked, confusion swirling in her mind. She had to think back, but she did remember it had been a bit of an ordeal. "Aye," she said at length. "You introduced her to Lord Ardee, but nothing really came of it."

Donal's brow creased. "Surely Earl Wyndham isn't still cross?"

Catríona's father laughed. "No, no. Nothin' like that. Quite the opposite, in fact." He leaned forward and rested his elbows on his knees. "Lord Ardee and Lady Aileen Wyndham-Quin are set to wed next month!"

Catríona's mouth fell open. "Ye're jokin'? After all this time!"

Her dad shrugged. "I kinda had a feelin' they'd be slow movers, but I'd seen a spark that night at the Queens."

"That's grand, Jimmy." Donal reached over and shook his hand as Donal Óg squealed happily.

Catríona's father grinned. "That's not even the best part." He paused dramatically, knowing he had Catríona and Donal eating out of the palm of his hand. "The earl is so chuffed with the match that he's sought me out for other advice as well."

Catríona inclined her head. "Other advice? What sort of advice?"

"Yer man's lookin' to expand his cattle and horse herds on his estate."

Donal's eyes widened. "Is that so?"

Her dad's brows danced up and down. "I showed him yer numbers and all the statistics on your stock, how ye've grown yer herd and how hardy the beasts are that ya breed." Another pause. "He wants you to be his exclusive cattleman."

Sara gasped. "Oh, a dhadí, that's wonderful!"

"He wants to contract you for two calves a year and at least one foal." He took a sip of tea, then continued, "And depending on how he's able to manage that, he may want more. The best part is, he wants to make sure ye're happy with the arrangement. Especially because he knows it was Catríona who really had the idea of matching young Ardee and the lady."

Catríona laughed. "What exactly does that mean?"

"It means"—he rocked in his seat gleefully—"that he's going to pay ya twenty percent over market value for each calf and foal for the next several years."

Catríona pressed her hand to her chest. "Muise."

Her dad beamed but kept his gaze pinned on Donal.

"Da," Sara said, her voice filled with wonder. "It's just like . . ."

Donal and Catríona finished the statement along with Sara. "The flowers in the fields."

Author's Note

Thank you so much for coming along to the Lisdoonvarna Matchmaking Festival with me. I hope you had as much fun experiencing it through Donal's and Catríona's eyes as I did. The matchmaking festival began in 1857, when the wealthy upper class would come and take the medicinal waters found in the natural spa wells scattered around the Lisdoonvarna town limits. They would "soak in the healing water while chit chatting about suitable matches for their children."[1] Social events, dances, outings, and more were organized in the hopes that—with some careful planning—marriages would eventually result.

Matchmaking has long been part of Ireland's history, and nowhere is this more prevalent than in Lisdoonvarna. Jimmy Daly was heavily inspired by Lisdoonvarna's current presiding matchmaker, Willie Daly—whom I honored by naming Willie Baggot after. And, yes, matchmaking still goes on in Lisdoonvarna to this day, as does the festival, which runs the entirety of the month of September.

1. Yolanda Evans, "Ditch Tinder to Flirt IRL at Europe's Biggest Matchmaking Festival," Thrillist, September 1, 2022, https://www.thrillist.com/travel/nation/visit-lisdoonvarna-matchmaking-festival-ireland.

Willie is a third-generation matchmaker, and he always carries a leatherbound book that holds records of every match ever made by Willie, his father, and his grandfather. Willie's memoir, *The Last Matchmaker: The Heartwarming True Story of the Man Who Brought Love to Ireland*, was an invaluable resource to me as I prepared to write this book. As was Willie himself, who was graciously willing to answer my questions about all things matchmaking. And while Catríona and Jimmy share Willie's surname, I'm afraid that's where the similarities end. Jimmy and Catríona are entirely fictitious creations of my imagination—as are Donal and Sara.

Not to worry, though, there are many historical characters who make an appearance. Thomas Wyndham, the fourth earl of Dunraven, was the landlord for County Clare in 1905, and his daughter Aileen May Wyndham-Quin really did marry Lord Ardee in 1908. To my knowledge, they were not matched up by a chance meeting with a matchmaker in Lisdoonvarna in 1905. And last but not least, Doctor Forster was actually a doctor in the area at the time as well.

The theme of love, of course, is woven throughout a story about matchmaking. But Donal and Catríona's story is about so much more. While today the matchmaking festival serves more as a party or monthlong stag party, my prayer is that through the pages of this book you've seen what True Love really is. And that you've been encouraged to lay your worries, doubts, and heartaches at the feet of the One who clothes the lilies of the field and feeds the birds of the air. He loves you so very much and has the very best in store for you.

Travel the Beautiful Land of Ireland in
Jennifer Deibel's
Next Historical Novel!

COMING SPRING 2025

1

The slap had hit its mark, leaving a burning outline Brianna was certain showed perfectly on her cheek. Despite the sting, she refused to press her hand against it. She wouldn't give Mistress Magee the satisfaction. As the woman continued to rail about Brianna's endless list of short-comings, Brianna plotted out the route for her afternoon treasure hunt. She'd never call it thus to Mistress Magee. No, to that woman it was a *daily constitutional*—a phrase that always conjured images of outhouses and pig slop rather than the walk of a proper lady. Not that it mattered much. Maureen Magee, headmistress of Ballymacool House and Boarding School for Girls, saw to it that Brianna was reminded of the depths of her station daily. Nothing befitting a lady befitted Brianna. But that didn't bother her. Not really. All she needed were her walks in the woods, her treasures, and the good Lord. A friend wouldn't hurt though. Not that Magee would ever allow it.

"Do you hear me, girl?" The headmistress's strident voice pierced Brianna's thoughts.

She swallowed a sigh. "Yes, marm."

"Then you know what you're to do?" The severe lines on the woman's face hardened with judgment, serving to further age her. "Well, child? Do you?" Mistress Magee straightened her posture, cupped her fingers together at her waist, and waited, impatience flashing in her steely eyes.

Child? Brianna was twenty, yet Mistress Magee perpetually treated her like she was still a snot-nosed five-year-old. "Aye, miss." At a spark of indignation from her guardian, Brianna corrected herself. "Yes, marm." In truth, Brianna had heard nothing of what the woman had instructed, but she didn't need to. Mistress Magee piled on the same litany of extra chores any time Brianna deigned to show her humanity. Today's egregious error? Not having the morning's porridge pot scrubbed and shining prior to the students finishing breakfast. Never mind that Brianna had been kept busy clearing dishes, wiping spills, and the like. That mattered not. All that mattered were Mistress Magee's ever-changing whims and Brianna's inability to meet them.

"Very well." Mistress Magee punctuated her thought with a sharp nod. "You know what's expected. See that you carry it out. Forthwith." She turned to leave, paused, then peered over her shoulder at Brianna, waiting.

"Yes, marm." Brianna swiped a sponge from the table and plunged it into a basin of water, then knelt and began scrubbing the massive copper pot.

Mistress Magee nodded again, a quiet "*humph*" escaping her lips before she swept from the hot, stuffy kitchen.

Once alone, Brianna plopped back onto her heels, finally allowing the deep sigh she'd been holding in to press out, releasing with it all the tension Mistress Magee's presence always cultivated. Tempted to let bitterness take root, she closed

JENNIFER DEIBEL

her eyes and imagined she was sitting at the base of her tree. She could almost feel the coolness of the damp earth seeping through her skirt, the gentle breeze tickling her skin, cooling the ache that still pulsed on her cheek from Mistress Magee's strike. Whispering a prayer for strength and endurance, she retrieved the sponge and resumed scrubbing.

As she worked the filth from the pot, her anger lightened and lifted away. A plunking sound and a gentle splash shook Brianna from her thoughts. Another leak? A quick glance at the ceiling revealed nothing. Peering into the pot, panic jolted her. She grasped at her neck and chest. *My pendant!* She plunged her hand into the murky water, ignoring the sludge collecting at the bottom, and worked until her fingers found what they sought. She curled them around the chain, then sloshed her prize a bit to clear the muck away and pulled it out of the water.

She wiped it as gently and as quickly as she could with her apron and then inspected it closely. All appeared to be intact—as intact as it had ever been, anyway. Clearly only a broken piece of a larger pendant, its edges worn by time, it was bordered with double lines accented with several fleurs-de-lis. Within the borders lay three stamped flowers. Brianna ran her thumb over the flowers, imagining her mother had once done the same. It was all she had that connected her to her family and long-forgotten past. She'd been left with it around her neck, even as a small infant, Mistress Magee had told her long ago. Before her hatred of Brianna had fully set in.

She clasped her hand around the shard and then opened it again to view the back of the trinket. Letters that seemed to have been hastily carved by hand stretched across the surface. Only part of a word. The *c*, *o*, and *n* were clearly visible. Another letter, or part of one, was slashed in half by the broken edge. How many hours had she spent daydreaming about what

303

those letters might spell? What they might mean? But there was no time for that now. If she was to have any hope of a walk in the woods today, she must hasten in finishing her tasks.

She worked the chain through her fingers until they reached the ends and refastened the clasp. The battered chain often came open and fell from her neck. And it had done so even more of late. Slipping it over her head, Brianna tucked the pendant into the bodice of her dress, praying it would stay. She needed a new chain. Since she did not receive any wages for her labors at the house—she was "earning her keep," according to Mistress Magee—the only way to procure one would be if she happened across one on one of her walks. But she knew better than to hope for such good fortune. Her years in the Ballymacool woods had taught her that treasure never reveals itself to the greedy, but rather the grateful. And so, as she plunged her hands into the now-cool water, she ran through her list of all that for which she was grateful.

———◦∞◦———

The library was dark and quiet—just how Michael preferred it. The fire that had been laid down that morning was now nothing more than an orange glow. The curtains were drawn, shadowing the room in the blissful gray of an indoor dusk. For any other household, that might seem odd at this time of day, but not for Castle Wray. Michael snorted at the name for the house situated in the heart of the Castlewray Estate. Although a grand five-bay, two-story stone house, it was not quite what he would consider a castle. And after a long morning of managing the sprawling property—one of the few ascendancy estates still in operation—a quiet afternoon with a good book was just what he needed.

Filling his lungs with the beloved musty scent of old books, stale tobacco, and a turf fire, he sauntered across the room to his favorite shelf. W. B. Yeats, George Moore, George William Russell, and others lined up like old friends ready to welcome Michael back into the folds of their confidence. Few things stirred Michael's heart and refreshed his spirit like an inspiring read, much to his mother's dismay. Other things more befitting a man of his age and station did so as well, though not to the same degree as words on the page. A bracing ride on his trusty steed, Cara, a rousing game of cards, or a well-brewed cup of tea or pint of ale all served to bolster his spirits after a trying day. But given his druthers, Michael would choose the quiet library—or a tree-canopied forest—and a familiar tome every time.

No sooner had he removed his book of choice from its spot than his parents spun into the room. His mother, equal parts the portrait of decorum and yet all a dither, fanned herself briefly before patting her hair and setting her shoulders, returning to the proper state of an ascendancy class lady of Letterkenny. Michael's father, tall and stoic as ever, clasped his hands behind his back and rocked forward and back on his toes once before settling his gaze on Michael.

"Good day, son," he greeted him. His words wished him well, but his tone implied something else altogether. *Wasting the day away reading again, I see?* is what Michael imagined his father truly meant to say. Michael absently wondered why his father went through the expense of having such an expansive library if it was so wasteful to use it.

Michael set the book on a nearby table. "Father. Mother." He closed the distance between them and placed a brief kiss on his mother's cheek, having to bend at the waist to reach her face. She pressed into the kiss, but then rubbed her fingers where his dark mustache and beard had tickled her.

His father cleared his throat and glanced at his wife, who

summoned the maid. With a flick of Mother's wrist, the maid scurried to the tall windows and tied back the curtains. Michael flinched at the bright afternoon sun and breech of his solitude. Opening the drapes felt like inviting the whole of the estate to gawk at the family's daily goings-on. At *his* goings-on. Michael would always choose to be out among the people, preferring the company of the down-to-earth farmers to the pompous showboats of high society. With rumblings of trouble brewing again in Germany, the men his father rubbed elbows with would be insufferable as the group passed around their self-proclaimed vast knowledge of world events and warfare. But there were times it just seemed easier to hide away from it all. And that had been his aim for today.

Gesturing to a settee in front of the fireplace, his father crossed the room and placed his hand on the thick wooden mantelpiece. "I've a job for you, Michael."

Michael sank onto the seat. "Oh?" It wasn't unusual for his father to give him tasks. It was, however, unusual for the job description to come with such a fuss and formality.

"Indeed." His father swiped at a speck of something on the mantel that wasn't really there, brushed his fingers together, and turned to face Michael and his mother. "It's your cousin. Adeline."

Michael fought to hide the wince that naturally contorted his face at the sound of his cousin's name. A fourteen-year-old spoiled brat, who seemed to have placed Michael on a pedestal. Whether it was childish infatuation or idolization of him and his stable home life, he didn't know. But he did know that Adeline succeeded in bringing utter chaos wherever she went. Managing to keep his composure, he responded, "What about Adeline?"

"It seems she's having some trouble settling in over at Bal-lymacool." His father paced slowly in front of the dying fire.

Michael swallowed a guffaw. "Settling in? Father, 'tis been nearly a year!"

Ignoring the comment, Father continued. "The other girls have been . . . less than welcoming."

Next to Michael, his mother *tsked*. "You know how young girls can be," she added, wagging her head.

I know how she *can be*. He blinked the thought away before it could escape his mouth.

"Adeline just needs some guidance," his mother added. "And a strong presence to deter any further . . ." She circled her hand in the air and studied the carpet beneath them as though searching for just the right word.

"Incidents," his father finished for her.

"Incidents?"

Mother sighed. "'Twould seem the girl has been somewhat . . . antagonistic . . . toward the other students."

"Truth is"—Father cleared his throat—"she's put somewhat of a target on her back and needs a watchful eye."

Michael rose and absently twisted the whiskers of his mustache. "I see." Though he didn't really. What had this to do with him? "What of Uncle Thomas? Can he not intercede?"

His father snatched the copy of Russell's *Awakening* from the table where Michael had left it a few moments ago and shoved the book on a shelf. The wrong shelf. "You know very well Thomas has his hands full with all the nonsense going on down there. Being so close to Dublin has increased the troubles on his estate a hundredfold compared to ours. It's the whole reason Adeline was sent to Ballymacool rather than Kylemore to begin with. I must continue with the duties of running Castlewray Estate, and your mother has her society engagements to keep up. So, it falls to you."

Michael tugged the book from its misplacement and settled

it in its rightful spot. *And what am I to know of the problems of a young girl?* He dismissed the thought as soon as it materialized. He knew full well any problems dear old Adeline was having were of her own making and not of the emotional variety. She didn't need a confidant. She needed a bodyguard. Since Adeline was Thomas's only child, she truly had no one to fill this purpose. Heaven forbid Father step away from his haughty circle of cigar-smoking pseudo-gentry to fulfill a true family obligation.

Gripping the bookshelf, Michael squeezed his eyes shut and whispered a silent prayer of forgiveness for having such a callous attitude toward his father. "Very well," he said on a sigh. He scratched at his beard and his mother winced. She hated that he refused to keep the clean-shaven face of a proper society man. The corner of his mouth turned up slightly, taking pleasure in the small rebellion. "When do I leave?"

"Directly."

Michael's jaw fell slack. "So soon? Is the situation so dire?"

"Not dire, but it requires expediency." His father's tone left no room for argument. "And you're to be there at least a fortnight. Perhaps longer."

Michael coughed. "*Stay* there? Father, Ballymacool 'tis only fifteen miles west. I can easily travel back and forth each day."

"You could, but you won't. Adeline needs someone there 'round the clock. And you're the man."

"Ballymacool House has some lovely cottages on their grounds for visiting family members and the like," Mother added. "They've got one already prepared for you, as they agree this is the best course of action."

Michael tried to ignore the fact that such plans would've taken quite some time to make. But since he couldn't stomach another debate, he chose to concede. "Very well."

"Aidan has your horse ready to go and your effects as well. Godspeed, son."

A puff of air blew from Michael's lips before he could stop it. At least his father had had the courtesy to allow Michael to use Cara instead of the blasted motorcar. He'd never trust those contraptions. At length, he shook his head, then accepted his father's outstretched hand and shook it. He ran his fingers through his thick hair and down the back of his neck before hugging his mother. "Good day, Mother. Father. I'll send word if I've need of anything."

Acknowledgments

Every book, I feel at a loss when it comes to writing the acknowledgments. Not because I don't feel there is anyone to acknowledge or thank but because there are so many! Writing is a largely solitary venture, but publishing a book truly takes a village. This book in particular was very challenging for me to write, and I'm not entirely sure why. Perhaps it has to do with the fact that I was wrestling with my own struggles of trusting God's provision throughout this particular writing process. I'm not sure. But what I do know is that I found myself stymied at almost every turn, slogging through writer's block like I've never known. Two weeks before this book was due, the first draft wasn't even halfway finished. But by the grace of God—and thanks to my intrepid Panera Girls (Liz Johnson, Lindsay Harrel, Sara Ella, Sara Popovich, Breana Johnson, Ruth Douthitt, Kim Wilkes, Erin McFarland, and Tari Faris) who helped me brainstorm some of the most key scenes of this story—I finished just before my due date, with time to read it back over before turning it in to my incredible editor, Rachel McRae.

Rachel, thank you for being so supportive, for lifting me up in prayer, and for reaching out with words of encouragement and affirmation when I needed them most. Thank you for trusting me to write these wacky stories with these crazy characters. I'm so grateful I get to be on this journey with you.

Cynthia Ruchti, agent extraordinaire—your guidance and leadership are invaluable to me, and I'm grateful every day to get to be on your team. Thank you for believing in me and for championing these stories.

Seth, my softhearted handyman. I see a lot of Donal in you—the way you carry the weight of providing for our family, the way you protect our children above everything, and at all costs, the way you wrestle with the daily grind because you want to grow in your faith while still being awed by the mystery of God's ways. Thank you for standing by my side (and sometimes behind me, pushing me—LOL) on this wild writing journey. I know when it gets crazy, a lot more falls on you and the kids. I cannot say how much I appreciate you supporting this dream of mine. I love you.

To my precious children, Hannah, Cailyn, and Isaac—talking through these stories with you is still one of my most favorite things. I love how you still get excited to share ideas and brainstorm with me. Thank you for understanding that this dream God's given me sometimes puts more responsibilities on your shoulders. I'm grateful that you all carry it with grace. And, girls, thanks for discovering that garlic parmesan pasta! That's going in the regular rotation.

To Mom, Bonnie Martin—my original and immediate beta reader. Thank you for dropping everything to read when I send you a fresh set of chapters. And thank you for being honest when things sound weird or just plain make no sense. I appreciate it more than you know.

To Dad, Jerry Martin—my original cheerleader. Thank you for celebrating me, praying for me, and encouraging me.

To Cheryl Deibel—I like this pattern we have going of spending so much time together around big milestones in my writing process. But maybe we aim for less medical drama next time, eh? LOL! I am so grateful to have had this time with you. Your quiet encouragement and whispered words of affirmation and strength do more for my heart than you could ever know.

Between teaching, raising kids, and writing, I'm fairly certain I'd already have been sent "back the way" if it weren't for my wonderful friends. Donna Carlson, Charity Verlander, Melissa Reagan, Missy Posey, Terri Logelin, Nancy Patton, Sara Walton, Lori Palmer, Julie Stiner, and Traci Bramlett—thank you so much for always checking on me, for all the coffees and hugs, and for asking how my progress is going. You keep me honest and feeling very, very loved!

Mark Anderson and Danielle Ware—the school year during which I wrote this book was . . . well . . . one for the books. The way you guys stand behind me and support me both in the classroom and out in the world is so wonderful. Thank you for understanding when my author world crosses over into my teacher world and for letting me take a day or two off here and there to take care of business.

To Robin Turici, line editor savant—my characters would be lost without you, and I'd have egg on my face more often than not without your keen eye for detail and unnatural knack for timelines and eye-color consistency.

And to the rest of my most wonderful team at Revell, Brianne Dekker, Karen Steele, everyone else on the marketing team, and our top-notch design team—you all are the real MVPs. The effortless way you make my books shine is humbling. Thank you for all you do and for how you walk this journey alongside me.

Father God, Jehovah-Jireh, thank You for all You've done for me. From bringing me into the folds of Your family to providing for us in such extravagant and creative ways. Thank You for creating the Great Story and for allowing me to share in the joys of story. I pray my words will always point the reader back to You.

And, finally, to you, my dear reader. I know it may sound trite, but I truly could not do this without you. There's no point in writing a book if there's no one to read it. Thank you for reading these stories, for loving my characters like I do, and for trusting me with your precious time.

Jennifer Deibel is the award-winning author of *A Dance in Donegal*, *The Lady of Galway Manor*, and *The Maid of Ballymacool*. With firsthand immersive experience abroad, Jennifer writes stories that help redefine home through the lens of culture, history, and family. After nearly a decade of living in Ireland and Austria, she now lives in Arizona with her husband and their three children. You can find her online at JenniferDeibel.com.

Deibel whisks the reader off to Ireland for a new kind of CINDERELLA STORY

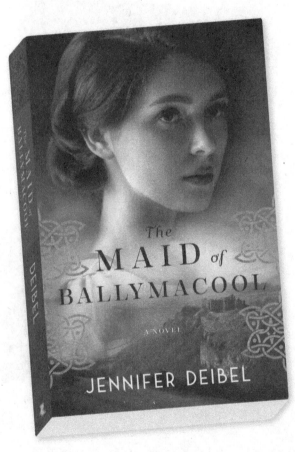

Revell
a division of Baker Publishing Group
RevellBooks.com

Explore the Emerald Isle in
The Lady of Galway Manor

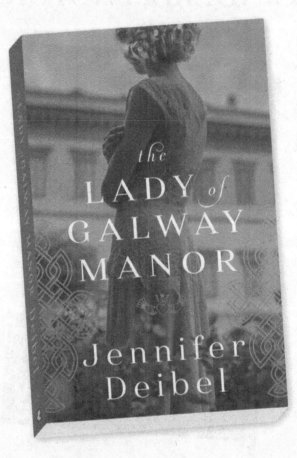

"An immersive read that left me feeling as though I had actually traveled to Ireland. Deibel is proving herself a master at taking readers from all over the world and throwing them into the culture and time of her stories. Pick up this book and be transported to 1920s Ireland, where folklore abounds, conflict is brimming, and love is in the air."

—RACHEL FORDHAM, author of *A Lady in Attendance*

Meet

Find Jennifer online at

JENNIFERDEIBEL.COM

and sign up for her newsletter to get the latest news and special updates delivered directly to your inbox.

Follow Jennifer on social media!

JenniferDeibelAuthor   ThisGalsJourney   JenniferDeibel_Author